YoYo
One Man's Decision to Become a Tree

Yo Yo

One Man's Decision to Become a Tree

Beijing – London quartet

Translated from the Chinese
by Callisto Searle

PalmArtPress
Berlin

ISBN: 978-3-96258-136-7

All rights reserved
First Edition, 2023, PalmArtPress, Berlin

Coverbild: YoYo
Cover Design / Edit: Catharine J. Nicely
Layout: NicelyMedia
Production: Schaltungsdienst Lange, Berlin
Printed in Deutschland

PalmArtPress
Pfalzburger Str. 69, 10719 Berlin
Publisher: Catharine J. Nicely
www.palmartpress.com

CONTENTS

A
THE REINCARNATION OF DREAMER | 9
小梦涅槃

B
WHO KNOWS | 77
无人知晓

C
DESIRE'S WINGS | 115
欲望的翅膀

D
ONE MAN'S DECISION TO BECOME A TREE | 219
决定做一棵树

A

THE REINCARNATION OF DREAMER

小梦涅槃

D reamer told me that one of the worst traits in humanity is confiding your problems in others.

Despite her young age she has a wealth of experience; she has this life all figured out. Once she told me, the moment that you start to tell someone your troubles, they will despise you, from the very marrow of their bones. On the surface they will pretend to sympathize with you, but really in their heart of hearts they are secretly laughing at you. They'll get sick of you by the third time you let it happen and start looking for reasons to put you down. To begin with, you started out here—she indicated a point above her head with her left hand—and when you start to talk about your problems—as she spoke her left hand dropped to a point below her belly button. Human empathy is an extremely limited thing; it is extremely fragile and there's nothing you can do about it. Don't rely on it, or you'll soon see things going against you. Dreamer stared at me with those child-like eyes of hers saying, remember: never ever confide in anyone. I'm telling you the truth, if you really can't take it you'd be better off dead than going to someone else about it. That's the price of respect. When you're dead people will remember a hundred wonderful things about you, they'll consider you worthy of respect.

I shook my head. Death is a rather steep price to pay to avoid telling someone your problems, that's too much!

Dreamer shook her head as well. It's worth it, it's a question of values. Dreamer spoke in all earnest.

I thought it very strange, Dreamer talking about values. In the few years I had known her, she'd given me the impression that she wasn't serious about anything; she laughed at beliefs, responsibilities. She would frequently criticize my attitude, the way I was always bringing up responsibilities, as if the responsibilities of the whole of mankind weighed upon my shoulders. If I had such a strong sense of social responsibility, why didn't I start by being responsible for myself? She had this strange theory that we must first love ourselves. That is terribly important. If you can't love yourself, you'll never be able to love anybody else. Of course, you can't become narcissistic either, that's just weird, she had added

Her odd theories really got to me sometimes. During the Cultural Revolution, the eight model plays were ubiquitous. The most representative of them is a scene in "The Legend of Red Lantern". The 'Jap devil' Hatoyama, leader of his troop, demonstrated the epitome of counter-revolutionary thinking by saying to the hero Li Yuhe, *If you don't please yourself, the world will stop turning.* At that time we weren't do anything in school all day, except sitting down together and having 'criticism meetings', uncovering each other's faults, criticizing precisely that kind of counter-revolutionary thought. Ever since I was a child I've been taught to be selfless, to think of the common good, to forget myself—how can I now decide to love only myself? And she says it is terribly important! Isn't that the same as the counter-revolutionary thoughts of Hatoyama? *That's one hundred percent individualism, it must be criticized more thoroughly!* Our ideas were like chalk and cheese. She went against everything I had been taught. I couldn't bear to listen to those theories of hers. I certainly couldn't debate the matter with her, I was no match for her way with words. I might as well just let her say her piece.

In order to avoid suicide, I must do my best not to talk about my problems. She looked at me, her face wreathed in smiles.

I was still afraid that she wouldn't leave it alone, so I didn't pursue the conversation. She was like a child in my eyes. To say she was a child was going a bit far, as she was only half a dozen years younger than me after all. Yet I clearly felt a degree of separation, as if we came from two completely different generations. I don't want to say we had a 'generation gap', that's a cliché. But we did have so many differences of opinion, fundamentally different in some ways: For example, parents bringing up their children; she seemed to think that was some kind of sacred right. If they aren't willing to support me, they shouldn't have gone and brought me into the world looking for a good time. I didn't ask to be born! If they're going to give birth to me, they've got a duty to raise me. You can't expect me to stand on my own two feet right as soon as I was born, what sort of freak of nature would that make me? What winds me up most is when my mum and dad are always telling me that they brought me up for nothing. As if I owed them something just for being born, were they bringing me up only in order to repay some kind of debt to them? The more they bring up that kind of talk, the more rebellious I get. I tell myself, I don't owe anyone anything. Returning a favor is something you do because you're willing. Keep reminding your daughter she's got to repay you; creating this psychological burden out of nothing. They're only hurting themselves. "You reap what you sow" as the saying goes. The only way for an unfilial daughter to change is if she feels guilty in and of herself, you can't make her. I don't want to be a mother as long as I live, just to save myself from always feeling that someone owes me something, always longing for them to repay me. What about you then, who's going to repay you for your trouble anyway?

A very tidy smile spread across her delicate features. It was nearly impossible to relate that impassioned speech to her delicate little face. Her expression was coolly lacking in all emotion. Against my instincts, I couldn't help but admire her, she was so self-centered and so logical.

One morning after a fall of snow, I lay in bed and began to think seriously about Dreamer's words. Did I want to be a mother? I've been married for more than eight years now.

Every month, when my period arrives, I greet it with an inner celebration, that once more I'd gotten away with it. At the same time, I always feel a little disappointed, secretly mourning that once more I've missed the chance to be a mother. The two feelings tied up together sometimes made me feel pretty depressed. Sometimes I feel I'm quite modern, full of confidence. I hoped I could be an intellectual female, not worn out by family affairs. I was going to be an iron lady fighting my way to victory, not only financially independent but emotionally independent, not needing some man to look after me. Spiritual independence is the only total independence. Then again, sometimes I really wish I were just simple and illiterate, with a pack of little ones. A picture of rustic living, throwing my whole heart into bringing up my children with my husband. What they call, "supporting your husband and raising his children." I think that maybe that would be a happy life as well.

As for happiness, everyone has their own ideas, don't they? Just like with beauty, which also has no fixed standard. Westerners like petite features: small nose, delicate eyes, small mouth, doll-like features—that's what they call classic Oriental beauty. A Western person will even go to great lengths to acquire tanned olive skin. That is the color of travel, a symbol of wealth, of being able to travel all over the world. It is seen as healthy and attractive. Most Chinese people think that big eyes, a high bridge of the nose and pale, white skin are the only standards of true beauty. "A white complexion compensates for ten faults", as they say. Those are two such different aesthetic styles. So I very rarely use the word, 'happiness'. Sometimes I'm not even sure that such a thing exists. Some people are happy just because they've eaten their fill, other people have all the luck in the world and want nothing more than to kill themselves. Like Marilyn Monroe, the epitome of beauty, most lower-class people would think that she was living in paradise. There are different standards for happiness; so there's really no telling what should make us happy.

I've let myself get carried away. This weighty question of being a mother has left me confused and undecided for some time now. Firstly, I'm afraid that I just wouldn't do a good job of raising a child. I'd be afraid that I don't have the money to provide a child with a good education. Just imagine if I gave birth to a genius (I've seen many mothers who believe that their child is a genius, children that spoke at three months, were composing poetry at the age of one, things like that). I was afraid that I would give birth to a little Mozart and not be able to afford a piano for them. I could destroy a genius—wouldn't that make you feel just awful for the rest of your life? In such a materialistic society everything is decided in terms of money. Of course it's not true that material objects can create a genius, but for poverty to destroy a genius is just as easy as that—if you couldn't give them a chance to flourish, or if they suffered an early death. And then again, I worry that I'd be too rough or simple with a child, that I'd be a failure as a mother. What if I enacted a vicious cycle of dissatisfaction and guilt, creating psychological impediments for the next generation. I might be like Dreamer's father, always complaining that my child is not filial, feeling that I'd brought a little thug into the world to be dealt with. What's the point of that? Every time I visit a colleague's home, I see their spoilt only-children bullying their parents. They use up their parents' time and energy. It terrifies me. Dreamer says that I am an 'idealist'. She doesn't really understand me. I am essentially selfish, I am not one to go making sacrifices, I'm not ready to give everything for a child, I'm afraid of taking on responsibilities. I'm afraid of not being able to properly educate the next generation. Or that I'll turn him or her into a little hooligan who'll do no good for me or the country as a whole. That would be a real weight on my conscience. I tell myself over and over: I have neither the patience nor the ability to be a good mother; I'd better just give up on the idea, otherwise I'll be the one to suffer the consequences. And yet my desire to become a mother grows stronger by the day. Perhaps it is purely biological. I can't go having a child purely for biological reasons, I'm a person not an animal. I have my rationale. But I am still a woman, it is natural for a woman to want to be a mother. When my maternal instincts flare up I can envisage just about anyone as the recipient of my mother's love, which just goes to show how deeply ingrained my desire to be a mother is. Even though I am constantly tortured by the nature of being female, I lack the required bravery. I'm just not ready, I'm not even sure what the exact connotations of "being ready" are. I don't know when I will really be able to give birth to such 'bravery'.

I'm not a mother yet.

I've imagined all sorts of possible figures of motherhood: a great mother, an insignificant mother. I find myself wandering uncertainly between the two extremes. As with any serious issue, I my hesitant character soon reveals itself. It's just one of my fatal flaws. One fatal flaw is quite enough for one person, but I have so many that make me miserable. It's really quite terrifying and I can't do anything about it. I always ponder far too much, and I'm slow to take action. For example, I know that idealism is a highly undesirable commodity nowadays, but whenever it comes to the crunch, it just pops up again! There's nothing I can do about it. I'm actually not an idealist. I don't know what I am. Perhaps this is what they mean when they say "your fate is decided by your character". Heaven knows.

Yes, I've been tormented pretty badly by this problem. As soon as it comes to mind, I'll be sleepless for a few nights. I'll be in a real state, as if I'd gotten sick with something. Dreamer makes fun of me saying I'm sitting on the fence. She says that I want to proudly uphold traditions and play at being modern at the same time. Doing neither all the way. What was I anyway?

I saw the heavy snow flying about outside, "I danced. My shadow tumbled after,"* I don't know why this line of Tang poetry should come to me just at that moment. The whiteness felt clean and sacred and maybe—oppressing. Snowy days always make me feel sentimental. My childhood years floated before my eyes: We didn't care about getting with the times then; we didn't care about the passing of time at all. We just ran about playing all day,

---

* From "Drinking Alone with the Moon" by Li Bai (701-62) the Chinese, Tang Dynasty poet.

nothing seemed to matter. There we were, having snow fights, playing games, the days passing by in a flash. How did I grow old so quickly? At that moment, the snowflakes grew pale and listless, dancing in the fathomless heavenly vaults. Snowflakes spinning, hopeless and helpless. Before long the ground was covered with a thick snowy eiderdown. I watched a few sweet children building snowmen under their parents' supervision. My brain went off on a stream of consciousness; I didn't mean to. I've never had any particularly literary leanings. Up until now the only book to move me to tears was, "The Song of Youth"*. That one really struck me. As a result, I decided not to touch the nerve of emotions too freely; it can be very painful. Why is it that today I've returned to that time that ought to be left well alone. As if sliding downhill, suddenly I remembered the first song I ever learned. I couldn't help beginning to hum it,

> *Snowman, Snowman, I want to know,*
> *How come you're so healthy,*
> *No clothes and no hat,*
> *you stand out there in the snow*

That's the first nursery rhyme my mother ever sang to me.

This year the Spring Festival passed with an eerie feeling. I wasn't in the mood at all. I wandered about on the streets with nothing to do, looking at the men and women, young and old, passing by in an endless stream of happy faces. I didn't

---

* 1958 Chinese novel by Yang Mo based in part on her personal experience of the Japanese invasion of China in 1937, before the Cultural Revolution.

know what they were so happy about, just because another perfectly unnecessary day had arrived. Do they think it's some big occasion? Brimming over with happiness? All of these days were invented by people. If we wanted to, we could come up with a special name for each and every day, and let people be lost in the festive spirit every single day. I don't know who I'm trying to convince. Indeed, festivals are a significant moment in our lives. At important moments they can bring a person back to life or renew their hope. Festivals are something that have stood up victorious to the test of time, as solid as a rock. Is the 'Ah Q' spirit deeply ingrained in our culture? I can't set about proving it. Anyhow, I'm usually happy with my lot. But today, I don't want a day, I want a day without days. I walked on the streets, with a blank expression, like a dog from a house of mourning. I had always enjoyed the firecrackers at New Year's; I liked hearing them go off and make the world turn dark—block out the sun and the moon, out with the old and in with the new and blessings on all. That was always a part of our ancient traditions. Yet for some reason they've been banned now. This year passed by the same as many others, the air empty and gray, no fireworks in the sky. I thought to myself the most long-winded saying of the bored youth of Beijing. – This is what we call entirely lacking in interest.

In all honesty, my rebellious years were over a long time ago. There was no reason for my feeling so down. It all comes

---

* Ah Q is a character from Lu Xun's novel *The True Story of Ah Q*, published in a newspaper in series between 1921-22. Ah Q is seen as a polemic of the flaws of the Chinese character, often engaging in self-talk to reframe failings and disappointments as victories.

down to my not being a mother, I'm sure. I always feel as if I haven't grown up yet, stuck in a rut and giving up on everything. My old classmate Jasmine Mo would say that of me. She's now wholly devoted to bringing up her only child. She doesn't have another thought in her head, her flushed face glowing with satisfaction. Her days are full and exciting, and she's always busy with something. The 24 hours roll on without pause. Today she's taking her son to an art class, tomorrow she's taking him to a violin lesson, the day after that she's taking her son to learn computer skills. She devotes herself to turning her son into a great talent. Every day she goes on about how she's so busy. I really admire her spirit of adventure. She rushes about all day every day with a great deal of interest in the smallest, most insignificant of matters. She's so full of beans, I feel in awe of her. I don't know if I was born with my decadent temperament, or if I acquired it later. There's no way to find out either, and no one to ask.

Dreamer vanished for three days and came back with the newest trend in haircuts. She appeared before me with her asymmetrical cut. I've invented that name for it, because I'm at all sure what this haircut is actually called. On the right, her hair fell to her earlobe, whilst on the left it was short like a crew cut. It looked as if something was missing—an ear or an arm, a leg? It was none of the above, but at any rate, something wasn't quite right. She looked out of proportion, an oddity that takes a little getting used to. We are accustomed to symmetry; asymmetry makes us feel unbalanced. Symmetry is what keeps the world going round.

I felt as if she came hobbling unevenly into my home.

That's only how it felt to me.

She said, you're alright, you haven't made a big deal out of nothing.

It's only that I'm not letting it show, I said.

She said, that's good enough for me.

Then she said, I've had a war with my family over this haircut, my father almost disowned me for it.

As serious as that? I asked.

Dreamer said, you have no idea how conservative my father is. He's got to the position he's in by suppressing himself and conforming to tradition. Even when he joined the revolution, he did it in the most cautious and frugal way possible. He can't even bring himself to spit out the pips when he eats a pear! He gives himself such a hard time. He'll use one toothbrush for five or six years without changing it. And you've never seen his washcloth—it's got five or six big holes in it and he still can't bear to throw it away. There's no telling him."

I knew that Dreamer liked to exaggerate. You had to take everything she said with a pinch of salt.

She went on excitedly, saying that I have no idea how her father lives. Love is precious but life is more so.* I have to live a good life. My father's generation put in a lifetime of hard work, but it's just not worth it. In this day and age, it's the bold that get ahead and the cowardly go hungry. My father's old-fashioned type will all be replaced sooner or later. My dad thinks the way I dress is the root of all our conflict. It's like class struggle, to the death, him or me. It drives me round the bend. We argue every day, there's not a moment's peace in our house. It's absolute torture.

Last summer, when it was in fashion to wear super mini-skirts and tight tops that revealed the tummy, Dreamer wore such a short top you could see her belly button. She was incomparably attractive and ran about just full of herself. She almost gave her father a heart attack. This time she'd just got in the house when her dad's mouth fell open and just stuck there. In the end he couldn't stop himself from flinging his chopsticks on the table in anger, and bellowing, you do yourself up like a freak one more time and you can get out of this house! Dreamer pulled a face as if she didn't care and said, fine, I'll live on the streets by begging and stealing and say it was you who drove me out. I'll say I've got a family that doesn't want me and that's why I'm homeless. The generation that came after the Cultural Revolution don't have it all sunshine and roses you know; sometimes we have to take the back door. My dad can't stand it when I act like I don't care. He came over to hit me but I leapt out of the way in a flash. I dodged him like a cat, then I went to a Karaoke bar and belted out a couple of numbers at the top of my voice. I'm not going to stay cross over him. But I'll have to stay with you for a few days, okay? Wait 'til the old man calms down a bit, then go

---

* From the Chinese translation of the Hungarian poem Liberty and love by Petőfi Sándor (1823-1849). This short revolutionary poem was translated and made popular amongst Chinese readers by Lu Xun.

back. He's making a lot of fuss out of nothing. As she spoke, she stuck her feet high up on the most expensive table in our home, as if she were head of the house. I feel both love and hate for that careless attitude of hers. It is what I lack, what I will never master as long as I live. I don't understand how we can be as different as people born in two different centuries when we were born only six years apart. Me myself—I'm neither classical nor modern, I like to move amongst the crowd neither outstanding nor entirely overlooked. I present a gray hue, the most conservative color of all. And so I sit on the fence, neither one thing or the other, Dreamer's always telling me off about it, she says you'll never achieve greatness that way. What day and age is it for you to be clinging onto your idealism? This is the age of the extinction of idealism, that kind of thing is way out of date. Still, you don't get a move on and find a new direction in life, be a bit more realistic. The idealism you were taught means to passionately pursue a bunch of ideals that can never ever come true. Practicality proves that those ideals are just empty words and nothing else. Their fragility has been proven, the times they are a-changing, idealism won't stand up to the might of materialism. In the process of its collapse, utilitarianism will show its power; people are all full of a terrible lust for material things. It is a terrible process changing from a poor person to a rich one. Just you remember: Desperate times call for desperate measures, and that's the truth. Someone like you shouldn't apply their conscience to everything: How much is your conscience by the pound, anyway? If the guys at the top are cheating people in business and everyone's being tricked, what morality is there left to speak of? Don't go acting stupid and always looking before you leap, as if you're afraid there's a tiger on your tail. Always thinking about how whatever you do may affect the group, even worrying if people will talk about you if you wear a new skirt—aren't you tired of it? You haven't the slightest sense of self. The tragedy lies in the fact that you are neither this nor that.

She went on and on, as if I was barely even human.

I never imagined that she was a theorist. It came in spiels. You'd never think there was so much going on in there, to look at those clear eyes of hers. I certainly looked at her with new eyes. Sometimes she really wound me up. I'd like to have a big argument with her, then never speak to her ever again. But there's nothing I can do about that laughing face and slippery tongue of hers. I just keep on putting up with it. I am a masochist, I deserve everything I get, I look for trouble. I've nothing to complain about.

One day, we were out shopping for groceries when she started laying into me again, saying my ideas were all wrong. What day and age was it to be trying to get rich by scrimping and saving?

I argued back, I don't want to get rich.

She went on regardless, you're always buying cheap food products, they'll only make you fat. You have to eat good quality foodstuffs or you'll just look stupid, don't you get it?

Her slender waist swayed as she walked down the street, turning the heads of several men. Their narrowed eyes sized her body up and down, and she was just thoroughly pleased with herself, her arm entwined with mine and blind to it all. A pair of beautiful almond-shaped Asian eyes stared at me as she said: The trends have changed now, just look at the rich foreigners, they're all lean, they eat health foods, if they're rich they go to the gym. A lucky egg is several times more expensive than an ordinary egg—do you know what a lucky egg is? She gave me a sideways look. I stared blankly at her and shook my head. She said a lucky egg contains no chemicals; the mother hens can run about just as they please, they are free and go wherever they'd like to go. They are eggs that aren't from chickens that are locked up in a cage, fed at set times and given steroids to make them put on weight. Only the eggs laid by chickens that eat only natural foodstuffs are called 'lucky eggs'. Her explanation was so deeply scientific; it left me speechless. Then she went on—she wasn't finished yet—only poor people are fat, because they eat too much rubbish and they don't know how to take care of themselves properly.

She told me pointedly, you'll never get rich on that little bit of money you save from going into your mouth. Your ideas are too old-fashioned, they must be changed.

She just went on and on until I was reeling, completely speechless. Sometimes she made me feel really ashamed of myself as if I was a real country bumpkin. Yet in fact I grew up walking on tarmac roads just like she did.

Just then she said she was feeling hungry. I went to the kitchen to fry an egg and cook some noodles. I especially fried some greens for her, in case she felt it was not a very nutritious meal. When I returned to the living room there were newspapers and magazines strewn all over the tea table, sofa and carpet. I said, Dreamer, pick those things up, don't just leave them lying about all over the place. She said, you keep the house so tidy it feels like a hotel, totally lacking in the personal touch. A bit of a mess gives a place the feeling of being lived in. She answered my request by having a go at me, I was utterly speechless. Sometimes I really don't know why I bother with her. I ought to drive her out of the house right now, just like her father did. I merely looked at her, my head bowed and speechless. She was sitting on the sofa eating with gusto. She flicked through a magazine as she ate the fried egg and slurped the soup and said, what are these idiots in the paper doing, always complaining about their own troubles. There's no end to the rubbish about the stupid Cultural Revolution. How they were forced to lead miserable lives, cheated by others—a right bunch of weak and pitiable women. Why don't they talk about how they're in the red now, or how well they got on under that system. They always have to make out that someone's out to get them, as if they were the worst off in the whole world. What is it with Chinese people, do you think they took the wrong medicine? Everyone wants to be the victim. Who's the one dishing it out then? No matter how they're getting along, they all bemoan their fate. This world leaves you with nowhere to turn, life is hard on me, indeed. Suddenly she began to sing a popular song, "Who are they? Who are they?" I found her overriding impression that she was the only one on earth worthy of respect quite unconscionable.

Her little face remained just as beautifully childlike and innocent as ever.

One evening, Dreamer came bursting in, steaming red in the face. As soon as she was in the door she was tripping over herself to get the words out: Tonight we're going to a concert, I had to really flutter my eyelashes to get hold of these two tickets. Her honesty was both adorable and terrifying, I don't know how to explain the feelings I had for her. Her eyes were sparkling. I could easily imagine how she had flirted. This little tart would balk at nothing to get what she wanted, I have absolutely no doubt of that.

I spoke politely but without a shred of sincerity; you really didn't have to go to all that trouble.

She narrowed her eyes as she smiled at me. I made a superhuman effort just so that I could introduce you to what is called modern music. This band is red-hot in Beijing right now, they are one of the most happening bands about. Just their name is enough to knock you out—Cobra! They're all girls, they're really cool. She was so excited she danced about. Tonight is a very special moment. I have to get ready. You go and change as well, do yourself up a bit, don't always embarrass me by dressing like an old waiting woman. As she spoke, she tore into the room she was staying in like a gust of wind. She spoke to me as if I were her Grandma. From the inner room a romantic and innocent little song wafted out:

See-saw dickory-door
They're singing a song at Grandma's house,
What are they singing about?
About all the bullshit in the beef buns.

I was shocked. She could pick up on whatever I was thinking, like an electronic signal. How would I be able to keep any secrets from now on?

I shook my head and walked into the kitchen to make some dinner. We could eat it when she came out, you can't go to a concert on an empty stomach after all.

Dreamer dithered about inside her room for a full two hours.

I shouted, Dreamer, it's time to eat; if you leave it any longer it'll get cold.

She replied from within her room, coming, coming.

She appeared in the doorway of the inner room and struck a pose with her legs spread apart. I was struck dumb. You're wearing that?

What about it, she said

I said, Dreamer, quite regardless of the weather, aren't you in the least worried about getting a rash?

The way she had done herself up was just terrifying to me. She had put on black lipstick and painted her fingernails black. She was topless beneath a black leather jacket with approximately one hundred zips upon it. The main zipper on the front was pulled up to just an inch above her navel and a pair of pert breasts were just visible. On her bottom half she was wearing a leather super-mini skirt, a pair of black stockings sheathed her straight legs, her feet were encased in a pair of heavy boots. Her hair was black and glossy, her face as smooth as marble; the contrast was striking. I thought she might be the only one of her kind in the whole city of Beijing. She was one of a kind, a unique being. She wouldn't stop until she'd shocked you into a stroke.

I said, Dreamer, I wouldn't dare walk down the street with you in this get-up.

She said, who cares if you don't go. I never imagined you were such a conservative type. Do you know what tonight is? A monster's ball, with all the local celebs, meeting for a moment to show off what they've got, and what am I? I'm just a small potato, that's all. I thought I'd show you something of the world, I had no idea you would be such a spoil sport.

She really told me off.

After a moment's pause, Dreamer turned to me and said, what about you, then?

I went obediently to my closet, took out a dress with sky blue dots on a white background, and walked to the bathroom. I changed my clothes, washed my face and even applied a little blusher. I brushed my hair and furtively applied a light red lipstick and secretively looked myself over in the mirror, I'd do, I thought. Going out with a hardened character like Dreamer you had to make the extra effort and do yourself up a bit, otherwise you'd be in for another telling off.

I walked into the living room full of a confident air. Dreamer was sitting on the sofa, one ankle propped up on the other knee like a young hoodlum, gazing about with a look of utter boredom. I had imagined that Dreamer would lavish praise on me for how nice I looked. Who would have thought that when she saw me come in she would just shake her head at me. This outfit is just too run of the mill. No, it won't do. She condemned me with all the cruelty of a judge passing sentence. She said that one must exhibit one's individuality in the clothes and makeup that one chooses. This get-up is much too mass culture. Not just common, but entirely tasteless. Come, come, come, let me help make you over a little. She walked straight up to my closet and opened the doors. Her eyes roved like a radar, up and down over the contents. She shot her hand in and drew out a raw silk, emerald green robe, sleeveless and neckless. She said, try this on.

I panicked, Dreamer, that's utterly impossible, this is a nightie that I bought for three *yuan* years ago. It's foreign leftovers! It's so low-cut, it's only a second meant for export. How could I wear this out on the street? Don't make me look a fool!

She said, don't worry about that. Then she spun round and rummaged for a long while in her own pile of clothes and pulled out a black silk waistcoat and made me put on. Then she ordered me to change into a pair of black high-heels. With a curious look on her face, she said, now, go look in the mirror.

When I looked at myself in the mirror I couldn't believe my eyes. Was that me? The long emerald nightie fell to my feet, it looked just right with the little black waistcoat. I looked elegant, not in the least over the top but just right, very much in tune with my character. Even a cheap three *yuan* nightie could become a ball gown with Dreamer's help! I could not help but admire her talent.

Dreamer stood with her arms akimbo as she continued in a snobbish voice. You usually do yourself up like nothing in particular, like a big country bumpkin. It's just so unnecessary. Look what a nice slim figure you have, why don't you show it off? Your clothes say something about your upbringing and character; they prove your individual style and taste. It's not about how much money you spend or how high class the clothes are. You have to understand the combination of colors and their interrelation; what clothes go with what shoes; what sort of bag and belt to match. These little details are of vital importance. If you slip up on these details it'll be instantly obvious that this person has no clue of aesthetics. There's so much to learn. I'll give you a proper lesson some other time. She made a flippant gesture, as if to say, that goes without mentioning.

Listening to this speech of Dreamer's was as good as attending ten years of lectures, I had no choice but to submit to her wisdom.

Following that, she made a generous sweep of her hand and said I'll give this waistcoat to you. In the future, don't always dress up like an army rat.

I felt thoroughly ashamed of myself, I nodded my head without pausing.

After what felt like a lot of wrangling, we finally left the house. The moment Dreamer appeared on the street she was greeted with a round of whistles from a bunch of little hooligans; I dragged her swiftly across the road.

She said, what are you afraid of? She walked on the street as if she were the only person there; she was eye-catching.

All the way along people were staring at us from all sides. I was accosted by all kinds of glances; I felt my scalp tingle and the muscles in my face twitch. Dreamer had her arm in mine and was striding on confidently. From this alone you could see that Dreamer and I were boxing in totally different weight categories.

When we reached the concert hall it was already packed out. People were thronging about; it was an experience like no other. Even in such a big concert hall, Dreamer was making waves, although there were several other alluring little creatures, Dreamer was top of the class. Her get-up was certainly unique. They broke the mold when they made her. She flitted about amongst the crowd, many men were leering at her like hungry wolves; she got more lingering looks than anyone else. Some gave her nasty looks as well, as if to show that they weren't in the least interested. It was just as well there was air conditioning in the concert hall, otherwise I'd have been seriously concerned about Dreamer passing out.

The concert was so modern, it was my first experience of such a thing. The music was deafening, cries filled the air. A few perfectly attractive little things were straining their voices on the stage, leaping about like little she-devils. They shouted so hard that the veins stood out on their necks and their faces turned red. It was clear that they were going to damage their vocal chords. I felt really sorry for them. Why couldn't they just sing nicely, instead of going and ruining their image. Their clothes were covered in gold sequins, they sparkled beneath the halogen lights, dazzling the eyes. I finally understood why Dreamer got herself done up like she did. She wanted to follow the pop stars, even to lead the trends of fashion. Actually, Dreamer had gone right ahead and outstripped the performers in her provocative attire. So, that is what they mean by the saying, 'the pupil outdoes the master.'

I had had quite enough of the concert. The thunderous crashing of drums and cymbals almost interrupted the rhythm of my heart. If the music had gone on any longer, I was afraid that my heart would have burst.

The concert finally wound up, but Dreamer was still full of excitement, she was jiggling all over. She walked over to me trembling from top to toe, and seemed full of herself as she asked me what I thought of it. It was as if she'd just stepped off stage herself. I replied in a despondent tone that I didn't think much of it, that there was nothing to get excited about. I went cruelly on, just to get my dissatisfaction well and truly off my chest; it would be more accurate to call it noise and not music. Dreamer could not believe her ears. She glared at me, then heaved a great sigh, oh, you're just beyond all help, there's absolutely nothing to be done with you. I'm so sorry I wasted that ticket on you, I could have given it to someone who gets it; this is modern music! Can you understand that you bitch? Are you a stuck-in-the-mud bitch or what! She began to raise her voice to me.

I said, Dreamer, watch your mouth, could you not keep calling me 'you bitch'.

I just can't stand that you're so entirely beyond help!

I don't want to understand this kind of modern music. I'd get more peace without it.

You're full of yourself.

You can't force someone to change their tastes.

You're being stubborn conservative.

If I am, then I am.

I hate stubborn conservatism; it is the sworn enemy of modern art.

She was so angry her face had grown several shades paler.

People on the street were looking right at us.

I said, Dreamer, let's not argue.

This is a matter of principle; I can't back down.

I knew that our bickering could go on and on. In the end, I capitulated, telling myself that I was a few years older than her, my views were different to hers. But I felt a weight on my heart.

I thought, she would rather die than try to understand why I'm so out of touch, so behind the times on everything. I'm such a disappointment to her.

That night we parted on bad terms. We each felt wronged by the other.

It was a beautiful day, the sky was blue with white clouds. Dreamer came and went in knee-high red boots, no one was telling her what to do. She had already been staying at my place for one and a half months. She was awfully busy every single day, even when she walked about she would have her headphones on and nod and move to the music. She was feeling good about herself. On a gloriously sunny morning, I told Dreamer she ought to move back to her place, or at least go and check in on her family. She turned her beautiful almond eyes upon me and stared at me for a long time, then said, I'm doing you a big favor by staying here, you know.

I asked her, whatever do you mean?

She continued without flinching, it's doing wonders for improving your self confidence. I think you've made a lot of progress, don't you?

I had not imagined that she would answer me like this. My voice died in my throat and I was silent for quite some time.

Finally I said, Dreamer, that's a bit rich coming from you.

It was obvious I was about to lose my temper, she immediately changed her tone of voice, saying, alright then Big Sis.

Just let me stay on a little longer. I'm going to pay you back eventually anyway.

I softened my tone, there's no need for that kind of generosity.

She opened her eyes wide and spoke seriously, surely you've noticed that I'm going to go far in this life, I've already seen that much myself.

I looked lost and said, no, I hadn't noticed, actually.

She pointed to her forehead with a solemn expression, have a good look. Have you ever seen such a full forehead? My lucky star's flying higher than anyone else's. I stared at myself in the mirror for ages last Wednesday, and I concluded that it's one of a kind. Just trust me, I wouldn't lie to you. A gentleman doesn't go back on his word, we'll just have to wait and see.

I stared at her blankly, I felt as if I were talking to a maniac.

Dreamer got up and spun round, saying she had something urgent to attend to and strutted off. Just as she was closing the door, she turned back and blew me a kiss.

Our discussion had ended.

That ridiculous conversation taught me a lesson: A dog's got no business trying to catch mice.

I didn't know whether I ought to laugh or cry over having invited such a precious creature into my house. As the proverb says, "it's easier to invite someone into your house, than to get them to leave."

Dreamer continued to come and go about the house as if she hadn't the least care in the world. I had to admire her callous disregard for what others thought of her. In order to preserve the excellent traditions of the Chinese people, I had no choice but to "accompany Buddha all the way to the Western Heavens." And so I decided not to say anything else. My husband said that Dreamer and I were starting to seem a bit gay. He actually hasn't the vaguest idea about homosexuality. It's just that he can't imagine how I could spend such a vast amount of patience on this relationship, and so he decides that it is homosexual in nature. Maybe there's something in that. Sometimes I will put my hand across quite unconsciously to touch her soft little face and the way her youthful body dances about before me makes me feel a little of the energy of youth again, but that's all. There's no actual sexual content. It's pushing it to say that I'm attracted to women. I just believe that women are there to be appreciated and men are there to be experienced. I don't think this harms my relationship with my husband in the slightest. We pass our days safely in peace and quiet; we live in a super-stable structure. My attitude towards Dreamer is the result of my primitive maternal desires acting up. I don't know why we always wind up hanging out together. I often feel as if she is at least two hundred years younger than me. She will always be like a child to me. Perhaps that is the drive of mother's love you mentioned? Who knows.

One day, I dreamt that my womb flew out of my body, it made a great big circle floating in midair. Inside it was springing full of wild grasses and lilies. Little boys and girls were playing hide n' seek inside and playing in the water. It was like a modern amusement park. I decided that there must be something wrong with my womb and I decided to go and see a doctor about it. I spent a whole three hours queuing in the gynecology department because I was waiting for the most experienced doctor there. The expert consultant came in wearing glasses, his hair salt and pepper white. He made me take off my trousers and lay down on the bed. To begin with I was a little embarrassed; it was the first time in my life I'd taken my clothes off in front of any man besides my husband. But I couldn't go getting any funny ideas in front of this doctor, that would be the lowest of the low. The old doctor was quiet and kind. When he was making a thorough investigation, he looked at me over his short-sightedness glasses as he washed his hands and told me that he had never seen such a smooth womb. He told me not to worry, I was positively burgeoning with fertility. I had always regarded my womb with fond regard. I thought of it as a rose: fresh, pink and overflowing with fragrance. I am often asked what brand of perfume I wear. I tell them I've never worn perfume in my life. What's more, my husband can't stand women that get themselves all done up. My plain and dowdy outfits, my mouse-like timidity and my cautious nature all suit him down to the ground.

I rode home beaming with the flush of youth and told my husband the good news.

His face was expressionless, he asked, was the doctor a man or a woman?

I answered, it was a man.

With a face as dark as iron he said that sometimes my behavior was so ridiculous that there were simply no words to describe it.

He seemed very angry, but he didn't explain why. I guessed he was probably upset because I took my clothes off in front of another man. He's very conservative and old-fashioned about that kind of thing. I thought to myself, one of the reasons he married me in the first place was because he could tell that my hymen was intact. We had sexual relations before marriage, and it didn't seem an especially holy experience. The first time when he found that I had bled, he simply jumped for joy. He held me in his arms and said it was just too beautiful, that he must make me his wife. Up until today I still remember the way his face was contorted with joy. We only did it that one time before marriage, then we organized a shotgun marriage, as if we were holding a solemn ceremony for my freshly broken hymen. We treated all of our friends and relatives in the town to drink themselves drunk for three days straight. He broke the bank, was it for my purity alone? Afterwards I thought, perhaps that time he was testing me to see if I was a virgin, and what if I wasn't? Would he have cast me off? Now that I think of it, it's rather detestable. Of course these are all things I thought of later. The me of eight years ago was pure and pathetic, with no idea about this thing called individuality. That whole affair is a secret wound in my heart. I can't talk about it to anyone. I cannot ask too much of life, after all you have to learn to be happy with what you've got. That's what my mother told me time after time. My husband demands that I remain faithful to him alone, and innocent. He says that, strictly speaking, it's for the sake of our home. He's said that to me on several occasions. Without his existence, this home would be nothing more than an abstract notion. He makes everything sound so official, so bound by rules. I never can find anything logical or clever to say back to him. However, I feel the presence of an indistinct threat lurking. Where does it come from? I don't know where to begin.

*Don't ask me where I come from, my fate is far, far away from here.**

As soon as I began to sing this song, Dreamer cried, oh please! You're caterwauling again!

She always gets right to the heart of things, she's just too sharp and crafty as a fox.

Dreamer didn't make an appearance at my house for a whole week. As previously when she'd stayed with me, she'd "go out fishing for three days then dry her nets for two", I once asked her out of friendly concern where she was going. She got in such a state, she turned quite pale. I didn't understand what I had done wrong. She said that Chinese people are completely ignorant about respecting a person's privacy, she doesn't have to tell me her private business. In the future I was not to go about blindly

---

* The 1979 song The Olive Tree sung by Taiwanese singer Qi Yu speaks about finding a sense of belonging when living in a foreign land. The lyrics were written by famous Taiwanese authoress San Mao, who spent time living in Spain.

asking questions about other people's private lives. I must learn how to respect a person's independence. There I was being told off by her again over nothing. I don't know where she got so many character flaws from; sometimes she could just drive you crazy. I'm not her mother, why should I be concerned with her. Her real mum and dad couldn't get anywhere with her, what chance did I stand? After that she was simply uncontrollable. She wore things that were so beyond the pale even I couldn't stand it. Usually I don't like to go making mountains out of molehills, especially when it comes to clothes. With Dreamer's encouragement I even imagined that I was becoming full of modern ideas. I liked to see young girls done up nicely making people glad to see them. Then Dreamer took a pair of jeans she'd just bought for over one hundred *yuan* and cut great big holes into them without even batting an eyelid. She had every intention of revealing her buttocks for everyone to see, what an idea!

Now, it's not that I don't know how to mind my own business, but that was going too far. She said that was a style, that's precisely the effect that she was going for. All the young artists abroad were doing it. You just don't get it, she said. I was just a rustic country bumpkin in her eyes. She's seen this "style" in several imported foreign movies, when in truth that style of dressing had already gone out of fashion abroad, and still she was full of it. If she wasn't there in front of me I wouldn't bother myself—out of sight out of mind.

Days without Dreamer in the house were astonishingly peaceful, my husband and I both left the house in the morning and came back in the evening, rising in the morning and going to bed at night. It was as if the atmosphere in our house had condensed. I almost felt that something was lacking and for several days I simply could not settle. I was always thinking about it on my way to work, I thought I ought to go and look for her. After all, she set out from my place, I am responsible for her actions. I had nowhere to go to ask after her movements because I didn't know a single one of her friends. All I could do was give Dreamer's father a call on my way to work one morning. He said that she had come home to pick up some clothes and there had been no trace of her since. I knew about that already, that had happened before she went off from mine.

Her father had asked where she was going.

She said to him, you told me to clear off. Now I will.

Her father sighed down the telephone, how could I have raised such a bad seed.

I mumbled a few words of comfort and hung up as soon as I could. I was getting worried as well. I didn't know where the little baggage could have gotten herself to. I stood staring off into space before the public telephone booth. Oh, how could we be so different when we are only six years apart in age? She's positively heartless. She just goes off, with no regard as to who might be worrying about her. The world does not exist for her and her alone. How could she do such a thing? She's so high and mighty! I really can't stand such selfish people, only concerned with their own happiness, with no thought for others. I resolved not to give her another thought from then on.

After Dreamer's disappearance, my life returned to normal. My husband was very happy with me during that period. He said when you were together with Dreamer you were always a bit crazy. Our house was always turned upside down as if it had been ransacked by the Red Guard. Now I had gotten the house spotlessly clean again. Every month I will be a bit of a clean freak for just a few days. For those few days I'll wash whatever I can get my hands on. I end up exhausted and aching all over, and then I get moody. Nothing suits me and I go crazy, emotionally fragile. I cry over nothing and my husband is victim to much of it. He doesn't know what to do with me, he's quite helpless. He makes it clear that he has no idea what to do about my abnormal behavior. He often says that women are monsters. For the first week of my period there is a constant ringing in my ears, a dark oppressive droning.

> *Fly away locust,*
> *Fly away and land again,*
> *Land and eat everything,*
> *Then fly away to who knows where* *

I was suddenly possessed by the notion that I was no longer human, I was a locust. I decided that I was a locust. Pushkin used this poem to make a veiled criticism about corruption in the days of Tsarist Russia. Although I'm by no means a corrupt official, I decided that I am, in fact, a locust. I get wrapped up in these hysterical thoughts sometimes. Whenever one of these moments is upon me I find myself wound up tight. I tell

---

* The Russian poet Alexander Pushkin sent to Odessa in 1823 to make a report on locusts, which were plaguing the area. The report was never produced, but he did write this poem based on his experiences there.

myself over and over again: I must control myself, I mustn't let myself go. However, this determination often works against me. I think to myself, I'm still a long way away from my menopause, and I'm already losing it, won't I just drive myself to death when I do reach that age. I'd do better putting an end to it all while I'm still young. Apart from the cleaning frenzy, the ringing in my ears and the hysteria; an even more terrifying phenomenon will occur. I will wage war on my hair, I will wash my hair and body innumerable times, as if I was getting myself nice and clean and ready for death. Naturally enough, some hairs will fall out when I wash my hair. Then I will crouch down on the floor and look for them, one by one, unwilling to let a single one of my lost hairs go. I crouch on the floor like a locust eating hairs, mumbling to myself as I go, where did all these hairs come from? On several occasions I have stood in front of the mirror, scissors in hand and been on the point of cutting all my hair off. That's a very dangerous thing to do! I'm really worried that one day I'll lose control and do something ill-conceived like that. When Dreamer was around I never experienced this periodically abnormal behavior. We were always arguing about something, she would always be snappy, and the time passed quickly. Annoying as she could be sometimes, you could say that we were pretty happy together. One time I brought home a calendar with pictures of the big stars on it. They were giving them out at work; I don't have enough money laying around to buy that sort of thing. It had big color pictures of movie stars printed bigger than life size. I flicked through looking intently at each one of the beautiful people. Dreamer came over to see what I was up to and I asked her which one she admired the most. She put her head on one side, pursed her lips and thought for a while, then said Pan Hong. I hadn't expected that at all. I asked her why. She said that she didn't think anything of her acting, she just liked the way she looked. I never imagined that Dreamer could appreciate that kind of sickly beauty, but it turned out to be quite the opposite to what I thought. She said she really liked that kind of melancholy beauty, it was tender and mournful, one couldn't help but be taken by it. Sometimes I really can't figure Dreamer out. There are many inharmonious facets to her character. According to her usual behavior she ought not to like that kind of image, she ought to go for the bold and daring type. I just couldn't understand it. She never complained about anything really, but one day her delicate eyes teared up in front of me. I asked her what was wrong, but she wouldn't say. To this day I don't know what upset her that day. Dreamer and I only ever talked about things of little importance, with no depth whatsoever. My husband came home late every night. He loved his job with a greater passion than he loved me. We'd been married for eight years and I've completely forgotten what it is like to feel jealous. I was already totally numb towards my marriage. It was as if we were two trees grown apart but so tangled together at the roots that we could never be separated out. It had already become second nature. I'm not sure if that's a good thing or not. Dreamer had one misconception: How could a person only have one love in this life, how boring! How could feelings be unchanging? The very idea of "Exclusivity" is old-fashioned, only by constantly changing can our feelings be said to be full of a modern awareness. The high divorce rate alone shows that people are developing a sense of self value, which is the mark of social progress. Sticking together when the feelings are gone is the real cruelty. When it came to love, Dreamer really could talk a load of nonsense. She believes that our generation's ideas about love are far outdated. She didn't think that getting into bed and sleeping with a man was any big thing. She said that men can separate sleeping together and love, women ought to be able to separate love and sex as well. If you go to bed with a man because you love him, it's easy to become a slave to your feelings. Only if you can get past that point will you be able to be master of your own emotions, now that is a true spiritual leap for a woman. She plays about with several boyfriends at once; she says that's the only way to allow herself to choose. On top of that, the equal division of emotions is the embodiment of universal love. It's nothing worth hanging yourself from a tree for.* The Chinese so-called honorable traditions say that growing old and gray together is the only form of true love, it's such a cliché, utter rubbish. It's repression of human nature through and through. People are three-dimensional, they have many facets. Some people's characters are naturally fractured and it would be awfully cruel to demand that they change. She also says that the idea of "trial marriage" invented in Western countries is highly scientific. That is to say, living together but not getting married.

---

* Referring to the cultural phenomenon of threatening or even executing suicidal acts in order to emotionally manipulate relationships, especially intimate ones.

If it works, then you can stay together, if it doesn't then you can just forget about it. If one morning you wake up and feel a need for belonging, it's never too late to go seek that out. She had a lot of funny ideas; I couldn't keep up with her at all. My husband and I stuck together like a pair of old cats, nothing much happened between us. There were lots of things I didn't tell him about, not because I had anything to hide from him, but because he wasn't interested in what I had to say, it was just a load of nagging women's stuff to him. He spent far more time with the computer than with me. I could barely keep myself from doing something really romantic, like throwing a great big boulder into the dead waters of our home and making some tidal waves. But I only have the heart of a criminal, not the guts of one.* I don't dare to make a move, not like Dreamer who dared to talk the talk and walk the walk. I'm too afraid of the consequences, I'm afraid of becoming the subject of gossip, of facing the criticism of others, of being irresponsible towards my home life. Why must I have such a strong sense of responsibility? Why can't I live as free and easy as Dreamer does? I find it very hard to explain these things. Our generation has been created to find it utterly impossible to be irresponsible. We simply couldn't live with ourselves if we were. And yet, there's only six years age difference between Dreamer and I! There must be some problem with me, that's all it could be. Nowadays whatever I do, I do it alone, my husband and I don't interfere with each other. Sometimes I feel as if my husband were a stranger, like a tree at the other end of the earth. He is very distant to

---

* The original Chinese phrase is "to have the heart of a criminal but not the gallbladder", because the gallbladder, traditionally, is the seat of courage and decisiveness.

me. I am very lonely. I don't like to use the word "lonely," it seems so sentimental. I wish I were a cold-blooded animal, no feelings, never defeated by my emotions. Dreamer says that that is right, it is of vital importance to maintain a distance with people, you can avoid a lot of unnecessary trouble that way. Maintaining a distance is the mark of civilization, that kind of inseparable, 'what's yours is mine and what's mine is yours' relationship, will only wind up in a battle to the death, with the closest of brothers becoming bitter enemies. You can see that sort of tragedy all over the place. Brothers add up their differences clearly—a discussion between gentlemen is as clear as water. These old Chinese sayings* are so cool! Therefore, shouldn't a husband and wife also keep some distance? That distance is absolutely necessary; it helps you to see the other person more clearly. You must have a sense of space. Leave a little corner of your heart, just for you and don't let anyone in there. It will be something that belongs to you yourself alone. That's the only way you can remain relatively independent, full of mystery, and more attractive. She made a frivolous gesture with her hand as she spoke. Privately I agreed with what she said, but I didn't let it show. She quite forgets herself when she knows she's in the right and I didn't want to encourage her bad ways. I really did learn a lot from her. I am truly grateful to her, and so she points out another of my faults, always being "grateful." That's not a good thing you know, you have to give it up. That kind of attitude will put you in a weak position. Imagine if you were always in a position of gratitude, people would look down on you. You'd never

---

* The two above phrases are traditional Chinese sayings of an idealistic nature, where family members are impartial to family affection and nepotism, and interaction between learned souls is never angry or convoluted. They give a hint to the kinds of phenomena that such ideals are intended to counter.

be on an equal footing with other people, and equality with others is very important. I asked her, surely you don't expect me to return bad for good? She said, you're really hopeless, can't you do anything properly? Do you have to take everything at face value, one good turn deserves another? Do you have to put yourself in such a low position? Don't be stupid! She told me off over and over again for being lacking in self awareness. I was just a serial failure in her eyes and it really wound her up. She said that people in this day and age are too practical-minded, they just take advantage and lack any imagination or romantic color. Did you know, there were poets before and artists who spent their lives drifting amongst the cream of society, who would support their artistic creativity, Wagner, Rilke, they were all the same. Nowadays the rich have no conscience. When I am rich I'll definitely give a lot of support to artists. I taunted her, maybe you'll be even worse than them when you get rich. She threw her head back and laughed. I could see right down into her stomach. There was an eye down in her stomach that was winking right at me, with a crystalline, sparkling blue light. I squatted down on the floor with a pasty look on my face; Dreamer didn't understand what was going on and quickly asked me what was wrong. I gulped out, I saw an eye in your stomach, it was blue. She started laughing again, and said, well maybe.

Then she said, these funny thoughts of yours have given me a good idea actually. What idea?

You should set up an Imagination Club. Every night everyone would get together to tell stories and the most ridiculous stories would be the best. We ought to set up a big scholarship fund in support of wild fantasies.

Then she clapped her hands in delight! I just can't stand to see her always so full of herself.

Oh, what's wrong with me? All I can think about is Dreamer —why can't I just think about myself instead? For example, that time there were promotions at work and salaries were increased and housing improved and things like that, all practical improvements. You could see some people giving gifts left, right and center, some people cried and threw a temper, some even announced that they would jump off a building, to seek a better life through death. You weren't in the least bothered, which is not necessarily to say that you are so very above all that, but that you know deep down that you're simply not good enough. You know that to struggle would be in vain, you might as well just act like you don't care, become a pacifist—that's where my cunning lies. Some thoughtful people tried to persuade me, saying that I had worked there for more than ten years, why shouldn't I try for it, I ought to get what's coming to me. It's not like I don't have a place to live, and we're quite happy where we are. One go-getter is enough for a household, if we were both that smart we would end up arguing with each other every other day. Why should I go looking for trouble? I'd only be trying for nothing anyway, going at it to the death with other people, making a great big pile of enemies, getting my knickers in a twist over nothing, and for what? I'd do better just taking the high road. And so some people decided for themselves that I was really removed from material interests. Dreamer said that she liked my calmness, but in fact that's no such thing. In truth, I'm at odds with the world over all sorts of different things, it's just that I'm not usually in a position to show it. No doubt when the time comes they'll all come pouring out and there'll be no stopping them. My colleagues at work think I am calm and helpless. If they knew how I go crazy at home they'd think differently. Very differently indeed.

Several months passed and I was lost in a state of wild imaginings. Dreamer had already disappeared completely from my sight. I didn't think of her anymore. I went about my business every day, showing no signs of being over-excited or upset. I rode my bike to work every day and home again at the end of the day. I was well-acquainted with the city, as familiar as I am with the organs of my own body. I could find my way home with my eyes closed.

Yesterday when I finished work, I suddenly rode off in the opposite direction of home as if on some strange mission. I rode about five stops when I saw a small restaurant, run down and without distinguishing features. I went in without knowing what I was doing. My hands were aching with the cold, my feet were numb, and I decided to have a hotpot. I started ordering a few things for the pot as if I were well-experienced at all that: Chinese cabbage, rice noodles, pickled tofu and a plate of raw lamb. Actually I like seafood, prawns and squid and things like that, but my purse wasn't fat enough for that, so I didn't dare to order them. The over-fed waitress, with the blood up in her face, answered me in sour Mandarin as if she couldn't really be bothered with serving me. Perhaps she was offended by my frugal order. I wasn't going to pay attention to any of it. I felt full after eating two mouthfuls. I looked up and everyone was in couples or in larger groups. I was the only one by myself and my status was a little unclear. I was neither at that age of lovely youth that attracts the careful attention of men, nor was I at the age of love's crisis, as a result I seemed more special, strange even. A few men at the next table were giving me sideways glances, as if I had come here on purpose looking for a bit of fun. If I were looking for that I think I'd have gone somewhere a bit higher class, like a five-star hotel, a three or four star would do—anywhere but this rough joint, those country bumpkins.

Actually, I very rarely eat out alone. I don't know why it was necessary for me to go so far out of my way to waste my money, the restaurant wasn't clean and had no atmosphere, the food was awful and I was being stared at to boot. I almost felt as if I was imitating Dreamer's style to some degree. Is it possible to imitate a style just as one chooses? It is a bit beyond the pale. I can no longer be held responsible for my actions! I was always so hard on myself, I needed to loosen up a bit. There—I found a perfectly good excuse for myself and my behavior.

The little restaurant was full of dark smoke, there was a cigarette hanging from the mouth of every man present. Smoke stung my eyes so that I could barely keep them open, but I still didn't want to go home. I saw everything around me in a haze;

the moon, the mist. My sense of self was on a once in a life-time high.

I got home very late. I made up a story as I went to tell my husband. I don't know why I told him a story; there was no reason for it whatsoever, but it just slipped right out.

I said, so-and-so's child was suddenly taken ill. It was quite serious, I went along with her to the emergency room, and that's why I came home late.

I was surprised by my talent for concocting stories, how could I possibly have created such a well-rounded tale at a moment's notice? I had never before realized before that I had such a talent. I felt as if I had discovered a buried treasure—I was wild with delight. I celebrated privately, in this instance at least I had gotten away with it, at the same time I felt a little guilty. But on the whole I was very pleased with myself for telling such a brilliant lie.

My husband didn't have the slightest shadow of a doubt. He just frowned and said that he hadn't had any dinner yet. And there I thought that I had escaped making dinner for one day, I hadn't imagined I'd still be stuck in that rut.

I shot into the kitchen and looked inside the fridge, only to find it empty. The only things left were two carrots from goodness knows when, already wrinkled almost beyond recognition, and an egg. And then I remembered that I had forgotten to go grocery shopping for at least a week. I had no idea how I was going to explain all this to my husband.

He spoke first, what is this modern rubbish you have been playing at? You've been all over the place recently. Look about you, the stove and pots are left standing cold—it just won't do. He looked about himself at our home, then stared at me without the least glimmer of light in his eyes, and said, a person ought to be clear about their position in life, you're at the age now when you ought to be well-settled*, why is it you seem to get more mixed up the older you get? Copying that crazy little tart Dreamer, are you made of that kind of stuff? Would you dare to go running about the streets with half your tits hanging out?

He told me off in a tone of voice that sounded as if he were telling off his grandson.**

I had no desire to answer back. At the pit of my stomach lay everything that I wanted to say, yet I remained exceptionally calm as I waited for the final judgment.

As husband and wife we're not very good at arguing. Whenever we disagree on something we fight each other with a nearly unbearable silence, I used the same weapon again this time.

He looked at me with impatience; I remained leaning against the kitchen door frame, still as a statue. He turned around and went into the bedroom without switching on the light.

I stood there struck dumb for a moment until I got tired of it, then I walked to the bedroom and lay down beside him.

I have always been good at making compromises. I never stick by my principles. That's my philosophy on life. It's a real mess.

---

* He refers to a quote from the *Analects* of Confucius, where 40 is the age at which one should be established in life.
** Grandson is considered a slur in Chinese, not because of any negative implications beyond that if you're the grandson you're low in the pecking order and must listen to your elders, who have the option of telling you off.

I didn't feel in the least sleepy. I lay with my eyes open, staring at the ceiling. The crisp winter moonlight shone in, turning the whole room a deep, melancholy blue, a spooky feeling filled the room. I gave an involuntary shiver.

He lay at my side and gently asked me what was wrong. So he hadn't gone to sleep either. I said nothing was wrong, he put out his hand and just like that we made up.

Every time we end up leaving things unsettled. It's not that I like to brush a problem away, it's just that I cannot take control of the situation.

He began to set forth a theory to me in all seriousness. He said that every person has a role to play in life. For starters you are whatever you act, and that will be very difficult to change. It could scar you for life.

What he meant was, if I wanted to change what I was, I'd have to destroy our home.

I have lived with him for many years, constantly accepting hints like that. I don't know if other couples are the same, but we have never had a single open and honest discussion. My powers of speech wilt before him. There is always some game behind his words, just like a bureaucrat playing political games, he was indescribably skilful with his words.

It's a bit mean of me to describe my husband like that; maybe I'm being too harsh.

Perhaps now you see that I am an odd character through and through?

I don't know what it's like to share a pillow with a man

yet dream my own dreams,* because no other man has ever appeared in my life up until now, so I have no means of comparison. He says I'm out of sorts. I only know that I've done a good enough job, that I'm basically satisfied with myself and that's a feeling I very rarely experience.

Lying. Going to restaurants alone. Showing a certain degree of independence, a bit of what I say goes—if Dreamer knew she would no doubt be pleased too.

Neither of us really know how to appreciate nature, we're obviously a very boring couple. We've never been for a walk at dusk, even though our home is right next to the canal. On summer evenings, silhouettes of lovers come and go until the depths of the night. If you looked down from our window, it's an exhibition of love: heated, sweet, moving, unforgettable. You couldn't help but get a little hot under the collar. In order to avoid such provocation, I very rarely go to the windowsill and look down below, that way I won't get over-excited. I don't remember the process of our falling in love at all, it's as if there was not one outing to the suburbs, not one picnic, no flowers or moonlight, only one practical examination and we became man and wife. There's no rationale to my complaints, and he's not entirely to blame. Even though I have certain desires, I never let them show. They are hidden in a particular corner, coming into effect from time to time, so that my husband and I remain distanced beneath our peaceable appearance, and I persistently refuse to talk about it. My husband isn't a saint, how could he know what it is that I want? I always try to make him be the first to express himself; in

---

* 'Same pillow different dreams' is a Chinese saying that is usually negative, that is to share a marital bed and have opposing, deceitful or secret ideas, but Yoyo subverts the traditional phrase here in the light of modern ideas of individuality.

matters of love it should be the man who makes the first move, but he is an introspective character, always lost deep in thought. I don't know why I insist on repressing myself. Nature? Yes, and then no. There is a terrible restlessness concealed beneath my peaceful appearance, sometimes I find it hard to contain and to control. It really puts me through it. I have revealed a little of my dissatisfaction to Dreamer in the past. Dreamer attacked me, saying that my ideas were outdated. She said the modern day is not the Qin Dynasty, men and women are the same as each other. Long ago, Chairman Mao proclaimed that women hold up half of heaven. How can you be so foolish? If I were to have my eye on someone I wouldn't pay any mind to two plus two makes four—I'd make an instant attack, keep pursuing them until they were mine, and when I'd had enough—I'd kick them to one side, that's called the liberation of women. We've got to as far as we can in the opposite direction to right the balance. Especially Chinese women, we have been oppressed by three big mountains*, as well as by the rights of our husbands and fathers. We need to go after it with all the more energy, to make up this lesson that we've missed. Of course it will require a certain amount of skill, you've been there you ought to understand—you don't need me to go on talking rubbish at you. But, when a person hasn't the courage to express their own emotions they're obviously just being timid; the very mark of a lack of self-confidence. So far as I've seen, this politeness between you and your husband is no good thing. There is a hidden danger present in it, pardon me, but you must have

* Revolutionary political rhetoric, standing for imperialism, feudalism, bureaucratic capitalism.

seen that too? Her questions had me tongue-tied. I came to myself after a moment, I respectfully replied, surely you don't expect us to come to blows over such things? She said how come you always take such a vulgar view of things, emotions are subtle. Having a fight wouldn't necessarily be a bad thing, not fighting is not necessarily a good thing either. It's a paradox. Something you both know but don't care to mention. You know it, he knows it, heaven and earth know it. You're a part of this, you're certainly clearer than me, so please don't fool yourself. She went straight for blood, catching me right where it hurt. But, afterwards I thought about it—Dreamer is still far too young. She's immature, she doesn't understand the subtle relationship between a husband and a wife, she sees things much too simply. I'm a part of it, and even I can't say whether it's happy or sad. A middling stance is the most prudent position, it's really all there is to it. Most couples preserve a spirit of compromise, cooperating with each other, overlooking some conflicts, avoiding some things. Coming to blows about a problem and letting everything out only ends up with both parties getting hurt. According to my own experience, there are no great truths to speak of between a husband and a wife. I only hope that the marriage question won't end in tears for Dreamer, I hope that she stays young and enjoys herself. She's too immature yet, she doesn't know how awful it is to be gossiped about, she doesn't understand how to keep a handle on the general situation, you have to know when to act if you want to be successful, slow and steady wins the race!

This speech makes me look as if I don't care for the big things in life or as if I understood the meaning of life—"Form itself is emptiness; emptiness itself is form." * The material world, heaven or hell; wherever you are, you've still got to take things one day at a time, I said to myself, spinning completely out of control. I began talking to myself about the house. I could only talk to myself, confirming my own ideas, otherwise I would go mad. I'm not one of those popular people at work that are good with words, so I had to find an outlet, traveling within myself, having crazy discourses with myself. My inner world was a crazy, fractured world. I lived and died within it. My inner world was an imaginary city, utterly void, yet full as a rich brocade. I walked in a city empty of people, in a desert that was a sea of people, with no conversation and no one to speak to. Only a woman who is quietly insane, who is only crazy when she is by herself, she is someone who dies in her fantasies.

I entirely forgot the existence of days. I decided that I did not want days. I didn't know whether it was winter or summer, maybe it was autumn or spring? The phenomenon of days ceased to exist. That doesn't prove that I was sick—I went to work and came home from work everyday as usual, I ate and slept everyday as usual. I couldn't remember if it was Monday or Sunday. I sat on the black corduroy sofa and stared at the ceiling, wracking my brains over what we would have for dinner that night. Just as I was straining to think, and getting

---

* A note of Zen Buddhist reductionism amongst the socio-political phrases that usually come to mind for the narrator. From the *Heart Sutra* or *Prajna Paramita Hrydaya Sutra*, a Buddhist text.

miserable about it, I suddenly felt a cool breeze behind me, the door was blown open gently and Dreamer appeared in a whoosh before my eyes. I was so startled that I cried out, I shrieked as if I had seen a ghost. Dreamer stood before me smiling radiantly, looking at me.

She spoke to me in a temperate voice, it's me, Dreamer.

Did you drop from the sky?

Think whatever you like.

She was as alluring as ever, entrancing, even though her hair had disappeared, every last hair, and her skull was dark and shiny. I saw that her heavenly eye was wide open, right down to her heels. Her whole body was translucent, her organs were entirely exposed. Her bald head was perfect in every way, like a fine, living dinosaur's egg. She had added the newest weaponry to her earlobes, there were hanging two huge earrings. I have never seen such big earrings in my life. They flashed with golden light under her earlobes, if it weren't for them it would be hard to tell discern her gender, anyhow it was either a lively young lad or a beautiful woman, unique and confident.

I seized Dreamer's shoulders and shook her back and forth, where did you go? You heartless creature.

She still greeted me with smiles, I went to the four corners of the earth, walking on clouds. She narrowed her eyes and gave me a flirtatious glance, she began to sing in a throaty voice, *the world outside is wonderful, the world outside leaves us no choice.**

---

* Lyrics by the grandfather of Chinese Rock and Roll, Cui Jian.

I interrupted her exaggerated performance. Dreamer, don't beat about the bush, hurry up and come out with it.

She looked at me seriously and said, do you really want to know?

My eyes shone with tears of earnest emotion, I nodded my head with all my might. She told me excitedly that she had gone off all by herself and joined a troupe, playing bit parts and generally helping out. They were met with a warm welcome wherever they went, and they didn't just go all over China, but also to Hong Kong, Japan, Singapore and Germany. Staying in big, fancy hotels, eating and drinking only the best, stuffing their pockets with money. As she spoke, she whipped out seven or eight notes. She went on to boast, from now on you don't need to go to work everyday, I'll look after you. I thought to myself, I would rather she were a pale and slender itinerant poet, drifting from place to place, driving a cart like a gypsy. Then I would walk through flames for her, I'd go to the very ends of the earth. Dreamer suddenly broke into a peal of laughter that made my hairs stand on end. She said, I know that your gross idealism is setting you off again, you're at the age you could be a mother now, how can you still be so innocent and childish. It's time you put away your useless romanticism and faced the facts, that's the only way to go. She was opening the case behind her as she spoke, and taking out beautiful articles of clothing and shaking them before me, saying that she was giving them all to me. There were all sorts of jewelry and valuables as well, I wondered if she had joined the Mafia, where could she have gotten such spoils? I was genuinely worried about her. I stood struck dumb, unable to speak, I wasn't sure if this was a person or a ghost standing before me. How could she read my thoughts so accurately? I would have to be careful, I ought to hide away. I was very worried, my hands and feet turned to ice. She said she was thirsty, she made me go and get her a glass of water, she was as good as ever at giving orders. I really did want to oppose her, but instead I found myself running to the kitchen in such a state of nerves that I turned over nearly all the glasses and bowls in the kitchen before I managed to pour half a bottle of water into a glass. There was absolutely no reason for my being in such a state of fright. I stumbled back into the living room carrying the glass. Dreamer took it and drained it in one gulp.

I stood struck dumb, unable to speak; I wasn't sure if this was a person or a ghost standing before me. How could she read my thoughts so accurately? I would have to be careful; I wanted to hide. I was very worried, my hands and feet were freezing. She said she was thirsty; she made me go and get her a glass of water. She was a good as ever at giving orders. I really did want to oppose her, but instead I found myself running to the kitchen in such a state of nerves that I turned over nearly all the glasses and bowls in the kitchen before I managed to pour half a bottle of water into a glass. There was absolutely no reason for my being in such a state of fright. I stumbled back into the living room carrying the glass. Dreamer took it and drained it in one gulp.

Then she said, why are you so pale?

Am I pale?

Yes.

You seem unwell.

Not in the least.

I can see your legs shaking.

That's my new hobby, I like to shake my legs from time to time.

So you are sick. And she put out her hand to touch my forehead.

Usually I would do anything for us to be close to each other, but at that moment I flinched hurriedly away from her touch and said tensely, Don't, don't, don't. As if I would turn into a piece of paper and fly away on the wind should she lay a finger on me. At that moment I could feel a gale rushing through my insides, it left me dazed, the world was spinning.

She gave me an odd look, I'm quite sure you're sick!

I said, Dreamer get out of here quickly. I was afraid she would start off again, it would be never-ending. All I could say was, I'll explain later. I opened the door, as if to say, after you. The movement was exactly the same as a scene in "The Last Tango in Paris." I'm not sure where I picked up this fake foreign style. I felt thoroughly disgusted with myself, but I was already past the point of no return; I could only put on a brave face and go on with it. I stood there bent over waiting for her to leave.

Dreamer looked at me in surprise and said, I've traveled thousands of miles to come and see you, who would have thought you would be so inconsiderate. Fine, fine, at least I won't feel like I owe you anything, there's nothing between us from now on. As she spoke, she put on a stately air, and walked out of the door with her head held high and full of righteousness.

Her song came floating out of the darkness,

Wahaha, Wahaha,
Our motherland is a garden,
The flowers in the garden are glorious,
The beautiful flowers are in full bloom
Every child has a smiling face,
A smiling face, a smiling face.*

I saw my own eyes, reflected in the glass, blossom into a smile.

I stood before the window. As I watched her figure moving into the distance I said to myself, Thank heavens.

But how was I ever going to explain this to her? Was I to say that I was having an episode of temporary insanity, a funny five minutes? They were obviously not very good reasons. Then what was I to say? Even I understood that I had acted foolishly. I immediately regretted driving Dreamer away. No, it wouldn't do, I'd have to go looking for her. I picked up a coat and rushed out of the door. I charged about without any clear motive for some time in the wind and rain, and then I found to my total surprise that I hadn't left the spot I was standing on, and yet I remembered running a long way. How could it be that I was still standing amongst a group of gray buildings? I put my hand over

---

* A 1956 Chinese children's song that was originally a Russian folk song and then translated into Chinese.

my heart and I could still feel it thumping away hard, this must be sufficient proof. And yet it seemed ridiculous and I didn't know where to turn. At the corner of one building I recognized the block where I lived. I climbed upstairs with my head hung in dejection, I was in low spirits. I just wanted to go to sleep. I saw a figure in the murky darkness and the fine hairs on my body stood on end, I thought I had seen a ghost. Then I heard a familiar voice say, where did you go running off to? When I got back the front door was wide open. I was in a state of shock. I said, absently, was it? He glared at me without uttering a word. I was thoroughly fed up with that look of his, as if I had done something so wrong that the earth would stop turning.

I turned my face away from him, and said Dreamer has come back.

No wonder, he said, in a peculiar tone of voice.

I said, what do you mean by that?

I drifted towards sleep like a sleepwalker. I walked straight to the bed and threw myself down upon it and then everything else was a blank.

At noon the next day a strange phenomenon appeared in the sky. According to ancient traditions, it is called 'the heavenly dog consuming the sun', scientifically it is known as an eclipse. This time it was not a total eclipse. Today the heavenly dog ate the greater half of the sun, leaving only a thin white rind, as if a tiny crescent moon had risen in broad daylight. Men and women of all ages were holding up pieces of glass in different colors and raising their heads to the skies. I have always been someone who follows the crowd and I too lifted my head to look. I looked until I saw stars. I hurriedly dropped my gaze to look at the surface of the road, many colors appeared on the floor that I had never seen before. I walked towards a shady avenue, the sunlight penetrated the shade of the trees, the shade of each leaf created a tiny crescent on the floor, the ground flashed with thousands of tiny moons. It was an awe-inspiring sight, the kind of thing only seen once in a thousand years. A strange thought suddenly appeared in my mind: Dreamer's in trouble. Today's omen is an inauspicious one. I have to go and look for her. I picked up my feet and ran towards a phone box at the side of the road and called Dreamer's father. At the first attempt it was engaged, after five minutes I called again. Those five minutes stretched like five centuries. At last this time I got through, a sharp and incisive voice came from the other end, who are you looking for? I gave out Dreamer's father's name. She replied in that same sharp voice, just a moment. I didn't know why my heart was beating so fiercely. A long time passed, maybe it wasn't so long, but to me every second I waited was like sitting on a bed of nails. I was unusually restless, I continually scuffed my feet on the floor of the phone booth. A raspy voice finally appeared at the other end of the line.

I asked, are you so-and-so?

Yes.

Has Dreamer been home recently?

What?

I raised my voice too and said, has your daughter Dreamer come home?

My daughter's name is Verdette,* not Dreamer.

What? That's impossible!

Whether you like it or not, that's my daughter's name.

Do you remember me phoning you before? I gave him my name.

They replied in a calm voice, no, I don't remember.

I tried to prompt his memory, you had a really hard time of it when Dreamer left.

Their voice became a little blank. What are you talking about, I don't understand at all, my daughter has never been away, she's been staying at home like a good girl.

I couldn't believe my ears, that's impossible. Why don't you try to remember?

They began to lose patience, saying, there's nothing to remember, this is ridiculous. And then he hung up most impolitely.

I was simply knocked out by this blow. I didn't know what to do. I stood in the phone booth for a while staring blankly; it was no good. I'd have to get to the bottom of this. So I phoned Dreamer's father back again. Even if he's not willing to admit that he is Dreamer's father, I wanted to have it out with him. The phone rang persistently at his end, a sound appeared; I repeated so-and-so's name once more, I waited again; the voice from before spoke again; I didn't bother to introduce

* A name shared by the maid to the legendary *Lady White Snake*

myself but burst out saying: It's very important, please tell me, where is Dreamer?

They got angry with me, what do you want? Is it extortion you're playing at?

I softened my tone, Mr So-and-so, please don't get angry, we've both been brought up and educated for many years in the Party; we know full well that when we have a problem we must remain calm. We mustn't lose our tempers; I simply have something to discuss with you: Would you please tell me honestly whether or not Dreamer is your daughter? I spoke to him in the business-like tone of a cadre.

He wasn't having any of it, instead he spoke in an ever more thunderous voice: Well, really, I've never heard the like! I've already told you in the clearest possible terms that my daughter is called Verdette, why do you keep bothering me? That said, he hung up the phone with a click.

I was fresh out of ideas, there was nothing else I could do. I looked at the handset in my hand, and shrugged my shoulders in a fake foreign gesture of helplessness, you watch the flowers bloom and die off and there's nothing you can do about it. I had never known the sky to be so dark before. I walked along slowly, beaten by the wind and the rain. A gale blew right through me, the sharp whistling of the wind was like the cries of a cat in heat, both rousing and piercing. I heard the sound of Dreamer singing a song in my ears, "It's not that I don't understand, it's only that the world changes so fast."* Yes—the world is becoming more and more messed up. I returned home and presented

* In Dreamer's absence, more of Cui Jian's rock lyrics make an appearance.

a front of undeterred calm in the face of troubles. I decided to make roast pork with pickled vegetables to cast off my bad luck. The whole building was filled with the enticing and mouth-watering fragrance. My husband threw down his briefcase as he came in, took off his coat and rolled up his sleeves, saying that he wanted to eat his fill tonight. Usually when he ate something he really liked, he would get excited and go red and emotional in the face. He relentlessly let rip with six or seven belches in a row, it was really disgusting. How could such wonderful food be transformed into such horrible sounds when they hit his stomach? There are always so many differences between us. Once Dreamer said to me in admiration, you've begun to develop a sense of self, you don't have to follow the man you marry, you've begun to understand your own value, that's very, very good. She was like a big boss, heaping praise upon me. Her endless instructions always resounded in my ears at just the right moment. I looked round then, at him, full of food and drink, already spread out on the sofa sleeping like a dead pig. Whenever Dreamer witnessed such a scene she would give a look of disgust, and say with dissatisfaction, just look at those manners. Dreamer said that that was the typical appearance of a glutton. I was just washing up and tidying in the kitchen by myself when he came in with a roll-up cigarette hanging from his mouth, his face rosy and brilliant with drink, he looked in quite good color.

I continued washing up as I said to him, something funny happened today, I called Dreamer's father and he wouldn't admit that Dreamer existed.

He said, what Dreamer?

I almost dropped the bowl I was holding onto the floor. What kind of worldwide joke* was this that everyone was in on?

Don't you remember Dreamer? Dreamer—the one who lived in our home for some time.

Who lived in our house for some time?

My temper flared up, what are you playing at? You only mentioned her yesterday, how can you not remember?

He said, what rubbish are you talking about? I don't understand you at all, I don't know anyone called Dreamer.

My chest tightened, he was saying exactly the same as Dreamer's father.

I began to shout, you were saying just yesterday that since Dreamer's come back I'll probably go crazy again. How can a grown man run out on the bill like that?

His face was blotchy red and white. He said, I think you have gone crazy.

Fine, fine, I'm crazy. Well, I think the whole world's gone mad. I slipped through the door with a twisted smile on my face.

I stood in the pitch dark looking all about me. I didn't understand what had happened, it was like a peal of thunder that came so quickly you had no time to cover your ears. I had to figure out if I was dreaming or awake. Why did they all deny the existence of Dreamer? Dreamer's existence had never hurt them in any way, why were they so afraid that she existed? I couldn't get my head around it. Surely it couldn't be

---

* Or "international joke". This is a common phrase in Chinese said to originate in Cold War times and refer to the kinds of rhetorical sophistication that nations and leaders use to cover up awkward situations. It carries the sense of conspiracy and corruption of information.

that she truly did not exist? That was absolutely impossible! I remember everything we did together as if it were only yesterday. It's all reliable and realistic, it couldn't possibly be made up. There is rational proof, it is hard as steel and just as resilient. In that moment, I could practically smell her scent. She was there, hidden in some corner, I could sense the warmth of her body, her breathing. How could such a concrete reality be untrue? There must be a mistake somewhere. She has been misunderstood, I've been misunderstood as well. We must save each other, we must come together from two different directions, from two different poles together to one point, we must draw ourselves together with our differences, otherwise there's no hope. Divided we'll fall. Everything we've tried for will be for nothing. You are not Dreamer, and I am not myself. We've got nothing to do with this world.

I'm just a locust. A locust. A locust.

I don't know how long I stood in the pitch black night. I don't recall what crazy ideas ran through my head. I only felt that my face was growing a little numb, my feet were getting a little swollen, the inky black sky was twinkling with innumerable stars. They were winking childishly, their gaze was just like Dreamer's—Dreamer's gaze.

I heard the whistling of the gale, picking up dust and gravel. I was blown about like a leaf on the wind, wild and primitive. I smelled baked potatoes; that was one of Dreamer's favorite snacks. I followed the scent, the night market was swarming with people; my every move was cool just like Dreamer's. I walked along confidently, singing as I went, not paying attention to all that. Several men looked at me, just as they would look at Dreamer, which gave my confidence a boost. Then, I felt as if I was Dreamer. I struck poses under the goose-down yellow of the streetlights; I threw flirtatious glances at some little hooligans out on the street, and won a barrage of shouts. I was certain now that I was in fact Dreamer!

I walked off in the direction of no direction with an air of pride. Some clever individual had said, there are no roads but those that are made by people walking them!* My imitation is proof of that. I no longer exist, Dreamer has turned me into another Dreamer. Is that even possible?

My rational mind brought me back down to earth. Suppose there were a hundred different possibilities, supposing Dreamer had gone missing? That would be a great blow to my self confidence. Supposing she really didn't exist, then I would have lost my mirror for reflection. Could everything between me and Dreamer be nothing but a dream? A one-sided hallucination? Surely Dreamer was not hidden between her and I? Nothing but another side of myself, another self? Another voice, another face, another soul? Leading and controlling me? Switching roles for the occasion, playing out her complex but pure self? Let's see just how many faces I have? How many false likenesses? How many realities? How many layers? Living the act on the stage of life and pretending the truth, both true and false, both false and true, changing the water but not the medicine,** just like

---

* To quote Antonio Machado
** A saying for when surface level changes are not genuine changes, as when one reboils the same Chinese herbal medicine, changing only the water but not the medicine. (Most Chinese herbal medicine is boiled twice before use).

the foolish old man who moved a mountain,* the innumerable sons and grandsons.** I overturned that theory, just as cleanly as overturning the three great mountains.* Dreamer had to have been real. She was real and lifelike, and so persuasive, she couldn't be a fictitious lie. From beginning to end I maintained that belief, if you don't share that belief then that's your own foolishness. I couldn't accept that reality. If Dreamer really didn't exist, I would lose my other half, I would be left with only a silhouette. I would be a person without a face, only a shadow. Such an idea was too frightening to conceive, I would be the first to deny it, to me that is a cruel reality. Could I really have tricked myself for so long? I couldn't accept that, I absolutely could not believe it. Was it true? No, it couldn't be. Turning over that theory was as easy as turning over my hand, it didn't require any great effort, I told myself bravely standing in the dark night. If you don't live for yourself, it's the end of the world. That's one of Dreamer's theories. Where else would I have picked up such an odd saying? It is absolutely in keeping with Dreamer's tone of voice. I strayed off the topic, once more I supposed that Dreamer had dissolved into my blood. I was Dreamer and I was myself. Is it possible to become two people at once? I could hold any situation in the palm of my hand, I could turn my thousand faces on any person. Isn't that the pinnacle of skill? I was rather pleased with the idea, if it were so, I would be able to get through this

* *The Old Fool Who Moved the Mountains* Is an ancient Chinese fable about a man whose perseverance allowed him to move a mountain: A strong-willed person who is not afraid of difficulties.
** In the fable, the old man who is viewed as a fool makes the very lucid argument that whilst he has innumerable sons and grandsons to continue his work, the mountain itself won't get any larger and will eventually be moved. The fable comes from the Daoist philosophical work *Liezi*.

tough time just as easy as that. Fine, from now on, no matter how anyone else denies Dreamer's existence, I have decided that Dreamer exists. Even if the whole of humanity were to deny it, my faith is unswerving. That way I'll be more honest, that will help to preserve me, I'll always be on the winning side. I'll achieve great things.

I walked on like a sleepwalker lost in a dream. I didn't know where in the city I was, I just said to myself, surely there's no longer any need to look for Dreamer? And yet I truly felt as if I were missing something. Had I lost my soul? My other mouth? My other eyes? No, none of them. Then what was it? It was nothing. I felt part of my face become wet; did I have to make things so absolute, so life and death? There was obviously no need. I ought to carry my emotions in my pocket, just like carrying a set of keys, being careful not to lose them. At that point, I subconsciously put my hand into my pocket, to feel if they were there or not. I didn't know whether what I put my hand on was my keys or my emotions. When I groped my way through the darkness back to the ninth floor, the instant I put the key into the keyhole I made up my mind: It shall be so. We were so happy that year when she left. She always told me, you have to be in charge of yourself, come and go without a trace.

During that dreamless night, Zhuangzi's dream of a butterfly walked into my dreams: Zhuangzi dreamt that he turned into a butterfly.* When he woke up he didn't know who had dreamt of who, whether he had dreamt of the butterfly or the

---

* The narrator refers back to the Cultural Revolution political rhetoric which calls Imperialism, Capitalism and Feudalism the three great mountains which are to be overturned, and links this imagery with the fable. See also p. 57

butterfly had dreamt of him? Had I dreamt of Dreamer, or had Dreamer dreamt of me? Had we both been part of someone else's dream? Or had Dreamer and I, from our own separate places, dreamed the same dream at once? Whether Dreamer was a dream or not is no longer important, it's a dream at any rate, what does it matter who dreamed of who?

The sun still rose in the East, it didn't rise in the West just because Dreamer had gone missing. In a morning of glorious sunlight, I opened a window and immediately a colorful butterfly flew in, dazzlingly beautiful. It flew and flew from this side to that, its joy was like a transformation of Dreamer's wild nature. I saw it all, I was utterly joyful.

I finally understood, Dreamer was a dream.
Was Dreamer a dream? I don't care anymore.
Am I dreaming or awake? What does it matter?
The height of dreams is endless glory.

---

* A classic piece of sophistry from the *Zhuangzi* within the Daoist school of philosophy.

B

Who Knows

无人知晓

I sat by a river, a river that stretched into the distance. I didn't know the name of the river—I didn't care, because it had nothing to do with me. I sat and thought about the distant past, so distant it seemed like another planet.

Bringing up their names, they were like things from another world, that nobody knows.

I concentrated on recollection, I thought of my neighbor, Taotao.

Taotao stayed in the same class as me from the first year of primary school to the last. When we had P.E. she always stood at the very last position at the very back of the group. She was so tall—her height was completely out of proportion with her age and unlike all the other children born in the 'Three Years of Natural Disaster'.** Back then we were all skinny and withered, bow-legged and pigeon-chested—a pathetic image of malnutrition. She alone had a face like peach blossom; she was tall and strong, as if excessively well fed.

* Taotao 桃桃 meaning Peaches
** The period of 1959-1961 in Communist China directly following Mao's "Great Leap Forward" policy were marked by famine and hardship. They are called either the "The Three Years of Hardship" or, as Yoyo has written, her protagonist calls it, the "The Three Years of Natural Disasters" (the discrepancy between the names used speaking volumes about the different political leanings and sympathies that exist towards this historic event).

All the older people around us called Taotao a natural born beauty.

Taotao's nature was just as gentle and sedate as her complexion and looks, which always gave me the impression of a well-ripened peach, so tender that it would spurt juices at the slightest touch. Sometimes I would feel certain that she was a figure from a painting that had just walked down off the wall. Her sedate nature gave me a sense of a fantasy world. I still cannot understand how a girl of twelve or thirteen could move with the grace of an eighty-year-old woman, even when she blinked it was a good three beats slower than the rest of us. When I was playing with my classmates—kicking the shuttlecock or skipping—she would be standing off to one side, with her mouth split in a dreamy smile. Her face was always wreathed in endless smiles—she just stood there smiling on and on, dreamily. Taotao only just scraped a pass in each of her classes. She exceeded every one of her classmates in her diligence—I would go so far as to say that the marks of her passes were extremely suspect. How could she fail to provoke sympathy in her teachers with her attitude towards study—none of them could possibly fail such a hard-working student. If I were the teacher, I too would see my way to awarding her a pass.

One afternoon when I was playing happily in the playground, Taotao came right up to me and said quietly, "There's blood on your trousers."

I looked down and searched all over, "Where? Where?"

With a solemn expression, she answered, "At the back."

I all but turned my head 360 degrees, but still I couldn't find it. I became flustered and upset, saying, "Go on, go away, go away! Stop frightening me."

Then I turned and pushed back into the crowd of people and continued our game of French skipping.

Taotao walked into the group again and grabbed my arm, saying, "No, it's no good."

I shrieked at her "What are you up to? Why won't you let me play? You big idiot!" My harsh words didn't infuriate Taotao in the least—she didn't say a word in reply—but she dragged me to the toilets, stubbornly hanging onto my arm. I was practically dragged kicking and screaming into the toilets—once inside, the smell of them stopped me from protesting more strongly. She just kept saying, "There's blood, there's blood there."

I was helplessly angry, having no choice I squatted down to pee—There was blood! I saw blood! I grew pale with fright —my bottom was bleeding. I didn't know where the blood was coming from, only that it was coming out of my body. I knew that blood was precious, you couldn't just go about bleeding all over the place; you could die if you lost a lot of blood. At that moment I thought I was going to die on the spot. I felt panicked, I felt wronged—I couldn't speak, I just cried bitterly until my nose ran. Taotao stood quietly to one side, watching me cry. At the time I loathed her, I decided on some subconscious level that Taotao must have performed some magic on me to make my bottom bleed! If not, why was she going after me so relentlessly? There was definitely something fishy about it.

I reasoned, by my absurd logic, that Taotao must have cast a spell on me.

Although I was still young then, the environment that we grew up in and our education taught us to be suspicious of everything from an early age. "Trust" was a strange and unfamiliar word to me. I learned hate earlier than I learned love. Our youthful spirits were soon tarnished. Suspicion and resentment became our first line of defence in protecting ourselves. I too adopted this naturally and without the least sense of shame.

Taotao waited until I was done crying, then she walked over to me, smiling meaningfully, and handed me something I'd never seen before—I took it unconsciously. I had no idea what to do with this snow white thing in my hand. Taotao took my hands and taught me how to use it, like a mother teaching her daughter, and she told me not to drink cold water, because that would make your tummy ache like an earthquake. I had to admire her wealth of experience, in a second my loathing for her turned to esteem. With that, Taotao removed her own jacket and draped it over me.

She said, "This will cover up the blood on your trousers." Taotao was a good half a head taller than me, and her jacket was like an overcoat, it covered up my bottom just right.

I was extremely surprised that she was so experienced; in my eyes Taotao had always been a girl who was physically well developed, but intellectually simple. In those days no one had to repeat a year, otherwise Taotao would have been left behind forever. It was hard to comprehend the heavy ponderousness of her motions, whatever game we played she would always come last. Her beauty and her stupidity were completely out of proportion to each other—the difference was astounding. In that moment when she removed her jacket, I saw the two mounds swelling out of Taotao's jumper—they were eye-catching and for a moment I felt fiercely embarrassed. I surreptitiously concealed the look in my eyes and subconsciously lowered my gaze to stare at my own flat chest. I thought those things of Taotao's were big and ugly, and she didn't even seem to feel embarrassed about them. As we walked out of the school toilets side by side, I consciously maintained a distance between us. Without knowing why, I thought that those things on her chest were terribly shameful, I felt that all of a sudden the whole universe had changed, I couldn't take another step forward, I felt that the whole world was staring at me, as if they knew my bottom had bled. As if I had committed the most heinous of crimes, I tucked my tail between my legs and ran all the way home.

Half a year after that, my body began to change in wild leaps and spurts. Like Taotao, two bumps grew on my chest, although they weren't as obvious as hers. I walked around hunching my back over, scared that someone would notice them.

One time my father said to me, "Tiddler, stand up straight, what's there to be embarrassed about a girl reaching puberty?"

In a flash I blushed all the way down to my belly button. How did my father know that I had reached puberty? Even more so, I hated him for talking about it—it sent me into a temper. But I had no right to get in a mood with my father, so I just hunched my back even more as I walked to show my silent resistance. Now I understood why Taotao would always stand still during P.E. class. I used to run as fast as a hare, I was the P.E. teacher's pride and joy—he said I had a chance at getting into a sports academy. Then, when during the sports assessment I didn't make the grade, the sports teacher couldn't understand why, and asked if I was sick. I made no attempt to explain. He was a male teacher, what could I say to him? As soon as I ran, the two little pears on my chest would take off like two little doves startled into flight, and I couldn't take another step. Ever since then, my relationship with Taotao underwent a major change: I was never again so impatient with her. I didn't think much of her before, because no matter what you taught her, she could study it ten times and still not understand it, she was remarkably stupid.

My modest intelligence made me feel proud of myself.

Now we started to exchange what are called 'confidences' in whispers between us. She told me that while you've got 'The Curse'* you mustn't eat ice-lollies, because the blood would

---

*Dao Mei 倒霉 is Beijing dialect for "meeting bad luck", similar to the English expression "The Curse", for having periods.

accumulate inside, and if the polluted blood didn't flow out then it could poison you.

I was dead scared.

I imagined I was bloated with dirty blood like a great balloon, ready to explode at a single touch, then the dirty blood would splatter over the sky and I'd never see my beloved parents ever again.

She would tell me these things in all solemnity—and you mustn't wash in cold water, you mustn't put your feet in cold water.

During summer, my greatest joy was to go and splash my plastic-sandalled feet under the cold water tap, and now I couldn't do it anymore?

Because of her medical knowledge, she became no less than a doctor in my view—all at once I looked at her with new eyes.

I heard the word 'The Curse' for the first time from her. I thought this word that she had invented was wonderful, describing the difficulty that a woman must face every month—it couldn't have been more accurate. In fact, I never found out whether or not she had invented that word herself. It wasn't important. What was important was that the first time I heard it was from her lips.

I would never again see Taotao as an idiot. My image of her grew in stature in a moment. She effectively became my personal medical advisor, and for the duration of the school day we were inseparable. And so I became friendlier towards Taotao, I often helped her to do her jobs about the house. Her mathematics was really unimaginably bad, she practically lacked all capacity for abstract thought. Those cells were missing from her brain, as if some part of her brain had been stuck together with glue, leaving her unable to think things through. I couldn't understand the difference in her mental age to mine, how could there be such a disparity? Every time I saw her sweating over a difficult math problem it would take her a good couple of hours to complete it, whereas to me it was as easy as blowing my nose. When it came down to it, I could strenuously explain to her for an age and she still wouldn't get it; I thought I might just as well dash them off for her and let that be an end to it. It would save trouble that way. So I decided to do the lot for her out of the goodness of my heart. From that moment on, our friendship became indestructible. On the way to and from school, Taotao would often produce snacks like a magician, producing a dried apricot and stuffing it into my hand or some jawbreakers; it was as if there were an Aladdin's cave in her pocket filled with an inexhaustible supply of sweets. I didn't understand why she should have so many tasty things to eat. Every time we had exams, she had boiled eggs, sweets and biscuits in her school bag. During that time her grandmother would provide nutritious food especially for her, to help her get good grades. In fact, Taotao's figure did not need any extra nutrition; already she had grown to look like a female deer—all body and no brains. I really wanted to tell her not to go blindly eating too many eggs during the exam period, the more you ate eggs, the more likely you were to carry a 'big duck's egg' back home.* But, because I was greedy, I tricked her: I didn't care about eating eggs myself, however many I ate, I'd never get a 'duck's egg' on an exam. But I was afraid if I said anything, that Taotao would blame her grandma and say, "it's all because of eating boiled eggs that I can't pass my exams." And then I could forget about sharing this treat with Taotao anymore.

As the saying goes, "One good turn deserves another."** So, soon enough I was helping her to cheat in class—whenever the time came around Taotao would look at me so pitifully. I couldn't bear to abandon her—I still had a conscience after all. So I did all that I could, passing notes, giving gestures, winking, anything I could do to help her through difficult times.

Around that time, if I didn't control my appetite, I could have eaten a whole cow in one meal. I was like a ravenous stone—I could put away anything. The subtle relationship developing between Taotao and I had one unwritten rule: I would do the brainwork for her and she would provide me with food, our relationship was, as the saying goes, based on 'cupboard love'.

* One of the many analogous images in Chinese is to "carry a duck egg" (get a zero) on a test, referring to the shape of the egg being similar to a zero. Conversely, one would eat an orange chengzi 橙子, because cheng 橙 sounds like part of the word to succeed cheng gong 成功. The prevalent and persisting belief in a kind of sympathetic magic where eating, carrying or using certain items can influence the result of life events like an exam is a part of the culture and appears in such areas as the arts, posters and marketing to this day. Although it may sound unfamiliar, it's as persistent and unexamined as practices such as touching wood to avoid bad luck - it preserves and continues cultural beliefs.
** A literal translation of the Chinese phrase is "Eating food from another makes your mouth (words) go easy on them; Receiving something from another makes your hand (actions) soft on them."

Taotao's grandma had bound feet. We all called her Grandma Fan. Actually Fan wasn't her surname, I'm afraid even she herself had forgotten her true last name. A long time ago she married into the Fan family, so everyone called her Grandma Fan.* Grandma Fan had a naturally luxurious appearance, she was nearly too obese to move. She said that if you drank cold water when you got old, you'd put on weight, just like people say you could get bloated by drinking cold water during your period. She had a pair of *three inch golden lotuses*** propping up her whole great body, when she walked she tottered as if she might fall. I often worried that she would go head over heels on the floor and never get up again. Her poor bound feet were like an overloaded truck, struggling under that overweight body, like a vehicle in motion with too great a load.

The first time I understood what a big deal bound feet were was when I saw Grandma Fan's. One day when we came home from school, I was going back to Taotao's as usual to do homework (whenever I did homework I would be looking about the room, my heart wasn't in it). Taotao completed her literacy homework one stroke at a time, then went to another room to do something, I didn't know what. After a while she came walking back in again and, with a mysterious expression she asked me, "Do you want to see how my Grandma binds her feet?"

I was curious, I nodded my head fiercely.

Taotao led me into a dim room; the odor inside was truly unpleasant, like the smell of rotting vegetables. At the time

---

* In China, women do not traditionally adopt the husband's surname upon marriage, but children are given the husband's surname.
** This phrase is a high-literary way to refer to the practice of bound feet, making them sound like delicate and precious flowers.

I was thinking of beating a hasty retreat, but I found I had no choice. Taotao had such a firm grip on my hand that I had no way to escape, I could only brace myself and follow her in. I saw Grandma Fan sitting cross-legged on the hard boards of a great wooden bed. She moved slowly, gradually undoing her foot bindings. The binding unwound from the ankle and as each layer was peeled away a weird smell emanated out. Grandma Fan leaned back slightly and took a deep breath in as if she wanted to suck all the horrible smell into her stomach—her expression, however, was one of utter intoxication. When Grandma Fan had completely removed the foot bindings I saw a grotesque pair of feet. The top of the foot bulged up high, the big toe buckled in towards the sole of the foot, and each of the other toes were disfigured too. It is said that when you bind feet, the bones on top of the foot must break, otherwise it won't become a proper bound foot. They were the single most ugly pair of feet I ever saw in my life. Grandma Fan was absorbed in staring at them. She inspected every detail with the greatest of care, as if appreciating valuable jewels. Afterwards, she gently wiped them with a wet towel and then gingerly wrapped them up again. The cloth began at the toes and gradually worked upwards, wrapping all the way up to her ankle. Grandma Fan was expert and dextrous in binding her feet, as if she were wrapping an antique and was afraid of doing it the least bit of damage. The whole process was as slow and sluggish as the most boring of North Korean films. My feet ached a little from standing there so long. I recalled the saying that "an old lady's binding cloth is long and smelly."*

* An analogy usually applied to overly long and boring essays, articles or movies.

I think that Grandma Fan's binding must have been white originally, now it's a grubby gray that could have been any color you liked to call it. It wasn't hard to see that that foot binding cloth itself was steeped in history.

I asked Grandma Fan curiously, "Why don't you leave your feet to relax this once?"

Grandma Fan smiled as she replied gently, "These little feet are hard enough to bind up. Once you let them loose, they'd grow like mad."

I had not yet emerged from my curiosity when Taotao put a word in from my side, saying "Grandma, you moan every day that your feet ache, why don't you give them a soak in hot water?"

Grandma Fan lifted a pair of turbid eyes and looked at us warmly. She said "Silly girl, as soon as I bathed them in hot water the blood would come back to life and then how would I ever get them back again?"

Taotao replied with dissatisfaction, "Grandma, that's the *four olds*,* you know that, don't you?"

Grandma Fan replied with an untroubled tone, "I'm old, I don't care about that lot. If you say it's four olds, then I am four olds."

Taotao's face blushed red all over, "Grandma, you're talking like a reactionary."

Grandma Fan didn't say anything more, but allowed her granddaughter to list her faults.

---

* Foot binding was indeed one of the "four old"s, aspects of traditional culture outlined as holding back the development of China as a modern state, by Mao Zedong. These were "old ideas, old culture, old practices and old habits", known as the "four old (things)", that the Red Guard were tasked with eliminating in 1966. A movement that resulted in the indiscriminate destruction of many cultural relics and practices.

Grandma Fan was the wife of a bureau director. Granddad Fan washed his hands of this human world when he was fifty-odd years old and Grandma Fan became a widow, relying on her monthly pension to get by. When Granddad Fan was still with us, the hall of the house was as busy as a marketplace. Now the tea gets cold as soon as you leave. The lonely widow lived in quite straightened circumstances, not a bit like the lifestyle of a real bureau director's wife. Grandma Fan was from a country village in Shanbei province, where suffering was not even worth mentioning. She was frugal and careful and kept all the best things for Taotao. In Taotao's mind, her Grandma could perform magic and who could always satisfy her every requirement. Of course, Taotao didn't have any outlandish requests; so long as her appetite was satisfied she felt perfectly content.

Taotao was untroubled by thoughts the whole day long. Like a pig, she ate then slept, slept then ate. Of course, I'm being a bit malicious to describe my classmate like this. But she really was just like tha—her ability to sleep was shocking, she could sleep thirty-two hours straight—she spent nearly the whole weekend in her bed. Every single time I went to call for her to play, her eyes were bleary with sleep.

Taotao was so lazy, but her Grandma never reproached her.

Grandma Fan had an amiable face and was sincere to others. She spoiled Taotao rotten. Taotao's parents had split up, so she had lived with her Grandma since she was little. Although you could say she hadn't had much fatherly or motherly love, her

Grandma gave her all the love she could. By the age of sixteen, Taotao was yet to wash a hanky or a single pair of socks. As a result, her fingernails were soft and fine as pieces of a silk coverlet.

The elders in their courtyard discussed the matter privately: If ever her Grandma were to kick the bucket, Taotao would be somewhat to blame.

Taotao lived a life of leisure and kept on growing like mad. The year she reached fifteen years of age, she had already grown to a height of 1.78 meters. She stood out in a group like a goose standing in a flock of chickens. She was really eye-catching, like someone born to play basketball. The sports academy had their eye on her from early on, but when they tried her out a few times they found that she couldn't be trained. You can't carve wood that's rotten through and through,* so they had to reluctantly give up on her.

By then I was attending a different secondary school and had no chance to spend time closely with Taotao like before. There was finally an end to our cupboard love relationship. I felt relieved, as if putting down a heavy load. I was so busy from dawn to dusk that I didn't know if I was coming or going, organizing blackboard bulletins and writing big character posters.**

I remember very clearly one morning in winter, we all reluctantly wanted to stay tucked up in our warm quilts a little

---

* A Confucian adage from the Analects, stating that you can't carve with rotten wood or make a wall from the wrong clay, alluding to the idea that a person's innate character will determine the results of any cultivation they attempt to practice. Similar to the idea that some people simply are not "cut out" for certain roles.

** Two forms of expression made popular in the revolutionary era, with characters and drawings arranged on blackboards, and posters pasted on walls with "big character" headlines.

longer, enjoying the very last moments of the sweetness of sleep. When all of a sudden a peal of piercing laughter rang through the courtyard. The kind of laugh that makes one's hair stand on end—a hysterical and hideous cackle that continued on for a good half an hour. When people couldn't contain their curiosity any longer, the windows of every household were pushed open and heads poked out to see what on earth was going on. I looked down from the second floor and was thoroughly surprised by what I saw going on. In the courtyard, Taotao had pulled up a row of poplars, roots and all, the trunks of which were each as thick as a dinner bowl! During the freezing weather of the very coldest days of winter the earth was frozen as hard as rock, it was really beyond the pale. There she was, screaming as she uprooted the fifth big tree. Everyone was scared silly by her inexhaustible strength. As a normal person's strength goes, three young lads would struggle to pull up one even of these trees, not to mention doing so in the ground of the Great Northwest, frozen solid down to a depth of at least three feet.

Taotao's Grandma told me afterwards, Taotao came down with hysteria on the day of her eighteenth birthday. When Grandma Fan cooked long-life noodles* as usual, the ordinarily greedy Taotao began to shout and yell, saying that her Grandma had put poison in her bowl. She smashed the whole pot of best quality noodles to the ground—and that was the entire 750g of noodles supplied to every household for special occasions and festivals!

---

* Long noodles are cooked and presented to someone having a birthday, to represent wishing them a long life.

Ever since then there had been no remission in Taotao's hysteria. She chased the children, as well as chicken and geese, in the courtyard. She ran about crazily like a whirlwind, kicking up all the dust in the yard—she really put a cat amongst the pigeons, there was no peace. In fact, Taotao was never one to hurt anyone; it's just that when she charged about, it was truly a terrifying sight. People differ in their capacity to deal with such overwhelming upheaval. After being pressured by everyone in the courtyard, Grandma Fan had to put Taotao into a mental health institution.

That day at noon, four big men in white suits arrived and indiscriminately dragged Taotao into a truck. Just like that she was taken away. Grandma Fan's face trembled in pain as she stared after the people taking Taotao away, but she was unable to help her.

For a while people were as pleased as if they'd seen off a pestilence, they were ecstatic and not one of them went to offer condolences to Grandma Fan. According to reason, I was once good friends with Taotao—that year Grandma Fan was really good to me, I often hung about to eat and drink at her home—since Grandma Fan had had such a shock to her system, I ought to have gone to ask after her. But I was indifferent, afraid that I might be infected with the rotten luck that beset her. Even at that young age I could be such a snob, I have to say it was a very poor quality in me. I feel repentant now, but it's meaningless; it's only a rather unsatisfactory way of comforting myself.

After that, every month when she received her pension payment, Grandma Fan would buy all sorts of good things to eat, put them in a big cloth bag and hang it from her walking stick as she made her doddery way out to the distant outer suburbs. The mental asylum where Taotao lived was a long way away from the city—Grandma Fan had to walk a great distance to see her. Every time she returned from visiting her she would say, with her face covered in tears, "My poor little girl."

After Taotao was sent to the asylum, Grandma Fan would sit alone at her kitchen window, just staring off into space from the misty break of day until sundown. Sometimes even when it was already thoroughly dark, Grandma Fan would still be found sitting there, stock still in that dark room.

One bright morning when I was rushing off to work at about six o'clock or so, I passed by the window of Grandma Fan's home and saw her sitting there, all alone before the half-covered window. Through the murky light I saw her gazing into the distance, but her expression was senseless and numb. I had already begun to hurry past when I felt a sensation like a knife piercing my heart. So I walked back again to Grandma Fan's window and called softly, "Grandma Fan."

She uttered a dazed reply, "Who is it?"

"It's me Tiddler."

"Oh, Tiddler, what are you doing going out so early?"

"Grandma Fan, it's chilly, you'd be better off going inside to lay down!"

"I'm old, I can't get myself off to sleep, so I got up to sit for a while and wait for Taotao to come home."

Without realizing it I had begun to cry, what could I say to her? Why should such a good person have such bitter luck?

After about a year and a half had passed, when Taotao was released from the mental asylum and her delicate features had changed completely. The blossom-like visage of before had vanished and grown into a puffy face like a great pancake. Her withered face was full of misery. Because of the steroids, she had grown large as a mother elephant. She became slovenly and filthy, and an unbearable stink constantly poured from her body. Her well-developed chest was like a milk cow's, filling out her top. Her buttonholes always gaped widely in an obscene fashion. Owing to the rapid increase in her weight, her trousers always seemed too tight for her. One leg was shorter than the other. She couldn't get the buttons done up and revealed her underwear for all to see—and she didn't feel shy or embarrassed in the least. Taotao's tender expression had disappeared. Now her eyes sent forth a savage expression. I was really shocked by the change in Taotao when I saw her—she looked like a wild animal.

It was summer; I was wearing a white polyester shirt when I saw Taotao sauntering about before her front door. I went up to her with the intention of striking up a conversation. Who'd have thought it, Taotao flung herself at me screaming,

I was too slow to dodge out of her way—Taotao grasped my neck tightly. I must have looked drained with fear at the time —I thought that was it for me. Taotao gave a piercing scream; there was a distance of only an inch between her face and mine, it seemed as if she wanted to swallow me up. I detected the smell of Formalin, the chemical corpses are soaked in. All of a sudden, Taotao released her grip and chuckled at me. I had only one thought in my head then: Run for your life.

I fled towards the stairs.

I could hear Taotao back there, calling my nickname, "Hey, Tiddler, do you want to eat some dried apricots? Ha ha ha."—she laughed the hearty laugh of a maniac.

That was the reward she used to give me when I finished her math homework.

Every time she would ask me, "What do you want to eat?"

I would answer without a shred of a doubt "Dried apricots."

Taotao still remembered that I loved to eat dried apricots.

I felt shaken.

That evening as I was reading by lamplight, Taotao's young face appeared on the pages, like the face of an angel. Whatever I did, I could not make any connection between her face now and her face then. I remembered that it was Taotao who looked after me when I had my first period. I kept it a secret for quite a long time, only Taotao and I knew, I didn't even tell my mum. Of course that's because of my girlish embarrassment, nothing else.

Very late someone came and knocked at the door. My mum pushed open the door to my room and said, "Grandma Fan's here to see you."

Grandma Fan was following at my mum's heels. She appeared weaker than usual in the dim light. I rushed to welcome Grandma Fan into my room. Grandma Fan repeated over and over, "I'm so sorry you had a shock today." As she spoke she falteringly drew a paper bag out of her pocket and handed it to me. "Taotao had me bring you these, she said you love to eat them."

For a moment I was tongue-tied with shame.

Taotao's grandma continued to explain, "They did Taotao wrong in the asylum. She takes fright now whenever she sees someone in a white coat. They used electroshock therapy on my girl. Taotao suffered a lot in the asylum. That place isn't fit for humans—they didn't see my little girl as a human being. I let my baby down, sending her to a place like that. I've been messing things up my whole life, I've made nothing but mistakes."

Thick and turbid tears rolled from Grandma Fan's eyes.

My mother and I both cried together with Grandma Fan.

Grandma Fan heaved a sigh and continued, "Oh, I've sinned! That year I encouraged my son in his engagement. Taotao's mother was my niece, there's a medical history of this in our family. Taotao's mother was twenty-something when she came down with this disease herself. I never thought that Taotao would go hysterical so soon. That bond of matrimony has destroyed two generations of my family. God is punishing me, what a terrible fate! Taotao's father won't forgive me as long as he lives. I destroyed his happiness—he won't ever see me again—he's my only son. Truly, I have sinned!"

By the light of the 18-Watt bulb, Grandma Fan's face looked like a picture of the suffering of Christ. Her pain seemed endless and inexhaustible.

The darkest hour comes before dawn.

I don't know if what is known as Heaven is the final resting place, but I think her grief goes far beyond what a person normally experiences—even after death she would still feel heaviness.

Now I understand why Taotao's grandma spoiled her so: She was atoning for her sins! But who could lighten her burden of misery?

That is all I knew about Taotao's family history. I felt no hatred towards the perpetrator of this tragedy but rather a boundless compassion for Taotao's grandma. There was no theoretical basis for this compassion, but by just seeing Taotao's grandma suffer more and more every day I couldn't even think of blaming her. There was no doubt that Taotao was an innocent victim. She had no idea what caused her disease. She was the product of incestuous coupling; she was a sacrifice. All day long she shouted to the crowd, "I'm not sick! I'm not sick!"

An insane person will never admit being insane.

Taotao's condition showed no signs of improvement after she came out of the hospital but rather continued to deteriorate. Her insanity grew ever more fierce—she refused to take medication—she said everyone wanted to harm her. She made herself up quite comically; she put her hair into a high ponytail and tied it with a red ribbon. All day long she looked at herself in the mirror, asking everyone who passed by, "Do I look nice? Do I look nice?" Whenever a man walked by, she kept smiling dumbly. If a man looked at her a little longer out of curiosity, she would go up behind him and put on a coy expression and give him a goofy grin.

Especially at the time of her month Taotao was like a cat in heat: relentlessly affectionate. There was a public toilet in our complex; as soon as she saw a man go in, she charged in after him regardless. After a while the entrance to the ladies toilet became desolate and overgrown by a thin layer of grass. During her period a nauseous stench poured out of her body. She didn't keep herself clean and tidy like she used to. There were several stains of blood on her trousers—so disgusting. Night after night, when Taotao was in high spirits, she lay awake crying and wailing, making such a noise that neighbours on either side couldn't get any peace. She got up early and ran about in the courtyard—jumping for joy—so that children from several streets ran over to see the excitement; they then shouted at her, "Looney! Looney!"

Taotao draped a flowery bed-sheet over her shoulders, paraded up and down the street, saying over and over, "I'm the most beautiful flower girl in the world! Pretty as a peach blossom; everybody loves me, and my name is Taotao."

The little children made fun of her, shouting, "Taotao, flutter your eyelashes for us!"

And she threw passionate flirtatious looks at everyone. Due to her chronic insomnia and uncontrollable emotions, her eyes flashed a bloody light, like a wildcat's gaze—it made one shudder. The local children ran a mile in fear, not daring to set even lightly a foot onto our complex.

Taotao became a target for ridicule in our complex. You only had to say that you lived in Huang Nisha No.4 – there wasn't a person within miles that didn't know—people said knowingly, "Oh, that's the complex with the lunatic."

As if we'd all become a synonym for a lunatic.

It even got to the point where some of us girls of marriageable age saw their fiancés break off the engagement precisely because of this; the reasoning being very simple: "A crazy girl in your complex poses a threat to me. I can't enter lightly. There's no way to go ahead with the marriage." There were more and more old maids in our complex, whilst all the young men rushed to find a wife and settle down.

According to a feng shui master, the yin energy in the complex was too strong and failed to stimulate the yang energy. If we wanted to change it, we'd have to dig three feet in the ground at the entrance, turn each building in the opposite direction and change the doors that face the mountain to face the river instead. A bunch of the old, weak, sick and crippled like us couldn't launch such a major offensive. Most of the people that lived in the buildings were retired or the lonely disabled living off their compensation money—and a crazy girl on top of that. Although Taotao was extremely strong, she couldn't help; she could only do disservice. We couldn't count on Taotao.

Taotao became a good-for-nothing—just another mouth to feed—and her appetite for destruction was immense. One time when she was unwell, she broke every bowl in the house all in one go. Standing on the ground dotted with shards of broken bowls, she said, "How nice"; she then used the shards to cut her arms, scaring Grandma Fan, who implored her to stop. Another time Taotao used her iron-like fists to smash all the windows in one block. She raised her dripping bloody fists and shrieked "Long Live Chairman Mao!" Even though Taotao was sick, she managed to preserve a clear political awareness. Even a crazy person loving the Great Helmsman so passionately shows how deeply the political climate had penetrated peoples' hearts. That she maintained such a strong political flair, even in her madness, was a special product of the time. We were all struck dumb—no one dared to stop her. Preventing a crazy person from shouting, "Long live Chairman Mao" could be punished with death. Taotao ran around our complex again and again with her raised blood-soaked fists, shouting loudly the slogan "Long live Chairman Mao", each time louder than the last. Grandma Fan almost fainted from pain as she stared in agony at her granddaughter's fresh blood dripping all over the ground.

Taotao was so obstinate, but Grandma Fan still took every pain to look after her.

Grandma Fan was always saying, "My little girl's sick."

Everyone in the area said that Grandma Fan had such bad luck. Even in her Golden Years, she still could not enjoy a single day's rest; she really had to suffer her entire life.

In order to prevent Taotao Fan from playing the same game again, every family in her building installed iron bars on their windows.

Huang Nisha No.4 grew even more gloomy—the very image of a great prison block.

I continued to live in the building as before. I had nowhere to go, and naturally I fell into the rank of the old ladies there. I had no other choice. I had the most boring profession in the world: accounting. Our leader made me, because they said my maths was good. All day I sat at the abacus, making an incessant clicking and clacking sound as I worked; I did sums until my mind and heart turned cold and all my feelings were repressed. I imagined that I was a glass figure; I had no sex organs. I could only sit before the abacus: my fingers moving swift as a shuttle, accurate and free of errors. I poured all my ability and feelings into the beads of the abacus. That year I won the citywide abacus accounting championship. I took home a gold-plated, plastic trophy and a big white porcelain vase with red characters printed on it: "Presented to a Progressive Worker". My mum was so happy; she couldn't stop smiling. Whenever she met someone, she would boast to them, saying, "My daughter brought home a trophy for me." Moreover, she kept it in the most eye-catching place in our house. The shape of this big trophy had a terrible association. I'm not a pervert (it was just like the country's most famous movie award, the "Golden Rooster", which is translated into English as the "Gold Cock", which means "a golden penis"). No matter how I tried, I couldn't help making that association. I don't know if they did it to be mischievous—the cup stood high up on our tallboy in the kitchen like some person's sex organ. It was extremely provocative to me. I thought that maybe I too have gone mad, like Taotao. Surely I don't have to be like this? My whole body felt sultry with rising heat and lingering sorrow.

From the beginning to end, Taotao never forgot our former relationship. There was a period of time where whenever she met someone she would tell them, "Our Tiddler's smart; she always used to come first in our class, all because I gave her eggs to eat; that's what made her so clever." No one believed it. They all thought she was raving—only I knew that it was the truth. But I wasn't brave enough to admit it—I wouldn't let myself be humiliated so easily.

I was not as genuine as a lunatic—there was a spot on my vanity.

The wind at dusk was warm; I was sitting on a bench in the Central Park, staring leisurely into the distance. The tired old sun dyed the sky into a stretch of mystery, inadvertently establishing a certain kind of atmosphere for the sentimental observer—just like how sensitive people always manage to perceive something that others aren't aware of. Although I'm not a sensitive person, I could see something a little different. As usual, I slumped on the bench, lazy and unwilling to move. A young boy rolled by with his iron hoop and ran past; the sound of the hoop's rolling made me feel very drowsy, but I knew I couldn't sleep there; that would mean I was a homeless hooligan. I had to put on the appearance of a civilized person enjoying the scenery in order to please my own vanity. The little vanities of women can be rather attractive—enough to entice a few men; some men are devoted to appreciating women's vanity. This is just a little trick, not worth blaming them for; it is one of the most important ways that men take control of the psychological balance. For example, men feel very proud if they have a pretty wife or girlfriend, what they call a "looker" in the capital—something to show off about. Or, another example: A man likes a woman to worship him. When a man knows a woman loves him close to mad intoxication, he has a reason for showing off. But it is impossible for an old woman to satisfy even this little vanity; I became the subject of everyone's discussions and attention, all without good intentions. Every day when I walked through the courtyard, the glances cast on me were exactly the same as those given to Taotao—I knew it. They said, "All old biddies are weird." In this society, old biddies are as those condemned to death; they face endless reproach. Even though I was a progressive worker, despite my best efforts, I could not get accommodation at the work unit. I raised the issue with our cadre, who told me that after top-level research into the matter, they decided not to award me a flat for a very legitimate reason: "Why would a single woman need a flat? As if we would give you the opportunity to misbehave!" There was nothing I could say. I thought it would be better to be like Taotao, crying and making a fuss whenever feelings overwhelmed me.

Why didn't I go mad? Whenever I felt unhappy, nobody pleased me. It felt like the whole world was against me. I didn't know which way to run to find my escape route. I always dreamt that one day I could escape from this establishment, this repressive and conservative, stagnant old city—the further I could run the better—I didn't care even if I had to run to the end of the earth. I always had a premonition; I would leave. This premonition gave me a little comfort. I didn't know where this premonition came from; it was a guiding light in the darkness, leading me in one direction. But at the end of the day I still didn't know what direction it was. I decided to talk to Taotao. It was as if she alone could explain my uncertainty. However, when I got up and walked towards Taotao's house, the spring wind was blowing all along the way. It felt like I was being rescued by a total reform. I felt an opportunity looming, as if I'd seen a ray of sunlight right ahead. As I walked into the complex, I was gradually able to perceive a faint glimmering light before Taotao's window that flickered like a spiritual light. In a flash I lost my courage again; my feet seemed to have taken root. I didn't move a single muscle, and that terrible thought vanished into thin air. My face was white as a sheet, like the dark side of the moon. I no longer needed secrecy, I was fed up with the darkness; it guided me through thirty-two long years. All my life a shadow covered me, followed me persistently—a faithful guard—wasn't that enough? My silence was like a brocade flag, fluttering in the wind, flying over mountains and seas, filling every corner. I was about to go mad with this silence. Was Taotao driven mad by the silence or was it the inherited genes that made her crazy? I rather believe the former. But medical experts believed it was 100% hereditary.

Do we believe in science? Or reality?
Of course the answer is science.

I couldn't resolve the dilemma, I was utterly unable, just as I was powerless to control my body. I couldn't hide the 50 kg. I couldn't eliminate my body nor my spirit, just as I couldn't conquer my desires. What was my desire? What was it that I wanted? It was hard to answer.

I wanted to run away, anywhere would do, just as long as I didn't stay in that bloody place. But, I continued to live there as without a bit of movement.

One year, the whole city launched a surge of major construction projects. A wave of rural labourers flooded the city being dug up—everywhere in real disorder like a post-war disaster. Not even a shred of empty space in front of our complex escaped the requisition.

Burly, heavily limbed country youngsters worked furiously in our complex, which made Taotao excited like a cat on a hot tin roof. As she paced back and forth, she stared at one lad, who wasn't bad looking, giggling the whole time. Quick as lightning, Taotao found out that his name was Little Lizi. Whenever he came into our courtyard, Taotao charged out of the house and hovered in front of him. Taotao's intentions were obvious. The workers around him made fun of Little Lizi, saying, "Hey, Little Lizi, that city girl has got her eye on you!" and Little Lizi blushed bright red, but didn't say a word. Come wind, rain or shine, wherever Little Lizi appeared, Taotao was standing there giggling.

At night Taotao stood watch outside the makeshift tents set up by the workers and laughed incessantly.

I only now recall how Taotao endlessly giggled when she was younger, already revealing her symptoms—only we never paid attention to it.

Taotao did nothing to hide her infatuation. During the Spring Festival holidays, all the country workers returned to their villages to celebrate the New Year. Little Lizi was no exception. Taotao gazed at the deserted and empty tents, bitterly calling Little Lizi's name, sometimes loudly, sometimes softly. Day and night the cries of "Little Lizi, Little Lizi" echoed through the sky above our complex. A normal person must truly feel inferior to the raging passionate emotions that a lunatic can express. When it comes to feelings, I guess I'm timid as a mouse. I could never be that brave, and I would never love with such intensity. I don't think I would—even if I was crazy.

After a fortnight, the workers returned with Little Lizi amongst them. Taotao revelled in happiness. She ran back home from the gate singing and shouting. Standing before the mirror, she tied a red ribbon in her hair, painted on a pair of red lips—her whole face painted in such a haphazard way—she looked a bit demonic. She spread her blood red lips, spun round on her heels and ran out of the house, shouting in a mad, frenzied joy, "Little Lizi's back, Little Lizi's back." When she bumped into Little Lizi, she swayed her fat figure for all she was worth, her reddened face laughing with an idiotic persistence. Taotao had her own unique way of expressing her special feelings. It's just a shame Little Lizi never reciprocated in the slightest. But Taotao wasn't angry; she only showed a determined patience. She followed Little Lizi as if she were his shadow—there wasn't anywhere she wouldn't go.

One day, Little Lizi finally couldn't stand it any longer; he scolded her loudly saying, "Stop following me!"

Taotao laughed heartily. Whenever she then bumped into someone she said, "He spoke to me, he spoke to me." Taotao took Little Lizi's indignation as a sign of love, and so her feelings grew ever more hot-blooded. She then stuffed an incomparably filthy hanky into Little Lizi's hand as a token of her favour. Little Lizi didn't even glance at it before flinging it to the ground.

Eleven months passed; it became apparent that the buildings would soon be finished, and the workers would move on to a different place—maybe another city, if the situation changed radically.

On one cold dusk, the usually reticent Little Lizi suddenly lifted his hand against Taotao. It is not clear why he hit her. He was probably fed up with Taotao always crowding him as well as the teasing from all the lads that worked with him, who were deliberately winding him up. Naturally, the hands used to working with bricks and tiles weren't light—his fist fell, and instantly Taotao's mouth and nose started bleeding. The bluish marks of four fingers were freshly printed upon her face. Taotao ran home crying and shouting. When Grandma Fan saw the state she was in, she was so angry that her hands shook; she said, "I was never cruel enough to hit my girl like that; it's against the law to hit people; I can't let this be the end."

The details of what actually happened next aren't very clear. Either way, after three weeks they were speedily married. Little Lizi became Taotao's legal husband.

It is said that Grandma Fan went and found Little Lizi herself. Their discussion lasted five hours when they finally reached an agreement: The Fan family would not pursue the matter legally if Little Lizi was willing to marry Taotao. They would change Little Lizi's residency status to the city, and Little Lizi would be a city dweller in name and law. With the conversion of his residency status to the city as his price, Little Lizi agreed to the marriage. For Little Lizi it was a great leap to go from eating agricultural grains to commercial food products. It was like reaching Heaven in one bound, leaving the lads who worked with him rubbing their hands, feeling utter disbelief that even a crazy city girl gets to eat fine food. But they didn't know that the price Little Lizi paid was that he could never divorce Taotao. If the fiancé knows his betrothed is insane before the marriage, then the law is on the side of the female party, unless Taotao were to die. At that time, Little Lizi also discussed his prerequisite conditions: First they would have to ensure that his status was changed, and only after that he would marry her. When the conditions are set, a gentleman cannot go back on his word. Grandma Fan took advantage of Grandpa Fan's old connections by visiting his old war buddies that were still in office with boxes of cakes and cigarettes. In those days getting in through the "back door" was still cheap; a few "fine" gifts would elicit a "fine, fine" response. Blame it on sympathy, but when his old war friends saw Grandma Fan, a lonely widow, they decided to help her out. After a few weeks, Little Lizi's resident status was smoothly and officially transferred to the city.

It put Grandma Fan's mind at rest to help Taotao and arrange her marriage.

Was she creating another lunatic?

Who knows.

She told the other elderly people in the complex that she could now rest in peace.

Taotao's marriage became the topic of conversation in every household for some time. They said, "old ginger is hottest!" "Grandma Fan really knows how to get a job done—little wonder as wife of an official—her path's been difficult enough. If even Taotao can find a husband then all the old maids in this complex have a chance of getting married off."

At that moment this seemed like an opportunity for me. By chance I started my own Long March. I didn't know what awaited me, all the undisclosed results, but I didn't pay attention—that is what I longed for. I couldn't hope to suddenly leave this both strange and familiar place to go far away. It's not that I wanted to go and do big things; I wasn't born with brains or great ambitions—I only wanted to escape. I'm not a driven person; I believed that wherever I went I would find a mediocrity that would attract the attention of no one. I appreciate blandness. Why couldn't I stand the blandness there? Am I not similarly repressed and suffocated now? I've always run to the ends of the Earth; there's now nowhere left to go.

Full of trepidation, I walk alone beneath the moon of a strange country; I cannot describe the stretch of earth beneath my feet—

nor can I feel its pulse nor touch its skin. I've become a wanderer, floating—forever floating.

Why?

Surely it cannot be fate?

I have paid a heavy price for this.

I think once more of Little Lizi. Who has paid the greater price, him or me?

Life punishes every one of us.

Just as the days punished Grandma Fan, so they have a lesson to teach you, me and everyone else.

But the days, once they pass, are never repeated.

The culture of my home runs in my blood, every single drop belongs to that place. In that earth where I was born and grew up, every tree, every blade of grass was familiar to me. Beneath the city walls there is a decrepit, old wooden chair; there are ancient incense burners in the temple ruins. Even in the dark, I could feel my way home from any corner of the city. That simple yet beautiful place is bound to me in countless and intricate ways; it is a knot so tangled it can not be severed. It wrapped itself around my heart, unwilling to leave—forever, forever.

Now I understand, saying to myself: "Someone like you won't be happy, no matter where they go—you shouldn't even have come to this world in the first place. That was your most basic mistake."

Can I, however, control my life? Could I have stopped myself from coming to this world? One has to ask "God" about these kinds of random coincidences. It's a shame I don't believe in any.

Maybe "God" doesn't have any answers.

Who knows.

When I got a letter from my mum saying that Grandma Fan had died, my first thought was, how would Taotao live?

Sometime later I received a letter from a classmate saying that Taotao had given birth to a baby girl. Her husband, who was strong as an ox, would beat her almost to death. He didn't really care if the pair of them, mother and daughter, lived or died. Taotao was in a really pitiable state.

I couldn't imagine how an insane woman could look after a baby.

I couldn't imagine how that child would grow up.

I could only make a wish to myself: If only this child could escape going mad when she grows up; if only she could avoid repeating this tragedy.

When Taotao's daughter grows up, will she or won't she go mad?

Who knows.

The moon hung high, cold as a blade.

I fell asleep by the strange river and dreamed of Taotao. I said, "Taotao, let's run away together."

"Where to? To Heaven?"

Who knows.

C

DESIRE'S WINGS

欲望的翅膀

I. *The Sunlight — A Symphonic Movement*

One Saturday morning, the sunlight came refracted through the dark green velvet curtains to fall upon the floor. The line of light formed a gently curving line, reminiscent of a surrealist oil painting; calm, peaceful, composed. From the quality of the light, you could tell that it was going to be fine weather.

Qu Shuang had chosen those heavy curtains precisely in order to prevent the morning sunlight from disturbing their dreams too early. She was a person who enjoyed her morning dreams, especially on the weekend. The half-light created by the emerald drop curtains felt as if it were a profound vault of heaven leading her into yet another illusion. She enjoyed the atmosphere it created; it allowed her to float gently off into the world of fantasy. She saw a pair of hands in the dim space, playing her body as if they were playing an ancient serenade, as her body released an intoxicating fragrance. She became absorbed in thoughts of her own body; she knew that her body was well shaped: elegant, like a fateful cello, with clear curves, a pure sound, upon which was bound to be played a surprising movement.

---

* Qu Shuang's surname – Qu, as an individual character can be taken to mean both "curved, twisted, crooked" as well as meaning a tune or a piece of music.

On this morning, the sunlight was like a movement in a symphony. It mercilessly invaded her territory, adding an air of undeniable enticement. Qu Shuang lay curled up in her husband's embrace, she did not want to get up, she longed to linger there a while longer. The soft bed, that unique body scent; they were reluctant to leave their bed in the benevolent morning. She allowed her hair to brush lightly against Luke's broad chest and his hand began to flow upon the stream of her body. Before long, the tide had risen over that pair of unconventional hands that surged wild and out of control in the rise and fall of the waters. His hands drew gradually nearer to that secret forest, where she was wet and trembling. He would be stuck in her quicksand if he wasn't careful. Luke knew that he was about to lose his way in that 'forest' once more. How many times had he warned himself not to play these games in the morning. It only made him feel listless for the rest of the day. There was no way he could hold himself back at that moment, he was bound to consume the fruit of temptation. Just as Adam and Eve burst into Eden and ate the forbidden fruit only to bring infinite trouble down upon their heads, and yet they could not help themselves either. He rolled wantonly over and pressed his body upon hers, licking her nipples that had grown erect with excitement. They were like pink cherries hanging on the branch, he had no choice but to pick them, to put them into his mouth, to swallow them down into his stomach and savor the fresh, wild taste of them. He laid his full weight upon her and she began to moan ecstatically.

That sound alone was enough to make him lose his last shred of reason. Luke could withstand her soulful cries no longer; he savagely thrust his scepter into the woman's concealed depths. The woman beneath him let out another pitiful cry, the sound that ignited their life-long passion. He was like a wild horse that had broken rein as he galloped within her body. He struck against her body fiercely, she responded by cleaving tightly to his movements, trembling up and down, in such harmony. He did not rush to finish, devising new games with his body language. He covered her. Underneath him she was like a beautiful eel, sliding beneath his body, twisting, struggling, gasping breathlessly. Gradually they were as water, water covering water, motionless. Suddenly a torrent ran through them, lighting struck, Luke could hold back no longer, his last defense finally broken down. He panted heavily, in the peace after the eruption. They collapsed onto the bed like a pool of water, and were silent.

The sunlight continued to gaze on them. Qu Shuang curled up in the soft bedding like a spoilt house cat falling back to sleep. After some time, Luke nudged her gently, "Hey, sleepyhead, it's time to get up."

She rolled over reluctantly, Luke put out a hand and rubbed her nose, "You fox spirit,* you've stolen my soul again." This joke made her feel unhappy in spite of herself. Luke had this ridiculous theory about lovemaking, that the man always lost out and the woman took advantage of him. It's not a business transaction, you can't talk about gains and losses, and

---

* In Chinese literature and folklore, such as *Strange Tales from a Chinese Studio* (Pu Songling c. 1766), a fox spirit is an evil feminine spirit, similar to a succubus or mermaid, that can steal a man's soul, or his vital energy through their dangerous beauty.

even if it were a transaction, it takes one to take the pain and one to dish it out. It's something both parties are willing to take part in. Wasn't using words like 'losing out' and 'taking advantage' just degrading yourself? She remained quiet, not wanting to ruin the atmosphere of the morning. She wanted to enjoy all that she could, that was the attitude Qu Shuang adopted throughout her life.

She rolled over and sat up, grabbed a robe that was to hand and draped it over herself. She walked barefoot upon oak floorboards. Despite the lightness of her body, the aged floorboards let out a creaking sound, like the old decking planks of a harbor, waiting for the youthful footsteps of sailors back from distant voyages. Treading the planks, they crossed from sea to land, joyously satisfying their thirst developed during a life at sea. She enjoyed their painful groaning, that spoke of the pleasure of being conquered. In bare feet, the energy of the earth penetrated the soles of her feet, and gave her a feeling of renewal. Qu Shuang's pride enticed her to put on all sorts of harmless little coquetries. Once a sculptor had told her that her feet were beautiful and had asked her to model for a sculpture. Ever since then, she would show off that superior part of her body, whether she was aware of what she was doing or not. She had a wonderful grasp of that. She had put herself through an extensive program of self-training, practicing her every move until it was just right. She always sat bolt upright like a noble lady; when she ate, she chewed her food so carefully that it gave one the impression that she was quite delicate. Her posture when smoking or her movements as she carried in a tray of tea all seemed to have been designed with the utmost care, including the deliberate elegance with which she walked down the street. Her affectations were deeply ingrained, to such a degree that you could no longer tell what was genuine and what was put on. This provoked, in some women, the irrepressible wish to imitate her and in some men, the irrational desire to protect her. She was not the kind of person to just obey what came naturally; she searched in earnest to be set apart. Entering her house, you experienced a peculiar feeling of exoticism that made you lose your bearings for just a moment. Being assaulted by too many feelings at once, it left you speechless, in a kind of dizzy blindness. Her home was an ambiguous middle ground that was difficult to define. All she wanted was to show herself off, and she was successful in doing so. Well and truly in character, she felt rather pleased with herself. She sought to show her particular feminine appeal in her everyday life, to show her character fully in every detail. She knew only too well the effect of the visual aspect on human psychology; you could see that just from looking at her eating and drinking habits: the exquisite coffee pot, the plate service that had to be pure white without any design—even the most everyday condiments were presented in bottles that were as decorative as vases. The kitchen was so clean it looked as if it had never been used, but was there only to be admired. The towels that hung in the bathroom were embroidered with a 'Q' in reference to her name;

the soaps were of the transparent fruit scented kind that can only be bought in specialist shops. No matter how simple a meal was, she would lay a tablecloth and use cloth napkins or at least paper ones. She pursued the "eating for form, not for function", in all its hollow fancy. The costly silver tableware she always used, the top-class French champagne, the highly polished stem glasses that rang out when touched together. One evening there was an old movie on the television called "A Nest of Gentry",* she had exclaimed that that was precisely the life she envied. In it there was a run down noble family whose master and mistress would still sit down at either end of a seemingly endless dinner table, even though the house was going to rack and ruin about them. The servants would run up and down carrying huge silver platters, opening the ornately carved lids to reveal a pitiful spread of a little cooked potato and a dry looking shrimp, and beside the potato and shrimp, a green salad leaf arranged decoratively to each side. The amount of food was minimal, barely enough to feed a cat. That is the highest level of formalism, not enough to fill your eyes, let alone your belly. That kind of decorative emptiness is precisely the kind of lifestyle dreamed of by those who make a pastime out of pride.

At that moment, a restrained smile spread across her features, and she walked slowly to the kitchen and made herself a pot of coffee. Then, choosing a seat by the window, she sat down and looked sideways out of the window. Her long, disheveled hair was coiled carelessly at the back of her head

* The 1969 award winning film adaptation by Andrey Konchalovsky, based on the 1859 novel by Ivan Turgenev.

with a strand or two trailing down the edge of her right ear. A black kimono with large golden flowers softly encased her body; her jade-white neck was like a scene from Swan Lake. The sunlight played intriguingly upon her body. Her shadow flung upon the orange floorboards, dappled and indistinct. She sat before the window absorbed in narcissistic self-interest, enjoying her shadow.

The room was full of the indolence of a Saturday. She sipped her coffee whilst gazing intently at a spider on the window. The crystalline red spider was working carefully on its creation. Qu Shuang held her breath and watched carefully, afraid that the slightest movement would disturb the spider's labors. The spider began in the center and went gradually spinning silk as it wove its web. The little spider slowly designed its image, from the small to the large, from the near to the distant. It gradually expanded, weaving in such a fine and careful way, the minute relationship between each thread was so precise it defied imagination, the joining of the threads was fragile, but perfect. Before long, the crystal-clear spider's web was hung at an angle between the window and the wall, invulnerably elaborate. Qu Shuang bore witness with surprise to this little wonder, human hands seem to fall far behind the wonders of nature. She thought to herself, what if relationships between people were that pure, then she would have no need to avoid the crowds. She looked away and stared off into the distance. At that moment Luke came into the kitchen, his satisfaction was obvious from the look in his eyes. He threw himself down into a chair and flicked through the day's papers, which rustled like falling rain in his hands. Qu Shuang gave him a sideways glance, and immediately he understood what it meant, he slowed his turning of the pages. They didn't need much language to pass between them to attain a spiritual connection. Their rapport was, at times, quite frightening, like a psychologist in control of someone else's central nervous system: A look, an expression, a movement, all were signs that could directly influence the psychology of the other. Luke was yet to come to a decision as to whether this sensory remote control of theirs was a good thing or not. At any rate, people had to be controlled by something, you might as well be a good husband as be trapped in an unyielding political system, and anyway his wife made lots of his friends jealous, that's something every man worth his salt ought to experience at some point. Of course, he sometimes complained to his mates about things at home, just for laughs, when in fact he never wearied of its joys.

Burst after burst of piano music floated up from downstairs, the inferior sounds of a grade five performance transformed the fluid sounds of Mozart into uneven notes, like an army on quick march. Qu Shuang stood up and said, critically, "Oh, there's always something disappointing in life." She shot into the bathroom and opened her robe before the mirror, the gold and black morning robe slid down her honeyed skin and fell at her feet. Her naked body was revealed before the bathroom mirror, and her eyes rested momentarily on her reflection, appreciating her body in a moment's self-inspection. She touched her figure lightly, the lines that comprised her were undulating curves, her slender waist drove many women to envy, several women had asked her in all seriousness what was her secret to keeping a willowy figure. To tell the truth she was a little on the thin side, her breasts were not full, but their contours were fine and they were slightly upturned, it made one think of a particular painting by Klimt; pallid and wild. It was precisely that touching delicacy that gave her a unique appeal. She was satisfied with her body; she knew that her body had a certain harmony that no one could imitate. With the taps gushing water behind her, she turned and poured in some herbal liquid, instantly turning the water a deep-sea blue, filling the bathroom with the scent of jasmine, she climbed joyfully into the water. She enjoyed the soft bubbles surrounding her, the beauty of the moment was almost enough to make her forget everything.

The midday sun was clear and direct, the blue of the sky made one feel expressive. It was already time for lunch, but Qu Shuang couldn't be bothered to go and make it. She hated cooking, her only standard for cooking was to fill her belly, she was not an aesthete in that sense. She was scared of putting on weight and she wanted to save money, the two went hand in hand together perfectly. She was accustomed to eating raw foods directly, like westerners do, she believed that that kind of food was very healthy, you didn't lose the vitamins and it was quick and easy, you only had to wash them and they were ready. Some health magazines said that cooking vegetables destroys the rich vitamins in them and could even produce carcinogens. Thereafter she deliberately became very careful about what she ate. When she went to the supermarket to buy groceries she would always painstakingly select slimming foods, with plenty of vitamins. She was typically superstitious in her belief in science. She unswervingly believed anything that was written in a book—an incurable dogmatist. She believed that the only way to preserve a woman's beauty was with a strict healthy diet. In fact, time was the greatest threat to beauty. A woman's beauty perished over time just as a tender flower is torn by a harsh wind. None could escape it; no woman of natural beauty could avoid the rules of nature, that was a well-established, if cruel fact. Who could possibly resist it? In Buddhism the classic saying, that "the four big stages all become meaningless" isn't some profound theory, but rather it means that there is a road that each person must walk. The specific four stages, "Birth, age, sickness and death" don't hold much mystery either, yet it sums up the whole of life's experience, whether one is rich or poor there is no escaping these things. They are the epitome of simplicity, and yet they ring with truth.

Qu Shuang made her way to the kitchen against her will, and removed boxes of ready-made food from the refrigerator, ham and salad. It was clearly stated on their boxes how many calories each contained, how much fat and how much of the different vitamins and such. And so, her mind was at peace as she put them on the table. Luke did not complain once, but set about chewing the tasteless yet expensive, basic fast food.

After lunch, Luke went to do some work as usual, he was absorbed in his designs. In his eyes, being an architect was the most ideal employment in the world. It demonstrated the creativity of an artist, yet called for a high level of training, perfectly combining modern technology with the visual arts. It was a thorough form of craftwork, not allowing for the least falsity. Once, he and Qu Shuang had gone some distance to see a friend's art exhibition. The exhibition hall was empty, the artist had just carved a few cracks onto the walls, and called it modern art. Many visitors whispered to each other, "Is this really modern art?" The confusion in their eyes was clear, yet they feared being found ignorant, and so they were quick to suppress their doubts and show how well they had understood this piece of modern art. Before long, Luke received a second invitation from the artist for another show, and it was those same few lines, just carved in different directions. Luke looked at it for a few minutes and simply walked out. Afterwards he discussed this artist of limited talent with Qu Shuang. Luke appreciated the daring of the gallery, that was in itself like a piece of performance art, which broke with the established idea of a gallery. In the past people felt that a gallery could only exhibit paintings which could be hung upon a wall, and this gallery had provided a space for the artist in an entirely different way than usual. This in itself was a conceptual revolution, and after all, changing long-held ideas is the only true form of artistic revolution! The problem is that you can only play that trick the once, after that it is just repetition, the creative process used was overly-simple, with no technical ability, anyone could copy it. Luke believed that the highest form of art was unique, it must demonstrate a high level of technical ability, otherwise anybody could be an artist; that would almost become criticism rather than art. The design of the Sydney Opera House for example, is the only one of its kind, an outstanding feature in its city. It has become a symbol for that city, leaving an indelible mark on architectural history. Luke had a dream too, he hoped that one day one of his designs would be used, and a piece of architecture could be built according to his design in London, New York, Paris or Beijing.

And yet today, Qu Shuang did not want to enter her studio at all, she wanted to enjoy the weekend sunshine to the fullest. They shared the belief that maintaining regular work schedules would enliven their marital relationship. Their work was, to each of them, like a kingdom of independence. Once you had climbed into your castle you were the king of it, able to give out orders to your obedient projects, which made the person giving orders feel masterful. In that sense, their work definitely gave them their independence. They each created an atmosphere in their separate occupations, which absorbed the shock of the complexity of human relations; that is the reason that they both chose freelance work. Freelance work is one of the most dangerous of all types of employment. All the risk is shouldered by the individual, who must have the courage to bear that weight. There are no medical or social benefits, and no company to buy life insurance for you. What's more, you'll never appreciate your holiday time as a full-time worker does, your wages are calculated by the hour, which can feel quite precarious at times. Usually the kind of person that chooses freelance work is the type who cannot be the boss and hates being given orders, but they also can't stand being bossed about by others, "You must do this, you must do that". Their only choice is to give their orders to themselves. Qu Shuang had to tell herself, "Today you must complete this, tomorrow you must complete that." No matter how unwilling she was, it had to be done. She had been scraping a living in a foreign country, if she didn't conform to Western ways she would simply die out, the only thing for it was to enter into the Western way of doing things. There was no other choice when it came to survival, that's the most practical way of looking at it. To die, or to live? It's your choice, no one's going to make the decision for you. Given the choice between life and death, naturally Qu Shuang chose to live. Life is beautiful, after all. They solved their problems from the most practical viewpoint—survival of the fittest! That's simple enough and those who strike while the iron's hot are the most successful. So they threw themselves with all their might into the traces. Their so-called means of survival being none other than to enter into the Western social system. It was very difficult getting started, they did jobs that they'd never done while they were in China, they painted walls, fitted floorboards, sawed wood, polished, sanded, fixed the boiler, laid roof tiles, from interior decorator to bricklayer, plumber, material supplies, there was no job too big or too small, and anything was possible. Now they had finally won for themselves a little rest, but every now and then they would feel the pressures of life. They still felt perpetually concerned about the future, they were very clear that this was what they had to do. Qu Shuang didn't dare to dream of winning the lottery, the possibility of getting rich overnight simply didn't exist. In that case taking pleasure as it comes seemed a pretty reasonable notion and Qu Shuang became more and more of a hedonist. Whenever they had some time off, and a bit of money in their pockets, they began to relax just like Westerners do, going to restaurants, pubs and bars. They were employed in all sorts of social events, going to concerts, watching the ballet, enjoying the mediocrity of middle-class life as fully as possible. The most significant quality of the middle classes was dumbing down. They thought that they were cultured, that they were the backbone of society, that their knowledge and skills enriched society, therefore they had a right to their banality. They liked life to be predictable, and seeing as the basis of society is a super-stable structure and they were the most stable of elements, they simply tried their best to achieve banality. Whether Qu Shuang realized it or not, she was trying to become one of them, because that is the safest way of living without losing a certain degree of taste. But, however hard she tried, she always felt that she was still an outsider, with no physical relation to this stretch of earth, with no close relationship to it. If she thought of it from an alternate point of view, it wasn't at all bad living life this way. It avoids a lot of trouble, a lot of excess bother. Then she thought of it as a blessing: She had no need to take part in troublesome elections, took no part in impassioned political debates. At any rate, they were foreigners there, no one was willing to take them seriously. They became peripheral objects, out and out anarchists. It was better to just leave them to themselves.

A leisurely weekend—a white canvas deck chair placed on the balcony, at her feet a stemmed wineglass and a chilled bottle of white wine. The slanting angle of the deck chair was quite comfortable enough to send one straight to sleep. The flowing lines of her body fit the deck chair perfectly, the sunglasses resting on her face magnified the indolent afternoon. It was already past four, but the sunlight had not yet drawn close to dusk, instead it was shining powerfully upon all creation. The sunlight threw its beams down on Qu Shuang's face, she was reading a recently published magazine about interior furnishings. It was obvious from this scene to see that she was thoroughly enjoying herself. She stretched out her hand, placed the magazine on the square stool to her left side, and lit a cigarette. Narrowing her eyes, she calmly watched the white clouds in the blue sky. Seen through her sunglasses, the clouds became a mysterious gray-blue color, great masses of clouds floating upon the seascape of the sky, ever-changing, not remaining still for a moment. One rosy cloud stood solidly against the sky, as if looking down upon all of creation below. Then Qu Shuang thought, if there is a God, maybe that is it. That said, she didn't need a god. Yet privately, she felt that some kind of a spirit did exist. What kind though? It was all so vacant and distant. She certainly had many unwritten rules in her life: She would not take a life; she knew that bad deeds would be punished. She had never killed a single animal in her life, not even tiny ones, (of course, she had swatted mosquitoes. When the natural world encroaches upon human comfort, people cease to be quite so friendly). Once she had opened the window to drive out a fly, causing a Chinese guest to poke fun at her, saying, "How can you be so childish?" Regardless, she believed that every life had a soul, and even if they didn't have a soul, life ought to be respected, life in itself has an innate value. Her neighbor treated her pet dog even better than if it were human itself. When it came to spending money on herself she counted every penny. In the shoe shop she would pick up a pair of shoes and turn them this way and that, and finally put them back on the shelf, saying to herself, "I really ought to buy a pair of shoes." Whereas in the supermarket buying food for her dog, she would go straight to the shelf and take down the most expensive tins of dog food, all the while saying to herself, "My Amzier loves this kind." Once when the old lady went to Italy, perhaps a relative of hers had died and she had no choice but to go, she asked Qu Shuang to look after her dog for a week, she made several long-distance phone calls just to ask how her Amzier was doing. The cost of the phone calls alone must have exceeded her usual daily expenditure. This left Qu Shuang feeling baffled, in some people's eyes it might be utter nonsense, but she believed it was simply a difference in cultural values.

Qu Shuang's neighbour treated her pet dog better than a human. When it came to spending money on herself she counted every penny. In the shoe store, she would pick up a pair of shoes, spin them around, and then finally put them back on the shelf, thinking, "I should really buy a pair of shoes." But when she was in the supermarket buying dog food, she went straight to the shelf and picked out the most expensive cans of dog food, telling herself, "My Amzier loves this kind." Once when the elderly woman went to Italy—a relative of hers had died and she had no choice but to go—she asked Qu Shuang to look after her dog for a week. She made several long-distance calls just to ask how her Amzier was doing. The cost of the phone calls alone must have exceeded her usual daily expenses. This left Qu Shuang baffled. In some people's eyes it might be utter nonsense, but it must have been a difference in cultural values.

The telephone began to ring, and rang very persistently.

She stood up reluctantly and went to answer it.

A voice of the opposite sex came from the telephone, and said that it wanted to speak to her.

Qu Shuang answered in the voice of a professional secretary, "Who's speaking please?"

"Don't you remember me? It's Thomas."

Qu Shuang experienced a feeling of shock, and a nearly forgotten memory rose again in her mind.

---

* Zhao Wuji was a Chinese painter of French nationality who was famous in Paris during the 1960s-1970s.

She had had a random encounter with Thomas.

They had bumped into each other for the first time at a friend's exhibition opening. Li Hai was a friend she had known when she was still in China. He was a graduate from an Arts Academy and painted traditional Chinese paintings. He was currently messing about with modern Chinese landscape brush paintings, which were selling quite well. He had several exhibitions at high-class galleries in London, and could live off his paintings, which was a kind of success. In Li Hai's paintings, there was a sense of exaggeration amongst the elegance. These ought to be two contradictory terms, they ought to be mutually exclusive, but Li Hai's paintings had their own logic. There was a tyrannical flavor to them (without invoking the derogatory sense of the word). It was full of powerful hidden messages. They might lead a certain kind of person into evil ways, and lead another kind of person into a palace of their imaginings! That must be what people refer to as the power of art. However, his paintings were a bit too like those of Zao Wou-ki.* Of course to say so would certainly have upset Li Hai. Repetition is the great forbidden of artists. To say that one person's work is like another's is not a very clever compliment to pay them.

Qu Shuang stood before a giant piece of freestyle modern ink and brushwork, almost two meters high and three meters wide. She was appreciating its vast size. The painting was both abstract and realistic. Its conflicting appearance took Qu Shuang away to a wasteland that was at once familiar

---

* Zao Wou-ki (1920-2013), a Chinese painter of French nationality who was famous in Paris during the 1960s-1970s.

and strange. That overworked piece of land had given birth to Qu Shuang and raised her; her love for and desire to escape from that land were like sisters that could not bear to be separated. She stood for a long time before that painting, analyzing it through her own eyes. Just then, someone interrupted her unbridled reverie. That person said he liked the painting too. His face spread into an ingratiating smile; a smile that turned Qu Shuang's stomach. No matter how knowledgeable the man before her might be, she couldn't be bothered to speak to him. To be fair, his features were very handsome, with a Greek-style sculpted nose. As far as Qu Shuang could see, the nose was an integral detail on a person's face, the nose was the symbol of intelligence, a stupid nose could never aspire to intelligence. Qu Shuang had previously examined the noses of several great writers, like Marcel Proust, James Joyce, Albert Camus, Samuel Beckett, Virginia Woolf, Anna Akhmatova and so on, all were endowed with indubitably unique noses. That thoroughly masculine man had skin with the rich sheen of olive oil, the bright eyes of a wild deer; his mouth had sexy curves, like a typical Michelangelo sculpture. He bowed when he spoke and Qu Shuang couldn't make out if he was trying to be gentlemanly or apologetic. His posture made Qu Shuang think of the scheming Dickensian villain, who said, "I am but a poor man", whilst hiding schemes in his wicked heart. His English was loaded with a heavy Indian accent. He began to talk enthusiastically to Qu Shuang, asking where she was from, who her family was, what she did here, and things like that, as if he wanted to find out everything about her in five minutes flat. When Qu Shuang told him that she made pottery, the man put his hands together and lent over saying, "That's wonderful."

Qu Shuang thought mournfully to herself, "Surely this is not the product of colonial culture?

Lots of people came that night, many of whom seemed familiar, as if she had seen them somewhere before. She looked up and caught sight of a cultural hobbyist well known in London, who was wearing an incomparably ugly hat. From the craftsmanship alone one could tell that the hat was not cheap, it was a royal sort of hat half covered in front with a birdcage veil, the sort you'd usually only wear for weddings and funerals. It seemed much too formal to be worn at an exhibition of paintings. As a result, her over-serious bearing made her look a bit odd. This respectable lady always did herself up to look like neither fish nor fowl and became the butt of other people's jokes, and the subject of their discussions. Her sense of color was all wrong, she would put red and purple together. Two decidedly inharmonious colors, mixed together they would make a thoroughly dirty hue, but she would still wear them together. She wasn't in the least selective about colors, she would wear anything. If she had the least idea of aesthetics she ought to know that some colors suited her, some colors could be worn occasionally, and some colors should not be thrown together at all. Wearing the wrong colors was like taking the wrong medication; it makes people feel unwell. However she dressed, she gave people the impression of a witch: Bright colors looked cheap and vulgar on her, middle tones looked suspiciously dark on her. In truth, at her age and with her looks, she only had to dress herself with dignity and that would be quite enough. She hadn't realized that, however, and so she put a lot of effort into getting done up, painting bold layers of rouge upon her face. However expensive the makeup, it did nothing to hide the naturally rough quality of her skin. She was always seen wearing all different famous brand items of clothing, but she had let it get so dirty that she looked rather like she had spent all day slaving over a hot stove, which didn't go with the brand name clothes at all. Just imagine, even the richest of superstars wouldn't wear brand name clothes in the kitchen. Qu Shuang looked at that ridiculous hat on her head and thought, that hat would look different on anybody else's head but hers. She exchanged a few sentences out of politeness with the zealous lady, and walked away. People were giving this oddly dressed woman sideways looks, and not to appreciate her style, but because they couldn't resist putting their heads together and gossiping about her surreptitiously.

The people in the gallery were walking to and fro, the well-trained waiters who were wearing swallow-tailed coats, frequently refreshed the guests' glasses of champagne. The scene was exceptionally lively, but the people there showed little interest in the exhibition itself. Rather the polite speech exchanged between guests grew ever more lively. It is a common ailment at art exhibitions, but, as a large crowd hints at the possibility of success, the artist can comfort himself with the thought of how many people had attended. Qu Shuang walked distractedly from one piece of work to another. In one corner of the gallery her gaze collided with the gaze of another; the collision was like a car crash, so swift that it left her no time to withdraw her gaze. It was a look that was scorching, a bizarre gaze, that unsettled her. She couldn't help but return his gaze for a moment or two longer. His eyes followed her everywhere, not letting her go; he was inescapable. She hurriedly brought her own eyes back to the paintings on the wall, yet she could still feel those eyes burning into her back. She lost control of her senses and the wine came spilling out of her glass for no apparent reason. The man dashed over and produced a handkerchief, which he passed to her. She stretched out her hand instinctively and their fingers met for the briefest moment, just a light brushing not lasting even a second. Yet it was sufficient to set both of their hearts racing. They looked uncomfortably at each other, obviously embarrassed, but that didn't affect the way they felt, they each felt that there was something uncommon about the person in front of them.

Their meeting was dramatic, it enticed them to wonder what might be.

The man introduced himself, saying "My name is Thomas Walter."

Qu Shuang looked at him with restraint, and introduced herself as well. By now she had already recovered her composure, and they began speaking to each other face to face.

She learned that he was in music, a cellist (Was that a sign? Qu Shuang always imagined her body as a cello). Naturally they began discussing music, and talked about many different musicians. When they came to speak of Schubert's Piano trio, Qu Shuang said that she had originally liked the piece very much, but that it was over-used now, she'd heard it as the theme in at least three different movies, it had become over-popularised, and popular music was too conventional. At that point, Thomas lifted his blue-gray eyes and stared blazingly at her, a gaze that flashed with a surprise that she had never seen before. Then Thomas asked her what she did, and she said that she played with clay.

His eyes filled with the light of confusion. His age was difficult to estimate, you could say he looked anything from thirty to fifty-or-so. The potential scope of his age was so great as to leave one feeling quite bewildered. On the one hand he looked quite mature, on the other he seemed young. At any rate he was not going bald, and he was not fat. Qu Shuang never felt good about balding men, in this sense she was on the side of most men that judged purely based on looks. She couldn't imagine making love with a bald man, with a great big, bald and shiny egg moving about in front of you, that's a ridiculous and laughable scene. She imagined that it would make her laugh uncontrollably. Even less could she imagine a great big belly pressing down on her body, that would certainly end in her breaking three lower ribs and winding up in the emergency room rather than enjoying the pleasures of sex.

Qu Shuang blushed subconsciously; she could not believe that she could experience such a direct train of thought.

She met his eyes once more, he was still searching, confused, so she explained to him what "playing with clay" meant. He began to laugh heartily, surprising all present. Everyone in the gallery turned their heads to look at them; it was as if they had known each other for hundreds of years. Then suddenly there was silence. He looked seriously at her, they were exchanging mysterious messages with their eyes. A subtle atmosphere developed between them. Qu Shuang cast a flustered look about her, it wasn't a very sophisticated means of cover, there was a pause of quite a few seconds, then she said that she had something to do, that she had to go.

They were both very clear that this was just an excuse.

Surprisingly, Thomas found himself admiring this excuse, it gave him a glimpse of her profundity. With his emotional experience, he found this woman intriguing. He didn't enjoy simple things. Sometimes he would make his life complicated, involving himself in complex triangles and getting his fingers burned. He sometimes hoped for a simple life, but things always went against his wishes, and he always courted curiosity and mystery. He could not alter his passionate nature, he had often told himself, "If I am to feel that I am alive, I ought not to repress my natural instincts." It was such a persuasive argument. He was always looking for passion; passion inflamed him. When he was tired out, his passion would also vanish, after that would come entanglement, pain, exhaustion, and guilt.

Qu Shuang was a practitioner of 'escapism'. She knew that at the key moment 'running away' was the smartest thing to do. Running away was simple and trouble-free, of all the plans in the book, walking out was plan A* It could always get one out of a tight spot. Qu Shuang walked towards a table near the window, put down her wineglass and went to say goodbye to the artist. She thanked Li Hai for the invitation, and explained over and over why Luke had not been able to make it. She said, Luke was indoors rushing to finish a design, his final deadline was tomorrow. Everyone that lives on the outside knows that the "final deadline" is the last chance, it was your meal ticket. And if you lost your meal ticket you had lost half of your life.

Liu Hai said expansively, "Yes, that's quite understandable." And then hurried off to continue his circuit. That night he was the star of the show, naturally he had his inescapable duties to attend to.

When Qu Shuang went to get her cape, Thomas said that he was leaving too, "We can go out together."

A perfectly normal sentence can have overtones under certain circumstances.

Qu Shuang looked at him strangely; she had no idea how to react to this situation that had arisen so unexpectedly.

They walked silently out onto the street, both acting a little restrained. Thomas said, "We could go to a bar nearby for a drink, if you don't mind."

She replied in a panic, "No, I have to go home."

---

* A Chinese saying, summing up the entire ancient book of Sun-tzu's *Art of War,* in the pithy aphorism, "Of all the 36 plots [in the Art of War], leaving is the best".

Despite her words, she stood silently on the spot without making a move to leave. They stood on the street looking at each other, having spoken a special language all night with their eyes, there passed between them a peculiar feeling of opportunity. It was a feeling that Qu Shuang had had very rarely since getting married.

Thomas' eyes burned as he asked her, "Can we see each other again?"

Qu Shuang shook her head, "I don't know."

They fell silent again. Thomas took a notebook out of his shoulder bag and wrote something down in it, after a minute he tore the page out and said, "This is my address and telephone number."

Those days absolutely everyone was using business cards, each time someone thrust a business card in her face she would be struck by the feeling that they were doing business of some kind, but not this time. Some intangible quality was added to her pleasure. Qu Shuang noticed that his bag was very stylish, made of rough leather, it was large and old-fashioned, even a little shabby, but not in the least cheap looking. Qu Shuang was very sensitive about the finer details in life; she was very concerned with matters of taste. She was filled with limitless feeling for this stranger before her; it was a feeling that could either vanish in a moment or be everlasting. She looked at him once more, and then she turned in the opposite direction and walked away quickly.

The streetlights had come on, the amber light transformed the ancient capital into a place of impenetrable mystery. A moist breeze brushed past and even though it wasn't raining, the surface of the road was wet. That is the special nature of London's climate, it lacks aridity, strength, everything exudes an extraordinary mediocrity, even the weather was restrained to an extraordinary gentility, without dramatic variations, nothing like the weather in Beijing where it was violently hot in the summer and exceptionally cold in the winter. Qu Shuang thought, perhaps the weather where one lives creates one's character. She did not know what kind of character Thomas had, she asked herself, was it really necessary for her to get to know him?

Qu Shuang turned the corner that led her home. From afar she saw that the lights at home were burning brightly, she knew that Luke was still working. When she reached for her keys, she unwittingly touched that piece of paper.

Luke was still buried in his work. She walked over and embraced him warmly, then went into the bedroom to hang up her cape. She remained facing the coat hangers for a while, then stretched out her hand and took out the piece of paper and unfolded it. There was the address and phone number written upon it, underneath the phone number he had drawn a black line and added a large exclamation mark. The exclamation mark was striking, Qu Shuang couldn't understand what it meant. It was one more thing to wonder about, did it indicate imagination, stubbornness, a kind of persistence? Usually she would have thrown away a piece of paper such as this without a second thought. This time, however, she stuffed the piece of paper back into her pocket. She believed that there was no more 'love at first sight' for married people; that was the right of young girls. People that are married with families have no right to that; they only have their marital responsibilities. She wasn't sure whether or not this was just an old and toothless theory. Ever since getting married, she automatically put her feelings and her soul into a 'safe'. It was as if she had everything she'd ever wanted, she shouldn't go getting ideas above her station, sometimes it made her feel disappointed. At that moment she heaved an involuntary sigh, and said to herself, "life is not perfect." Did she want to experience pain on top of imperfection? One glance that day had stirred her desires, was it "love at first sight?" She was afraid to even think of the phrase, and yet she was in love with the idea of it. And looking back, at what point had her own love life not been a case of love at first sight? It left one feeling dizzy, shaken, excited and it was unforgettable, what a rare heartache! She almost admired this form of self torture.

The next day when Luke asked her over the dinner table about the exhibition the night before, Qu Shuang gave him the barest of descriptions, and didn't mention Thomas. Usually she'd go on about the smallest matter for ages to Luke. She liked chatting with him, she felt that he was not only her husband but also her closest friend, there was nothing kept hidden between them. This time she hid something from him, even though nothing had actually happened, it became a tiny private matter.

Her life up until that point had been a stream upon which her sailboat sailed smoothly. She was happy with the current situation. Sometimes she would feel an intangible frustration, she did not know what kind of innate desire it was; what was it that she was hoping for? She wasn't at all sure. She believed that there were many coincidences in a person's life, like opportunities. The fact that some people were unsuccessful was not necessarily because they were not clever, but because they were not lucky. Some people's luck was entirely dependent on opportunity. Maybe that's what people often refer to as 'fate'. Was it possible that her chance meeting with this stranger was a matter of coincidence? She could not fully believe that she had some inescapable connexion with that foreign stranger. She would rather let it become a memory, a comet in the night, that came and went.

Several days later she had a dream—she dreamt of him. She dreamt that she was standing on a towering precipice, when a hand pushed her off. She fell down and down, she thought that it was the end for her. Just as she was about to hit the bottom she was caught quite unexpectedly. She opened her eyes to see that strange man; he ran his hands softly over her body and she turned into a cello, and he played her. The bow leapt upon her body, his fingers played with the strings of her body, stroking them softly, creating elegant notes. He continued looking expectantly at her. She smelt the particular scent of his body, the smell of camphor and peppermint mixed together, the smell that only men have. Some people say that one cannot perceive smells in dreams, but she really truly smelt that scent in hers; she could not explain that mysterious fragrance. Suddenly the cellist opened his arms and the cello blew into a ravine upon a gust of wind, and broke to pieces on a pile of stones. She woke up from her dream covered in sweat; her panting breaths woke Luke who was sleeping by her side. Luke held her tightly, and asked her about her bad dream. Usually she would describe every detail of her dream to him, and Luke would listen and laugh and say, "Why don't you just write it into a novel, it'd do even better than your artwork." But this time she only said that she was afraid, and dared not elaborate further. She was frightened senseless by that wild fantasy of a dream. The dream then also became a part of her secret. She could not believe that it was mere coincidence.

The fragrance from the dream continued to entwine itself about her.

The day after the dream, she took the piece of paper and carefully hid it in her diary like a fanciful schoolgirl. When she opened her diary, it was like the quill of memory describing two worlds: a real world and a world of fantasy. She had to keep these two separate, it was as if her life had become full of meaning and gave her the courage to evade the other reality. It was as if she understood now the source of her burning desires. She must have always been searching for a fantasy world, to draw a line between it and the mundane world of reality, a release for her naturally nonconformist soul. That way she could enlarge her encounter with that strange man into a rich world of imagination; the stranger to her he was the better; the more distant the better. That only served to increase the space for her imaginings. She could fantasize without limits, creating her fantasy world with scarcely any restraints; embellishing her bland reality, weaving garlands of beautiful roses, making them variegated and colorful, heavy and intoxicating, covered with the light of her desire. She became a poet of the imagination, regardless whether she was in the realms of reality or fantasy, she had attained a kind of perfection. She looked at that piece of paper, she thought to herself that there was no need to call him, she would not allow her wings of desire to become real, they only took her for flights in her dreams, charging, rising, turning, dancing wildly, making her giddy, shaken, free. That was enough, that was what she thought.

The summer in London was full of tenderness, while its streets were tumultuous. Young lovers kissed passionately in the street, people hurrying home could not help but slow their pace, while drunkards cursed at the tops of their voices. The city that won't sleep, not until the dawn. Everyone was competing to enjoy London's brief summer as fully as possible. Qu Shuang and Luke were driven outside by this unseen passion along with everyone else; almost every weekend was spent in pubs and cinemas or at concerts, where they would enjoy life in the capital to the fullest. Occasionally they would go to friends' gatherings. There were many names for the parties: moving parties, welcome home parties and parties for seeing off friends, a party for the end of the barbecue season; another if someone had had another child. Since there was no limit on the number of children you could have here, some clever Chinese individuals were pushing on with the 'great production drive',* and using it as an excuse to apply for permanent residency. On these grounds, if they were refused it would seem suspiciously inhumane. Of course, for the most part, it was birthday parties, everyone has a day of birth, having a party was the best way to show that you care about yourself, therefore birthday parties seemed especially important.

At dusk that day, Qu Shuang and Luke were due to attend a friend's birthday party. As soon as they walked through the door, Qu Shuang saw that Thomas was there too, their eyes met again in that instant. Qu Shuang experienced a moment of apprehension. She didn't really want to see him, she had long since relegated him to her dream world. She had no reason to be nervous, and so she tried her best to appear calm, not approaching Thomas directly, instead she spent a long while chatting with other people. Despite this, she could feel a pair of eyes pursuing her throughout. Then, out of the corner of her eye, she caught sight of Thomas chatting with her husband and grew very nervous. She hadn't done anything wrong, and yet she trembled as if she were a thief. She walked over to the table strewn with plates and glasses and poured herself a glass of red wine. As if the wine in her hand

* Borrowing a term from Cultural Revolution China, c. 1940.

would embolden her, she walked towards the two men, holding her wine in her hand. Before the two men she consciously chose a position that was a little distance away from Luke, she didn't want Luke to show too much closeness in front of this stranger, such ancient little tricks from the arena of love came gently back to her.

Luke introduced her to Thomas in a straightforward fashion, "This is my wife, Qu Shuang."

Thomas extended his hand, "Nice to meet you, Qi Sang." He pronounced her name all wrong.

They merely exchanged a knowing smile.

Luke could tell from the way they looked at each other that they had previously met. He asked them casually, "Have you met already?"

Qu Shuang did not reply, but turned her head to the side and looked blankly into the distance.

Thomas replied openly, "Yes, we met at the exhibition last time."

A ray of light shot through Qu Shuang's mind, she could not bring herself to be so frank, but she liked men to be so. Her eyes threw out a tender light, and she smiled gently at Thomas, to show her gratitude. He bowed slightly to show that he was delighted to be of service. These subtle actions were apparent only to the two of them.

Luke told Qu Shuang with enthusiasm that he and Thomas had many friends in common, which must mean that to some extent they were all in the same circle.

"It's a small world isn't it?" Thomas asked Qu Shuang with a sideways look.

Qu Shuang looked at him coolly, her reticence that evening had a profound significance. The three of them went on about these friends that they had in common, hearing from each other that so-and-so had moved to another city, who had got a nice new job, who had split up with who, et cetera. At any rate no one getting a divorce in their friendship group was a miracle nowadays, someone was getting divorced every five minutes. There was some intangible game at work in that atmosphere. Thomas didn't pay the least attention to Luke's presence, but continued to cast very sensual looks at her. While Qu Shuang felt tense and nervous but didn't want to stir anything up in front of other people. Having drunk some wine, everybody was feeling chatty, as the room temperature gradually crept up. Qu Shuang said that it was too hot inside and with that as an excuse, she left. She walked into the back garden that was small and untidy. In one corner were several wobbly chairs and a table with rotten legs. At a glance you could see that the owner was not a traditional British housewife, she didn't seem to care in the least for growing plants and flowers or any other form of horticulture. Although the garden was messy and desolate, that did not alter the fact that it offered a chance to get some fresh air. There were several people there already talking away in twos and threes. Qu Shuang stood beside the fence where the weeds were growing riotously and looked blankly at the sky. An inexplicable emptiness left her feeling quite helpless. She could not understand where this restlessness had come from. She stood enervated under the night sky, as time coagulated beneath her feet. Suddenly she was aware of a stream of air at her back, the warm stream of air circled about her head and her sixth sense told her that it was Thomas, yet she did not turn. Thomas stood quietly behind her for a while, then walked up to her side.

"Here you are." He said.

"It's cool here." She raised her head to look at him.

"You look beautiful tonight." Thomas said.

Qu Shuang knew that it was a comment made out of politeness, to which she made no response. That night she was wearing a light gauze dress that fell right down to her feet. A light purple gauze set upon a deep purple fabric, the patterns underneath were just visible. The deep purple gauze clung to her body like a wrap of mist: It was complementary and just allowed one to make out the lines of her body; it was revealing but not excessive. There were several gashes in the pale gauze, whereas the sleeves were a light purple mist through which one could easily make out the curves of her arms. The unique style of dress lent her the look of the immortals.

That night, she was like a fresh bunch of lilacs under the moonlight.

"You are really beautiful." Thomas looked straight at her, and repeated himself.

The words of praise at the second repetition seemed full of some profound message. She did not respond to his signals, and they fell silent, catching each other in their eyes, but deliberately saying nothing. Thomas looked embarrassed; he seemed to be searching for something to say, when he said, "When did we see each other last? Spring has already been and gone, and yet this flower is yet to open."

Qu Shuang gave him an odd, sideways look, she was afraid that she had misunderstood his words.

That night the moonlight was dim and mysterious, only adding to their helplessness. They continued to stand silently in the dark. That night she was particularly reticent, she felt that everything was out of place, he ought to have remained in her dreams, and here he was stubbornly making an appearance in the real world, it made her feel miserable. She felt as if there were some unseen force leading them on, the further she pulled away, the closer it drew to her, a mysterious force that was beyond her control. She had no idea what kind of power it was, that filled her with excitement and fear. At that moment, they were standing very close to each other and she grew aware of his breathing. She smelt the scent from her dream, all of a sudden her blood rushed to her head, she stepped backwards as if she was going to fall. Thomas quickly put out his hand to catch her, but in the instant that his hand touched her, she vanished like a shadow. Thomas barely had time to react when he found she had already turned and left.

When she re-entered the room, she saw Luke looking all over for her. She walked straight over to him and said that she wanted to go home. Luke looked at his watch and said that it was still early, that they could stay a little longer. "Why leave so early?" Luke asked her, a little confused.

Qu Shuang said that she was tired and insisted that they leave. Luke didn't have much choice but to go along with her. As usual, there was a long round of enthusiastic but empty 'farewells', repeated on a loop to friends new and old alike, half-hearted discussions of the possibility of meeting again. Luke showed great patience in this matter, whereas Qu Shuang was already sick and tired of it, she hid away to one side, looking detached, hoping that they could quickly bring the scene to an end.

Just then she noticed Luke exchanging addresses with Thomas.

The two men shook hands earnestly and said goodbye!

On the drive home, Luke seemed a bit drunk. He drove as if he were dancing. The car swung back and forth down the center of the road and he appeared to be in the mood for a quarrel. Qu Shuang who was sitting beside him warned him that the police wouldn't be in bed just because it was the weekend. He didn't pay the least attention, but spoke loudly as if he were sitting next to a deaf man. That night, Qu Shuang felt as if everything was messed up.

After that night, Qu Shuang felt uneasy. She would lay around and not feel like doing anything, as if she had come down with something. Luke asked her if she wanted to see a doctor, but she said there was no need. She was only feeling depressed and miserable. Several times she had been on the point of just asking Luke what he thought about Thomas, but she always managed to contain herself in the end. She decided that those were two worlds that could not be brought together. That was an imaginary distance, her own space could not contain those two worlds. She had had enough of wild days, she craved peace; why was she so down in the dumps then? A clear answer never came to her.

Qu Shuang was intelligent, she did not want to get stuck in this unnecessary complication. It took her a long time to reconcile her feelings. After that, she felt much better, but a telephone call that afternoon churned up her carefully smoothed out feelings. She involuntarily lowered her voice, looking quite guilty, and rambled on at her end of the telephone not knowing what to say, whilst the voice at the other end grew ecstatic. He said that he was so lucky that she had answered the phone. Only then did she force herself to regain a little composure, she asked, "And what if it hadn't been me who answered, what would have happened then?"

"Who says I can't call other people?" the other end of the telephone replied.

Qu Shuang could not resist laughing, "You're a crafty character."

As soon as the words left her, she knew that she had made a mistake. That sentence reduced the distance between them, which was not what she wanted at all.

"Not everyone understands my craftiness." The other end said with obvious pride.

She was not sure how to continue the conversation, and grew silent.

The other end said, "Why don't we go for a drink sometime?" He was always talking about "going for a drink" as if it was an alcoholic he was asking out, rather than a lady.

"I'm not sure if I have time." Qu Shuang's tone of voice was hesitant.

"You will have, if you want to." It was as if he had seen through her thoughts.

"And what if I don't want to?" Qu Shuang instantly began to play the devil's advocate.

"How about this then, we'll meet at the Half-moon Bar at 7.00 Tuesday night, okay?"

This stranger always managed to read her thoughts. She had always been attached to the moon, she was enamored of the pallor of the moon (of course the idea of the moon looking sickly pale is just a human idea pasted onto a natural phenomenon). She liked the sickle moon, half-concealed and radiant. She enjoyed a cryptic half moon even more. Walks under the moon's silver light made one seem mysterious; it heightened a romantic mood. The name of the bar at least made it worth paying a visit. She turned the matter over in her mind. She did not want to prevaricate too long over the phone, Luke was in the room next door, he might come in at any moment. In order to bring the phone conversation to as swift an end as possible, she hurriedly agreed to meet him on Tuesday night, at the Half-moon Bar as he had suggested.

After she had hung up the phone, Qu Shuang still felt hesitant. She could not understand why she had agreed to the meeting so readily, when it went against her intentions. She felt as if she was being led on by something that left her no choice.

At dinner, Luke asked who had just telephoned, Qu Shuang made a vague reply that it was nothing important. She thought that that would not count as being dishonest, and saved them the trouble. She did not want to speak of Thomas at the dinner table, it was as if his name was forbidden territory between husband and wife. It was like a needle that touched upon the tip of the nerves of their household. Perhaps that is an exaggeration, but whenever his name came up, she experienced the uneasy sensation that she had ulterior motives at heart.

The streets outside the window stared at her with evil intent.

She waited for the arrival of *that* moment with a heart ill at ease.

II. *The Silhouettes Overlap*

It was ever so slightly chilly that night. She deliberately did not particularly make herself up; if anything, she was more careless than usual. A pair of fitted brown jodhpurs revealed her long legs, a light beige silk shirt tucked into an exquisite leather belt, to enhance her striking waist, a camel colored cashmere sweater not worn but casually draped over her shoulders, as if jumpers were made only to be draped and not worn. She didn't look at all as if she were going to a rendezvous, but rather as if she were going for a day at the races. Her dress was always unique, different from the crowd. She was never one to follow fashion. It was difficult to describe her attire, simple yet exaggerated, casual yet weighty, with no lace or trims at the edges, a bit like the style of the dancer Duncan. To use the jargon of artists, her attire belonged to the school of the "Neoclassical". She always went to extremes in her attire; her skirts would either be long enough to sweep the floor or as short as short could be, but never in the middle. Getting ready that night was a painstaking process, she could not be accused of dressing to reveal or seduce, nor was she overdone or flirty, but she looked, one had to admit, one hundred percent attractive.

The night before she had performed a complex beautifying massage procedure on herself; the following day she certainly was glowing. Just before she left she applied light make-up to her face that would have taken a well-trained eye to detect. However, this light makeup was entirely different to her wearing none at all—like the difference between cotton and silk, it was a difference of intrinsic qualities.

After leaving the house, she deliberately avoided taking the tube, because then she would have arrived punctually. She preferred to leave a man to get hot under the collar waiting for her rather than arrive even one minute early. She always arrived casually late for her appointments with the opposite sex, that was her established style. She boarded the route 76 bus and climbed to the upper deck, choosing a seat in the first row. The glass of the windscreen was bright and broad, her field of vision stretched far into the distance. The rosy clouds of sunset were reflected in row upon row of skyscrapers and tall buildings, the ancient city was dyed beautifully in the colors of the summer evening. She looked at the distant setting sun, it was huge and red. Strictly speaking it was not bright red, but the indescribable red of a sunset, incomparably glorious. It made her think of the English painter Turner's work. Turner's skies were bright and mysterious, but always transitory, his brush created a frenzied whirlwind, was he describing the sky or himself? Those crazed eyes of his expressed an age of omnipresent danger.

The bus was exceptionally quiet, the only other person on board was a sagging, middle-aged woman sitting on the opposite side to her. Her hair was a straw-like blond, her mouth painted bright red. She wore a low-cut dress, revealing her soft full breasts, so that anyone could become well-acquainted with her intimate places. She sat there quite openly. Qu Shuang saw that the skin on her bosom was wrinkled, and could not help but remarking to herself that women are a wreck when they age. From the remains of her appearance, she felt certain that the woman opposite her must have been appealing in her youth. She possessed the common standards of beauty: blond hair, blue eyes and a large bosom. And yet time had cruelly taken away her beauty, leaving even her breasts wrinkled. The magic mirror of time really was devoid of all pity. Fear of aging hit her in that moment. Life is short, she had no reason to tie herself down, she ought to enjoy all that she could. With that thought in mind it was as if she had found sufficient bravery for her present mission.

As dusk was drawing to a close, she found the pub in the place Thomas had described on the telephone with no trouble at all. It was beside the river, in a quiet location. It turned out to be a unique pub after all, the outer walls were painted an enticing shade of violet, the name "The Half-Moon" was written in golden letters on the wall, and the letters were elegantly curved, like delicate crescent moons. The unusual design alone enticed one in to have a drink. Her muscles that were taut with tension relaxed as a result of the personable surroundings, she prepared herself for just a moment and walked in. Inside the pub, the lights were dim, the shadows fell in layers upon the wall. She saw a pair of hands in the darkness motioning to her, before she had absolutely realized what was going on, Thomas was suddenly standing before her. He laid a well-mannered kiss upon her cheek and when he stood aside to let her by, his hand rested lightly upon her waist, just like the touch of a lover. Ordinarily she would have seen this as an instance of pure sexual harassment, yet at that moment she felt differently; she didn't mind it, she desired it even. She felt as if she had come here for that harmless touch alone. They both walked intuitively to the same table in the corner, it was a clear and deliberate choice. After they were seated, he asked her what she would like to drink and she said that she would have a gin and tonic with lemon. A drink made of a traditional British spirit mixed with a soft drink, the slightest bitterness mingled with the sweetness makes it delicious.

While the waiter busied himself with the drinks, she took the chance to look about her, it was a rather traditional pub, with chandeliers of embossed, colored glass, an example of thoroughly ancient handicrafts, of which there are many copies nowadays, whose level of craftsmanship never meet the standard of the genuine older pieces. Although the oil paintings on the wall were not masterpieces, they were masterfully executed and well-aged, well-suited to the Georgian building. The best feature of the pub was its peaceful atmosphere, unlike some pubs that were raucous with voices competing with deafening music. Of course, it was obvious from the sparse customers that the pub did not do very good business. A small blue and white porcelain vase was placed on each table, with a spare-looking spray of white tuberose, giving off bursts of uplifting fragrance, which gave the pub an atmosphere of nostalgia out of nowhere. It made Qu Shuang drift into thoughts of the pensive quality of Venice, of that briefly glorious Austro-Hungarian empire now lost forever, its glory already history, where old people rely on their memories to survive— a capital permeated by a languishing, pensive air.

She was just losing herself when Thomas interrupted the train of thought that took her far far away. He gave her an extremely meaningful look and said, "It's great that you've come." She wasn't in the least accustomed to the wide eyes of Westerners. Whenever they're keen on someone, the light in their eyes is enough to burn you. She had very rarely seen an Asian person's eyes look so bold and daring, that kind of look gave her a start whenever she was faced with it. She did not know how to avoid those eyes that were like a bolt of lightning, they followed her into her dreams, where they would have new encounters. Thomas was staring at her with such eyes at that moment, she felt uncomfortable all over, she felt as if every single part of her body was superfluous, she did not know what to do with them. She laid her hands awkwardly on the table, she did not know where to look. She was flustered as a schoolgirl innocent of worldly matters. Thomas said that he liked the way that Oriental women have.

She carried on talking quite out of place and asked, "What way?"

Thomas did not reply, but snatched up her hands in his in the heat of the moment. In an instant she no longer felt flustered and calmed down completely, her hands which had no place to go a moment ago had found a fitting place, her hands in his large damp hands seemed to mean something. Her palms began to perspire as well, yet they were icy cold. A pair of icy hands like a ball of cold fire, burning them. They were both very clear that this was a sign of danger, the flames danced, and gradually leapt out of where they belonged. They did not say a thing to each other, they followed each other with their eyes, as if trying to get to the bottom of something, as if they were determined to solve the riddle. It was a riddle without an answer, yet all the while they both labored in vain searching for answers. The touching of their hands was definitely a moment of enlightenment. The candlelight leapt in their eyes, their black silhouettes flashed about on the wall, sometimes overlapping, sometimes parting, acting out a mime of love.

They did not say much that night, they just looked quietly at each other, having one drink after another, passing love letters to each other with their eyes. Unspoken, they were all the more meaningful, more attractive than endless chatter.

By now, the people in the pub had grown even fewer and they too walked out onto the street. Just as they were leaving, Thomas turned swiftly and pinned her to the corner of the building, roughly forcing her hands behind her, kissing her violently. To begin with, she tried to resist, but gradually she began to respond to him, their tongues wrestled with each other in their mouths. She could hear his heavy breathing and the furious beating of their two hearts. Once more she became aware of the scent from her dream. As his body pressed against her for all he was worth, she turned her head aside and muttered softly, "You're going to crush me into the wall." He pressed harder against her, as he panted out the words, "I don't just want to crush you into the wall, I want to press you into my flesh". His naked insolence stirred her desire, they rubbed against each other, only separated by the thin layers of their summer clothing, panting, the unsatisfied desire shot like lightning through the marrow of their bones.

The sky was pitch black. Venus, the first star to rise, was piercingly bright. All the stars in the heavens were spying on their transgression, but she didn't care any longer. His hands slipped over every part of her body, they kissed without pause, their bodies twisted licentiously together. She felt waves of heat rising within her. They each wished to be hunted down by the other. If only they could linger on in some other place, some other time—Qu Shuang pushed him away and said she had to go. Thomas looked confused, but remained silent, and continued to stare straight at her. She lowered her head, Thomas said that his home was not far away, they only had to pass through the haunted public gardens to reach it, they could go in for a drink. Qu Shuang shook her head, she said that she was already nearly drunk as it was, that she couldn't drink anymore. Thomas said that he'd see her back home then, but she refused to let him. Just then a black cab swept past on the road, one of the unique features of London. Her hand shot up, the cab stopped to her left and she jumped into the cab in a drunken haze, with it taking her further and further away. Thomas became a black dot left behind her, they melted away from each other in the night. She did not know whether they would get in touch again, they had not arranged another meeting when they parted ways. Still their bodies retained sufficient signals, even though they had not broken through the final barrier, the force of them had already torn through many boundaries. A passion that she had not felt for a long time beat against her like waves, at that moment she could still feel waves of titillation rushing through her body. Despite this she had to preserve her calm, it was precisely this that men who had contact with her found unimaginable and that made women hate her; her restraint undoubtedly made her all the more attractive, forcing men to persist in pursuing her. Women saw it as a pretentious show of coquetry, and yet her restraint did not stem from modesty at all, but rather from haughty pride. Perhaps that was the reason that she encountered such envious hate in people. You could say that she was a lonely figure amongst women. Women didn't really like her, even her best female friends gave up on her. She couldn't explain it clearly, she was only vaguely aware that women never really trusted her, their judgmental gaze pushed her out to a distant periphery, she was always a lonely individual.

Qu Shuang groped her way furtively up the stairs, she was half-drunk. Relying on the buoyancy of the drink, she had strung together a perfect web of lies on her way home. Whatever questions Luke might ask she would be able to make a seamless flow of answers. She walked carefully into the bedroom, afraid of startling Luke. She didn't switch on the light, but crept quietly into bed. In their room, lights flashed dimly in the gloom. There was something creepy about the dim light, which made her feel guilty and afraid. At that moment, she heard Luke's even snores, quiet, steady and calming, the breathing she was so familiar with, which gave her a feeling of safety that no one else could replace. It was as if she had taken a pacifying drug, she no longer felt panicky. Feeling as if she was walking on clouds, she lay down in her bed. Recent scenes retreated like a surrealist oil painting hung on the wall of a gallery somewhere. She hung alone on the branches, her body painted in a deep blue mysticism. She was crooked, perverse, deformed. She didn't know whether it was an after-effect of the alcohol or a nightmare.

At breakfast the next day, she waited anxiously for Luke's questioning to begin, but to her disappointment he didn't ask her a single thing, not even a vague inquiry. Qu Shuang couldn't help but feel a little let down. She was good at playing the little tricks that women play, she understood her place in the house. Luke's regard was crucial to her, she liked to be spoiled by a man. She felt a little let down that Luke had not displayed the jealousy that her pride demanded, even though she was extremely worried about Luke growing suspicious of her. If Luke got caught up in this, it would put her in a very awkward position indeed. She was caught in a provocative mood; she asked herself, did Luke not care about her? She could not understand how her life could have turned into a game overnight. She had not yet realized quite how dangerous the situation was, or how great a price she would have to pay.

In the days that followed, Qu Shuang forced herself to remain on an even keel. She undertook no action, she was waiting, waiting for the summons that kept her in suspense. When the telephone rang but once she was there in a shot, whereas she was usually disinterested in telephone calls. Normally she couldn't be bothered to answer it. It wasn't that Luke hadn't noticed, but that chose not to say a word. His silence tortured Qu Shuang. Qu Shuang was caught between suspicion and suspense, even though she didn't feel that she had done anything wrong. She wanted to tell herself that that night did not exist, she tried to get through by lying to herself. The more she wished she didn't have such thoughts, the more the strange thought appeared like a poisonous dart stuck in her brain. One day, two days, a week, two weeks passed—there was no word from him. She snatched up the telephone several times only to put it back down again, her restraint and pride would not allow her to call him. Strictly speaking, it was her vanity that prevented her from doing so. She did all that she could to cover up her restlessness, afraid that Luke would notice the least little thing. She had no reason to hurt him. And yet her absentmindedness grew obvious. It was a contest, a contest between the games of man and woman. At the same time, she felt another self going further and further away from her, that person dissolved at liberty in the sky, whilst she created her own prison of velvet and locked herself inside of it. She imagined her home as a beautiful prison, she was unable to escape from her delightful predicament. She really did want to open up and discuss her state of mind with Luke. She didn't know whether men torment themselves over this sort of predicament as well. She couldn't really be sure about the way men thought, especially the man on her mind—they had only had a few instances of contact that only went skin deep, it really only amounted to primitive desires. She had always believed so strongly in spiritual interaction. She had no trouble with her sexual desire, and she had a good sex life with her husband. Why should this primitive urge have such a tight hold over her and refuse to let her go? It seemed overly simplistic to explain it away in terms of novelty or excitement. It didn't get to the root of the problem—what was it? Should instinct prevail over sense? Or sense over instinct? Which was the more important? She knew that it would be too cruel to discuss this with Luke, and yet she knew so well that he was the most suitable person to discuss it with. The way in which their knowledge of each other extended to the very marrow of their bones was difficult to describe. A look, a movement, they were perfectly attuned and it made people around them quite jealous. They had previously discussed what to do in the event of polygamy, affairs and taking separate lovers just as friends would. They were both very open-minded. Luke felt that it wasn't unimaginable for either the husband or wife to take a lover. The problem was what would happen to that loving couple? Of course it was a bit sentimental to use a word like "loving", people aren't accustomed to use such old-fashioned language anymore. Whoever uses such words is bound to become a laughing stock, people will think that you are entirely behind the times.

On a drowsy afternoon, the telephone began to ring violently, making Qu Shuang start in fear. She felt instinctively that this was no ordinary phone call. She seized the phone. There was a stream of air at the other end like a bolt of lightning, she lost her bearings, she wanted to hang up the phone straight away. She didn't want to put herself in a ridiculous position again, she did not need him in her life, she had already told herself hundreds of times over. The receiver nestled close to her skin, controlling her in a way she had never experienced before. That rushing sound of air was so intimate, possessed of its own great power, as if it were caressing her skin through the receiver. Desire was transmitted throughout her body, she did need him! At the other end he was saying, "Hello, hello," and she found that she did not have the courage to throw down the receiver and ignore him. At the other end, he was frantically giving all sorts of reasons why he hadn't been in touch. He had been performing in a few Eastern European countries, it was a disaster trying to make international calls from there, it was impossible to get through. He had tried no less than a hundred times. Whenever he came across a phone booth he'd dive in and give it another go, but in the end he just gave up! He said that at that moment he felt absolutely bereft of hope! It was simply the end of the world! He explained down the phone.

He swore down the phone, damn those backward countries!

His explanations, along with his sincerity, renewed her faith. Her accustomed pride returned. She said that she hadn't been waiting for his call. She landed herself in it with that foolish sentence. She regretted it as soon as it slipped out. But it was as if he hadn't noticed, instead he continued with his endless explanations. He said he missed her very much, that he must see her immediately, that he couldn't wait any longer. When Qu Shuang heard that, she softened, that was precisely the reason for her being so frantic over the last few days: She couldn't be sure whether he was thinking of her or not. She hated herself for giving herself away so easily and silently warned herself that she must never do such a stupid thing again. That sentence was exactly what she had wanted to hear; she found herself beginning to collude. And yet she went on without thinking, to say,

"I don't want to do the things I do, I don't want to say the things I say, and I can't say what I want to." Her tone was full of obvious hurt.

Thomas was already well accustomed to her way of speaking, that always had a hidden meaning. He believed that she always said the opposite of what she thought. He was deeply intrigued by the equivocations of this oriental woman. He felt that it would be the best proof of his intelligence.

However, what he did not realize was that this time she was telling the truth.

Both ends of the telephone were silent for a long time, Qu Shuang did not want to be the first to speak just then. She waited patiently for his instructions. He arranged for them to meet in the evening with an undeniable tone of request. He invited her to his house. She muttered down the phone that she wasn't sure whether or not that would be suitable. He closed in on her asking, what was unsuitable about it? Goading her on turned out to be effective, Qu Shuang said fine, and quickly hung up the phone. She felt a bit flustered. At that moment she only wanted to leave the room as quickly as possible and go somewhere where there was no telephone. And yet for days she had been glued to her spot bedside the telephone afraid that she wouldn't be there to take the only call she was waiting for. Now she could go out, to get away from the call that made her tremble with nerves.

She walked dazedly out onto the street, without knowing which direction she should take. Luckily, there was a cafe at a nearby street corner. She needed to go there and sit for a while, to rearrange her jumble of emotions, but before she had reached the café, she found herself walking into a pub in spite of herself. In London you can find a pub on even the most far-flung of corners, as if the British can live without restaurants, but they cannot do without their pubs. Some poor Brits have drunk their noses red and their faces ashen, and they still don't stop drinking. Theirs is a culture puffed up by its soaking in alcohol! She was thinking that alcohol would be the best solvent for conflicts and she needed to forget things for a while.

The pub had an atmosphere of death. The cheap, florid carpet; the filthy old newsprint wallpaper; a row of customers, all pensioners, holding up the bar, their bodies giving off a queer smell made of body odor gone a long time without a wash. They stared at her with a look of astonishment in their eyes. It was obviously not a pub that young people frequent. Ordinarily she would not choose this kind of pub, generally speaking she was far too concerned with ambience, but she had no place for such concerns now. She only wanted to sit down and have a drink. A glass of fine Scottish Whisky slipped down her throat, warming her insides, entering her body like a fresh spring. For a moment she felt much more relaxed. Just like a man, she said to herself, "the wonders of drink!" She had never understood how men could get steaming drunk. Now she could understand a little at least, although she still felt distaste for the unappealing flaws that appeared in people when they were drunk. She remembered her mother saying to her when she was still very young, that the best proof of a man's character is to see him after he's been drinking, you want nothing to do with a man that goes crazy on drink. She did not know then how deeply this would affect her subconscious. She half-consciously examined the state of her boyfriends when they drank. Each of them had been as quiet as a mouse, her husband was especially sweet when he drank; he just smiled broadly and followed her arrangements.

She paid the bill and walked out onto the street, through a graveyard. It was one of London's oldest graveyards and one of the earliest hangouts for homosexuals. She could still see a few solitary men loitering about, they sat pensively upon the benches by the graves, looking as if they were there to keep those at rest beneath the sod company, rather than to wait for the call of the living. Coming to London nothing shocked Qu Shuang more deeply about the difference between the two cultures than the discrepancy in their attitudes towards death. In China, a graveyard is a terrifying place, set far away from crowds of people, the gravestones a mess, a place where spirits come and go; they symbolize darkness and bad luck and worse. No one would be willing to go for a stroll there; no one would go there at all unless they were going specifically to tidy up the grave of a relative. It made Qu Shuang think of something interesting, two friends of hers had just gotten married and had bought a classical English house in a district of London, with a little garden overgrown with creepers, a really nice atmosphere, the street was quite clearly called "Lovers Lane." Yet it was situated right beside a graveyard. Whenever they invited Chinese friends over, they would mutter to themselves, "Why would they want to buy a house next to a graveyard? It's so unlucky!" Some of these friends even visited less, fearing that they would catch the bad luck. Yet, that friend lived more happily than the lot of them, winning the lottery and going traveling, he lived a good life. It must be at least eighty percent down to the excellent *Feng Shui* of that spot, bringing them good luck, there was no other explanation. In all her experience in China, she had never seen a cemetery in a city center. And yet from far-off New Zealand, to central cities like Paris, Rome and London, there were centrally-located cemeteries everywhere. There were always flowers in bloom; they had a pleasant atmosphere and weren't in the least terrifying. They were seen as a fine place for a walk or to spend one's time, and a symbol of history. Sometimes they were even seen as the pride of the city and a famous historical site, with so many famous people buried there, they created beautiful bone-yards. Several times Qu Shuang had been led by enthusiastic friends into different graveyards to admire their history. They believed that a cemetery contained the historical remains of a city. A friend had once proudly led her to the cemetery in central Vienna. Beethoven, Mozart and Brahms were all buried there. There were many unremarkable people buried there, as well as famous people. They were called cemeteries, and they were markedly different to the Ancient Mausoleums,* Sun Yatsen's Memorial, Mao Zedong's Memorial Hall, which were the resting places of glorious leaders. There you had to hold your breath and pass by on tiptoe, with a serious expression on your face, revering them. You couldn't let slip the least sign of happiness, you must be mournful, otherwise people would think you were being disrespectful. Of course it was even more unthinkable to see such places as a diversion like an amusement park. She remembered back, when she was still in China, to a reverential trip to Chairman Mao's Mausoleum. Everyone lined up, wearing a serious expression, to enter the hall wherein lay the crystal coffin. One unworldly youngster went in scuffing his feet on the marble floor, saying "This place would make a pretty good dance hall." The next day a report was made and he was tracked down and given a telling off. He returned to the office where he worked, swearing and blinding, "I don't know which one of you lot told tales on me, come on and stand up to me if you're tough enough!" Recalling the scene, she laughed out loud. Distant memories made her head feel much clearer; she looked at her watch, it was getting late. She rushed back home and washed her face. She made herself up, but not too dramatically. She believed that as a woman approached middle age, it was ridiculous to rely on makeup to affect others, especially in this kind of situation, that was even more ridiculous. In order to avoid any suspicions that she was out to attract, the smartest thing to do would be to rely on her natural beauty as a woman, her inner modesty; she was very

* Changling and Dingling, two mausoleums outside of Beijing

smart when it came to that. Luke hadn't come home yet; she left him a note saying that she would be home late. She didn't say why she would be home late. She thought it was better that way. She didn't want to resort to lying to Luke too readily. She knew that that was forbidden ground between husband and wife. She believed that whatever happened, their marital relationship was built upon a foundation of trust, she would only resort to that plan B when there was nothing else for it, that was her expedient plan.

She recovered her usual calm. Casually locking the door after her, she walked out onto the street feeling in no hurry. She consciously slowed her steps, enjoying the scenery on the street. The nerves of a few hours ago, the fear were all swept clean away; they just vanished to who knows where. Her heart was filled with an ambiguous peace. She no longer asked herself whether it was right or wrong, she had found a perfect excuse: She wanted to enjoy life to the fullest; experience is a kind of wealth in itself. It was as if she had found her confidence, she explained it away to herself all the way there, easily finding her way to Thomas' address. It was an old-fashioned apartment building, its brownred bricks different to the other buildings, with sculptured friezes, black wrought iron balconies that jutted out of the face of the building at regular intervals, the type of balcony that looks delicate and fine, best suited to an elegant eighteenth or nineteenth century maiden standing there gracefully, holding a fan. Qu Shuang could not help but begin to rhapsodize: The ancients truly created life around the concept of beauty. The remains of their architecture create a clear contrast to modern designs. Our antecedents knew more about life than those that came after them, their standard of beauty held a much greater value than that of modern man. At least Qu Shuang thought so. She was craftily filling her mind with thoughts of tradition, as she opened the door of immorality; it was one of life's jokes.

When the street name and house number matched the street name and house number on the slip of paper in Qu Shuang's hand, she found herself poised, about to personally destroy the realm of dreams she had created, to destroy the beautiful dream! And tumble into chaotic reality. It was natural that she would feel a little afraid. Her finger hesitated in midair for a second, and finally pressed the doorbell, speaking to the receiver hesitantly, "It's me." The strange thing was the direct way in which she addressed it, rather than saying "Hello," or I am so-and-so, it was the subtlest tone of voice.

Thomas' voice came through the speaker, "Please come up to the third floor." It was that jubilant voice, once more.

The door buzzed and opened automatically. Qu Shuang went straight up to the third floor. The doors to either side of the stairs were tightly closed, whilst the door diagonally opposite the stairs was left ajar. She was just considering whether or not she ought to push that door open, when a large hand stretched out of it and dragged her inside. Before she was quite sure what was going on, her face had been smothered with kisses. She did not resist, but neither did she respond. She hadn't expected it to happen so quickly—there was no preamble, he got straight to the point. She stood coldly in the doorway, unmoved. Thomas didn't pay the least bit of attention, but went on kissing her as if there were no tomorrow. His tongue stubbornly forced its way into her mouth, pushing against her teeth and gums. His tongue was sweet and large inside her mouth. However she resisted, it could not be made to leave. Before long it had ignited the energy of her own body. Her hands went against her and grasped his neck, whilst his hands mercilessly gouged her waist. Still they said nothing, but remained pressed together in the narrow corridor. Her legs entwined lasciviously about Thomas' waist. She felt herself become wet and sticky, something burning and large swelled between Thomas' hip bones, pressing up and down against her. His movements were violent and powerful, they did not have time to take off their clothes, they just went at it frantically. They flung themselves upon each other as if they had been walking in the desert for ages and found a patch of sweet dew. Desperate with thirst, there was no escape, they had no choice but to give it their all and plunge towards their deaths. It was as if they were not making love, but wrestling. They fell onto the carpet on the living room floor; half-crawling, half-rolling. They knelt on the carpet tearing each other's clothes off. There was nothing holding them back, two bodies unrestrained and naked under the warm candlelight. They threw themselves into the slaughter, striking each other, as if they wanted to murder each other, a fight to the death. They toppled over everything that was on the carpet, the scene was catastrophic. Although the storm came in violence, it was unstoppable, hopeless, and vulnerable. Such wild actions occur only when one stakes everything on one roll of the dice. Inside their bodies, that were rubbing together furiously, there burned a hopeless flame; it was dangerous, it stripped them of their sense of security. Like a stick of dynamite that might go off at a single touch and blow them both to pieces. A sex act performed without any safety measures, it felt all the more powerful and exhilarating as a result.

Their crazed passion lasted a long time. They clung together, like a pair of orphans who had lost their mother and found each other in the darkness, afraid to lose each other again, clinging to each other for dear life, as if dependent upon each other for life, as if they could not help themselves, they were indivisible. Sometimes they were rough, sometimes like a stream of water, they responded to each other, as if they wanted to swallow each other, their tender flowing madness. She cried out from under his body, a repressed and painful sound, like the groans of someone struck down with a mortal illness. At times her body was bent tight like a bow, her legs stuck straight out. Thomas' body strained all over, striking like lightning, he suddenly opened his mouth and began to cry, an uncontrolled howling, like the roar of a lion in a primitive forest. His arrow finally shot, piercing her most vulnerable part, they both lay panting as, tired to death, they collapsed into a pool of water. The thunderous act of love between man and a woman left them feeling ecstatic.

The storm had finally passed. They looked at each other for a long while in a state of peace. Neither of them tried to explain; their bodies had already written everything. Thomas' body curled up in a fetal position, encircling her. She shrank comfortably within the embrace, and yet she was aware that it was not an island of safety, she had turned the unreal into reality and this reality would ruin her. This temporary harmony would soon be smashed by the tidal wave of reality. She was standing on a precipice, no matter how many happy moments they enjoyed, this feeling of presentiment continued to strike her.

In the moment of daybreak, that elegy will disappear in the first light.

She waited in a hopeless mood for that moment.

Only when they had grown quiet did Qu Shuang have the opportunity to observe the room. It was a large room, the ceiling was quite extravagant in its height, engraved all over with Classical Baroque patterns. The few items of old-fashioned furniture were casually placed in the corners about the room: a heavy sofa faced the fireplace. Sitting all alone in the center of the room, a coffee table like a coffin stood covered with all kinds of books, magazines and cups. Only the cello looked poetic, standing at an angle in the corner near the window. Sheet music lay scattered on the floor, where they had kicked over the music stand in their violence. All kinds of wineglasses and candle-holders lay on the floorboards, two arm chairs also lay knocked over, this scene of disorder was the spoils of their recent conquest. A set of high-class speakers were arranged on the right hand side of the room, filling it with an old French folk song, Edith Piaf's husky voice enhanced the night's romance. Their two naked bodies in the dark room were like two roses blooming evilly, separated by night and day.

Qu Shuang lay on her back on the carpet and looked up, admiring the ceiling. She liked the tall ceiling; the sense of space was pleasurable. She seemed to appreciate the spacious room, almost devoid of furniture, that showed the boldness of its owner's aesthetic principles. Her gaze traversed the unfamiliar space, at that moment she felt as if she was nowhere at all, she had already floated away, she had flown away to a desert island, she didn't need anybody.

At that moment, she was feeling fine.

Thomas got up and went to the kitchen and poured out two glasses of white Burgundy wine, passing one glass to her, he raised his glass saying, "Cheers! To our new movement!"

She stared into his gray-blue eyes and with the word, "No," she drained the glass in one mouthful.

Suddenly she felt wounded. She said that she didn't know what she was doing. That was drôle! She'd already gone and done everything, and there she was saying that she didn't know what she was doing. She said that she hadn't intended for things to turn out that way, that she had no wish to play with fire. She said she had a family, and she said, "You know that. My marriage is not bad." The expression on her face was a heavy one, it showed not the slightest sign that she could be joking.

The worst part was that Thomas was not in the least enraged by her talking nonsense. He merely said very quietly that he apologized, that it was not his intention to hurt anybody.

The scene before her was risible. A minute ago they had done the boldest, most illogical act, and now they were speaking logically about it. What had they been doing a moment before? It had to be a piece of satire. It was ridiculous.

Qu Shuang said that she hadn't meant to blame him, that she was only feeling guilty, she felt as if she had committed a crime. She hadn't wanted to let things get so far, that was not what she had wanted. But things had gone in the opposite direction, and got more and more out of hand. She was already past the point of no return. As Qu Shuang said this, she was aware that it was only a half-truth. The beauty of a lie far outweighs that of the truth. It was all within her expectations, she had hoped that this crime would take place (we'll call it a crime for want of a better word, until we find a more suitable word to replace it).

Thomas regarded the Oriental woman before him, thinking to himself, that concealed behind her delicate appearance there was such a wild potential. In the emotional games between a man and a woman, Thomas had already perceived her complexity. In that sense, you could say that Thomas understood the woman before him.

As their conversation drew to a close, Qu Shuang lowered her head and looked at her naked body as it stood discussing serious topics with a naked man's body. She couldn't help but find it ridiculous and laughable. She quickly got dressed with an odd expression on her face. Her internal thermometer dropped to below zero in an instant. She said she wanted to go. She was always like that, the one to leave. It was the most irresponsible attitude to adopt, and the simplest solution available.

Thomas wanted to keep her longer, but she insisted on leaving. Thomas had no choice but to get dressed. He said that he could see her back home and she said there was no need. Her attitude was cool, with a look designed to keep him well away from her. Thomas was confused by this sudden refusal, he walked downstairs with her dazedly. They walked out together, the early autumn night full of the scent of the rambling rose and the moon lit them up affectionately. They walked quietly to Thomas' car, it was an old-fashioned SAAB. It appeared silvery gray in the moonlight, that mysterious silver-gray color that she had always adored. Thomas pulled out his keys and opened the car door. Just as she was about to climb into the car, Thomas pinned her down again, their bodies pressed together incorrigibly. They were so hungry for each other's body. They desired each other as if they were possessed, the heat of desire impossible to suppress. Once more they were exploring each other through their body language. That terrible excitement had ignited into a raging fire once more, turning them from dry kindling, into a blaze and then into spent ashes. They crushed themselves into the car, once inside the car they threw themselves upon each other wildly, trembling as they heaved up and down. Thomas thrust against her savagely, it felt as if they almost turned the car over with their movements. It seemed that their lovemaking would always be a scene of violence. They used every ounce of their strength to describe this one stroke of the pen, as if they had to engrave it on both flesh and soul, never to be forgotten for the rest of their lives. Their physical expression was eloquent, whilst their linguistic expression lagged behind it, imbecile, idiotic. Neither of them dared speak a word of truth, their bodies experienced all that was true, while their language was false, they dared not face up to reality. It was as if they could be irresponsible for their actions, but not for their words, words in reality were the more fearful thing. Thomas knew that he was faced with a married woman, it wasn't appropriate to speak to her of 'love', that would be irresponsible towards her, and towards himself. And Qu Shuang had even less reason to use the word 'love' to him. She didn't even dare to tell the man before her that she loved her husband. When they were together they always chose their words carefully, afraid that they might slip into a linguistic trap. Just like when she told him, "You know, my marriage is not bad," she chose the neutral phrase "not bad", meaning that she was hiding something in her story, waiting for him to search it out, to discover it. Thomas understood what it meant of course. They carefully wove a path through the minefield of language; avoiding making contact with sensitive regions. They were very cautious about the power of language, in contrast their behavior was extraordinarily bold. They didn't care about what they did, they had found a good excuse for it: It was instinctive, instincts were not controlled by language, they were not responsible for reality. Their caution with language was paradoxical. Theoretically speaking, Qu Shuang could accept the idea of loving two people at once, but when theory was put into practice she felt thoroughly guilty, she felt a pain she could not unburden herself of with words. She was assaulted by the feeling of everything going to pieces, there was no way for her to go but down. The problem was that when it came down to reality, she could not be sure that she loved this man. Their conversation was simply too limited, he was still a stranger to her. She could even go so far as to say that she didn't understand this foreign man at all. The strange thing was that she didn't feel that she wanted to understand him too deeply, they put everything into their physical expression alone.

They didn't have the courage to say that word.

When did people become so false?

So Qu Shuang returned home once more with feelings of guilt and confusion.

The lonely night time streets amplified the beating of her heart. She lingered for a long time at the foot of her building, afraid to climb the stairs. She could see lights on in all of the windows and Luke's silhouette passing between them. She knew that Luke was worried and waiting for her, how could she explain it all to him? She really wanted to just sit down and get it all off her chest. She wanted to confess to Luke as the faithful to a priest—would that make her feel better? She didn't know. She knew that if she told him, it would cause Luke a great deal of hurt. She thought to herself, she had no reason to cause Luke so much pain. Hurting the one you love is a real crime, an unforgivable crime! Therefore, she decided to say nothing. She didn't want to say anything to Luke, it was her private secret; after all, how pitiful it was to be a person without a secret. She would not willingly reveal this secret to anyone, it was 100% her own private property, no one could infringe upon that right. This decision allowed her to recover her courage a little, she subconsciously gave her miniskirt a tug down, pulled out the compact from her handbag and looked in the mirror under the light of the streetlight. She carefully redid her hair and walked off into the dark night ahead of her.

She took each stair with a self-condemning stride, her legs feeling heavy as if they were filled with lead. When she reached her door, she paused for a moment. Without knowing why, when her hand touched the door-key her heart trembled, the hand that held the key was trembling as well. She closed her eyes tightly and had to take a deep breath before she was able to put the key into the lock. When she opened the front door, Luke was standing in the doorway, with an expression that was heavy but controlled. He waited for her to speak. Qu Shuang murmured weakly, that she was really hungry and shot into the kitchen, opening the fridge and looking for something to eat. She was afraid that Luke would notice that she was flustered, panicked; but Luke did not follow her into the kitchen, she tried hard to calm herself as she heated up some food. When the food was ready, she carried her bowl into Luke's study. Luke had his back to the door, sitting bolt upright at the table, as if he bore it a grudge. She walked up to him and ruffled his hair with her right hand. She asked him if he had found her note, as if that were an explanation. Luke said that he had seen it, in a muffled voice, and continued to hold his silence. Luke was not especially gifted at rhetoric, but he had that dignity particular to him, he was usually able to control himself, and at a key moment he could maintain a fearsome cool. That coolness was terrifying, it far exceeded the power of a great explosion. Qu Shuang knew that once this cold attitude was set off, there was no stopping it. It was more effective than noisy fury or shouting, you could forget about invoking the least change in him then, when he had made up his mind he was harder than steel, when things had got to that stage there was no turning back, Qu Shuang couldn't be clearer about that.

That night Qu Shuang was infinitely affectionate to Luke. Behind her tenderness she felt that she was dirty. Whenever she got close to Luke she would pause, this was the body that had been twisting under another man's body just an hour ago.

She began to hate herself a little. She inwardly swore to herself never to become entangled with that man again, in any way. When she closed her eyes, Thomas' body was demon-like lifting her, throwing her down, spinning, flying, galloping like a fine steed in the darkness, he traversed the plains and the seas, mountains and ridges, forests and the earth, he burst out of the universe, flying towards a height beyond the sky. This sexual hallucination was the first of its kind that she had experienced, she could not help but begin to moan, she cried out like a true Jezebel. Sylvia Plath wrote:

old whore petticoats.
To Paradise.

Her poems are the bible for narcissistic women.

III. *Coda*

The affair had infiltrated Qu Shuang's body like a drug.

This unprecedented creeping about was incomparably exciting. Who could have imagined that playing at being a Casanova could be so interesting. She had thought that she would put a timely end to the affair. Who could have predicted that instead it would leave her feeling so hung up on him. When she went without seeing Thomas for a few days she would feel so infatuated with him that she didn't know what to do with herself. She couldn't stay still when she was at home, she was all over the place, replying only absentmind-edly to Luke's questions. The number of phone cards in her handbag secretly increased, public phone boxes became the hotline for their emotional communications. If she was on the phone at home, when Luke came in she would speak in code, Luke didn't understand a word of it, or she would whisper something and look flustered. Her behavior was becoming stranger and stranger, she would often disappear unexpect-edly, Luke would have just seen her quite clearly sitting in her studio, and she had just disappeared the next second! Before, she would always tell Luke clearly where she was going when she went out, she might even tell him at what time she would return down to the hour and minute. Nowadays, she didn't even speak to him, or she would write a note saying, "Just popping out, back soon" and be gone for hours. Luke did not want to argue. They had always had their own separate rooms, and didn't interrupt each other while they were working. You could say that they were a rather modern couple. They had unspoken rules, for example, they never opened each other's letters, if a letter was addressed to Luke, Qu Shuang wouldn't dream of opening it. They didn't question each other too much over their comings and goings. They didn't want their family life to impinge too greatly on themselves as individuals. They each had sufficient space to be themselves and felt that their life as a household should not put fetters on their individual rights. However, Qu Shuang's recent behavior had gone beyond the usual limits of their established household life. She was too mysterious about her movements, going out with no explanation whatsoever, she seemed beyond all control, and often came home at the dead of night—she could hardly avoid attracting Luke's attention. Whenever Luke asked she always said that she had gone to a bar with some friends. Luke asked, with not a little sarcasm, where had so many friends come from all of a sudden? Within this vicious circle even when Qu Shuang had a legitimate excuse for going out, Luke would stare at her with mistrust. During that time, Luke suspected that his wife's every action had ulterior and unspeakable motives. But he did not want to look into it, he was waiting. They had both reached the age when they were entirely able to fool themselves, the age that demands things to be crystal clear and flawless had already passed them by never to return.

Once, when Luke was due to go out on a business trip about one of his designs, he watched Qu Shuang struggle to control her excitement. He felt thoroughly dejected, but there was nothing he could do. He felt just like the dumb man who had taken a bitter medicine but was unable to speak of its taste. He had originally decided to wait until he came back from his business trip to have a long talk with Qu Shuang. He wanted to get to the bottom of things, even though it went against his wishes, even though he felt that a disaster was approaching, there was nothing he could do to stop it. Accurately speaking, Luke's home was his only refuge, he was happy with his wife, he felt that his wife was woman enough for him. If Qu Shuang occasionally made eyes at someone else, such harmless little things didn't hurt his feelings, in fact they satisfied his male pride, it proved that his wife was attractive. He was not usually a petty man, he was pretty magnanimous, but with things the way they were, he felt he was left with no choice.

A fortnight later when he returned, Qu Shuang was happy as a little bird, chattering away to him about this and that, taking out her latest porcelain models to show him. Later on she made him *jiaozi*,* which was something that only happened once in a blue moon. He hadn't eaten *jiaozi* for three years, it made him feel as if he had returned to the warmth of his home, that he was head of the house. He forgot about laying his cards on the table, he felt delighted, he sent the lingering remainder of the shade at his door away to beyond the furthest horizon. He was in good spirits as he drank and did not forget to enjoy some overdue fun and frolics with his wife whom he hadn't seen for some days. Qu Shuang was as loving as possible, Luke could see that she was faithfully welcoming him home, her happiness showed in her every move. This all supported Luke's feeling of sovereignty.

But it wasn't as simple as Luke thought.

Meetings between Qu Shuang and Thomas continued to occur on the streets of London, in all sorts of cafés, music halls, bars, cinemas, and of course, more usually, at Thomas' apartment. Qu Shuang was constantly warning herself that it couldn't go on like this, yet she continued to arrange the next place that they would meet. Desire and denial held her from both sides in their jaws. Enticement surged through

---

* A boiled dumpling usually containing a filling of meat and vegetables most common in Northern China but available throughout. They are usually eaten on high holidays and mark a celebration as well as being labor intensive to prepare, making them more of a food for special occasions.

their every nerve. They arranged to watch movies together, to go to concerts, to go for strolls in the country, to go out to dinner; just like a real couple enjoying the pleasure of falling in love. Each secret meeting was an exploration, exciting their every nerve, they behaved like undercover agents in a movie. Wherever they went, they first cast each other a look, a knowing greeting and stood still on the spot and didn't move. Then they looked about to see if there was anyone they knew, only then would they rush off to a more private spot. Such concerns came mostly from Qu Shuang, she was always terrified of bumping into someone she knew. They really didn't know that many people in London, and London was such a big city. Nevertheless, she was very nervous about it. Qu Shuang was always worried that one day she would raise her head to see Luke standing there. She maintained a low profile, always assuming an equivocal attitude towards Thomas, which concealed another truth. Supposing she had bared her soul in the very beginning, she was afraid things would be very different to the way they were now. On a tender afternoon after they had taken a stroll together, Thomas grasped her right hand, opened her fingers and placed a bunch of keys in the palm of her hand. This action did not surprise her in the least, but it did put her in a difficult position. It meant that they had gone beyond the bounds of an everyday relationship, it was a sign that she could enter into Thomas' life whenever she wanted to. She felt moved and sad at the same time. At this crucial juncture she was as indecisive as a man would be in the same situation. She could not decide what it was that she wanted. What was it that she wanted out of Thomas? Surely it couldn't be that love was just a matter of hormones? That would be simply too depressing an answer.

On a night where the moonlight fell bright as a snow scene, Thomas sat on the balcony playing a Fantasia by Schumann for her. The cello's sound was highly expressive, slipping gracefully from between his fingers, which pressed the strings harshly, the rasping of the bow created the unique timbre of the cello. Thomas held the cello in an embrace, as if he were embracing a lover; facing the solitary member of his audience, he seemed intoxicated. The cello notes melted together with the moonlight, the music was painfully beautiful, the whole of the night sky stood still for the expressive and pensive sound. It was a moment of fantasy, a kind of sublimation. Her eyes lingered tenderly upon him, her entire body stretched out peacefully, a moment of floating vacuity; that kind of transcendence was a feeling that she had never experienced before, she had never been as intoxicated as she was that night, she felt she could just melt under her lover's cello strings. Qu Shuang found to her surprise that it was completely different to listening to music in a concert hall. That was a rational experience, executed in an orderly fashion following the commands of the conductor; and this was a purely individual performance. He dissolved himself in the music, recreating the music, expressing his emotions through the music. At that moment, they were at one with the music, drunk in its fantasy.

One day, they discovered in conversation that they both worshiped the same musician—Pablo Casals—the greatest cellist for them both. Qu Shuang looked intoxicated as she said, "each morning I dress to Casals".

Thomas kissed her tenderly. He could hear Casals notes within her skin. He responded that, "a day without listening to Casals would leave him spiritually impoverished." He said that his fate was entwined with that of the great man because of the instrument they both played.

Music took them to a new height. There was a new tone to their clandestine meetings, they were no longer frenzied. There was a new cadence to their physicality, soft, slow, a gentle merging containing an unspeakable torment, a stroke that could only be accomplished without words. Qu Shuang never asked Thomas if he saw other women; it was Thomas who told her in the very beginning that he had a girlfriend in America. Qu Shuang was not in the least surprised, in fact it made her feel better, she felt that it was fairer this way. She was mindlessly destroying her home, there was no need to be the cause of anyone else breaking up. It was more logical this way, both parties were on an equal footing, no one was indebted to the other.

And she never asked him "What should we do?", "What will happen in the future?", "Do you love me?" or any other stupid question that would have dropped her into the tangle of emotions. She adopted the attitude that she would remain drunk all the time there was wine on the table. She became a reckless devil, even if Thomas were to ask such questions, she would skirt around the issue and refuse to answer head-on. She even felt a little afraid of him expressing himself too clearly. In her subconscious she felt that she had no right to accept his love, she was afraid that his love would destroy her home, that it would destroy a man who was four years her junior.

After several meetings between them, Thomas had asked her about her age, only then did she discover that Thomas was younger than her. Thomas found it surprising that she was actually much older than he had imagined, he said, he knew that Asian people always appeared youthful, but she just looked so young.

Thomas described the history of his love affairs to her. He said he didn't know why, but he always seemed to fall for women that were older than him. When he was nineteen he fell in love with the same woman as his father, even though the woman was older than his own mother.

Qu Shuang didn't ask him any stupid questions, like, "Do you regret that?" as other women would have, she only sighed gently. She wasn't sighing for him, she was just sighing for their endless future.

Afterwards Qu Shuang asked him, is that the 'Oedipal complex' that is referred to in Freud?

He said, maybe it is.

Qu Shuang said, "I don't want to be a mother to you."

He said, "You're not my mother, you're my Eastern Queen."

Qu Shuang said, "I don't want to be a queen either, I want to escape."

Those were words spoken in truth, she basically wanted to escape from Thomas, but the more she wished to escape from him, the closer she was to him. She couldn't understand it, it was incomprehensible, whatever kind of union it was, her every meeting with Thomas was like a trap, into which she fell deeper and deeper, unable to free herself. On the way to their meetings she would tell herself innumerable times, "This must be the last time, it can't go on like this. I am going to tell him tonight that I can't take it, my self-reproach is like a sledgehammer striking me, every day guilt clutches my heart like a vice, I am like a criminal, I live like a thief every day, I don't want to live like this. Let's end this terrible relationship and just be friends." She repeated the words to herself over and over. She knew that saying "let's just be friends" was an excuse. The second they came face to face their bodies would be flung together desperately, suffocated in kisses, entangled in caresses. They knew that they didn't have many chances to be together, that their time was short. The only way they could express their co-dependence was through their bodies. The brevity of time added unlimited levels of excitement to their games in bed. They each tried to give their all to the other, protecting each other's weaknesses, taking as much pleasure as they could from each other. This was very different to living with Luke: That was relaxed, natural, with nothing to hide, nothing dramatic, nothing exciting; it was one great legally protected safety net. She and Thomas together were responsive, primitive, they were a symphony, first came the entry, the opening, the overture, the climax, the lingering note, the ebbing, the return, only then came the coda. Thomas' performance in bed was exceptional, he used every trick in the book. He was repeatedly amazed by the softness of this Asian woman's body, how it flowed and slipped beneath his own, the way her nipples revealed a bashful red aura when excited, the way her skin emanated a fine gauze like dew after they had met with particular passion, which stimulated ever greater desire in him. Their every coupling was full of dangerous currents, the excitement of cheating, which gave them greater pleasure, from their sight to scent, from touch to perception; their condemned madness burst with a clinging hopeless air. Gradually she realized that it was not a game, that there was definitely some mysterious power forcing her to become so entangled with that foreign man. Thomas was not the playboy with a roving eye as she had imagined. If he were, things would not have ended up like this. If there was more of the game about it, they would feel more relaxed, their spiritual pressure would be lessened somewhat. The more serious they were, the more complex the situation became and the more pain it caused them. It often followed that after their forgetting themselves in their passion, they would suddenly be assaulted by an intangible sorrow. They would both feel so pained that they couldn't bear to utter a word, then they would each search out the other with their eyes, searching for their refuge in that bottomless soul. They would lean together for long periods of time, as if when the night had passed they were to be parted forever. Such dramatic scenes weren't deliberately sought by either of them, they were simply caught up in the moment.

After a long silence, Thomas said to Qu Shuang that he hadn't contacted his girlfriend for a long time.

Qu Shuang was very clear what that meant, she didn't ask anything further, she turned away and said, "That's not good."

Thomas said, "It can easily be dealt with."

Qu Shuang understood his hidden agenda, she feared such hints, she was afraid he would put her under more pressure. When Thomas had finished speaking, she did not know how to reply to him, she felt stuck between a rock and a hard place. Thomas understood that it would be impossible to make Qu Shuang leave Luke, although he wasn't sure exactly why. He didn't want to be the first to bring it up and so he waited for Qu Shuang to mention it. And Qu Shuang refused to speak of it, she was so cautious to protect the interests of her home. She had never brought Thomas to her home, even when Luke was not there. She defended her home as if it were her castle. She felt as if that way she was being respectful to Luke, it gave her conscience a little peace. The trouble was that she realized more and more how much she needed Thomas. She had turned the unreal into reality, she had thought that the two layers of this world could be separated, the "unreal" and the "real", when two layers are made into one world it inevitably creates a mess, leaving her mentally and physically exhausted, and full of self-reproach. She found it impossible to choose between or reject one of the two men. All of a sudden, she realized how difficult it would be to sever herself from either one of them. She weighed the advantages and disadvantages, beset by problems on either side. Giving up Luke would be like giving up half of herself, her connection with Luke was based on a cultural homeland stronger than blood relations, to sever that relationship would be equal to cutting her off from her past, it was unimaginable, unacceptable. She couldn't imagine speaking to someone every day in a language she only half knew, then again she and Thomas were saved a lot of trouble because their linguistic expression was incomplete, they had never argued, their language had not reached a sufficient level to do so. An indistinct tone lent proceedings a more romantic atmosphere, but at the same time, because their speech was not completely clear, they lost that level of attraction. When Qu Shuang told Thomas a Chinese joke, he merely stared at her in confusion, and asked her three times in a row, "Beg your pardon?" Even the most hilarious jokes became boring in an instant. It made Qu Shuang feel dejected. At such times, Thomas would once more express his wish to learn Chinese, but Qu Shuang knew that understanding what lies behind language is the result of a long-term immersion in that land, and could not be picked up in a day or two. She was linked to her mother tongue as she was to air and water. Luke was like a symbol, their harmonious language brought much joy to their everyday lives, sometimes just a word or a witty joke would make them rock with laughter, they were both able to appreciate the magic of each other's native language. She could never obtain that from Thomas. She cared so much about the potential of language, she wasn't sure at all how this would turn out.

Qu Shuang had tied herself down fast between the two of them.

Whenever she thought of it, she would give an involuntary shudder.

That night the moon was incomparably large. It hung detachedly in the sky, golden coloured, a startling color, as if a giant sun had risen in the night sky. It looked even more bizarre than if the sun had risen in the west. People stood and looked on at the spectacle, there was certainly something unusual about it.

Qu Shuang had just left the house when she raised her head and saw the miracle in the sky, and shouted, as if waking from the middle of a dream, "It's Mid-Autumn Festival!"

And that night, the moon was round and bright just as it ought to be.

She had always loved that night, it was the most poetic of all the traditional festivals. On that night everyone would stare dumbly at the moon in the sky, their compatriots would be looking towards each other from all corners of the globe, thinking of their distant relatives.* Just that image alone was deeply moving. Our ancestors truly understood this beautiful phenomenon of the natural world, and gave it such a lovely name, to remind their descendants not to overlook this lovely night-scene, which further strengthened its poetic nature. Every time this date came around, her heart was filled with a swelling tide. She was not a poet, she did not have the soul of a poet, yet she felt she had something to express, this heightened her repressed passions, making her feel inconsolable.

But tonight was different to other festival nights. The moon in the wilderness was huge and perfect in the beginning, frighteningly bright. Gradually two thirds of it were covered by a dark cloud, the contours of the moon were only just visible through the veil of cloud and before long a mysterious darkness had covered the moon completely, leaving only a crescent shaped gold edge. The lit edge like a golden thread flickered with a rose color, it was a rarely seen total lunar eclipse, the earth's shadow cast strangely upon the moon, that created this sight.

That night's eclipse had been predicted in ancient texts long ago.

How could there be a Mid-Autumn Festival with no moon? Because of a rarely seen total eclipse?!

What did it mean? She secretly asked herself.

At that moment, Qu Shuang was on her way to Thomas' home. She saw a fibrous silver color cast on the lawns, dogs were barking wildly and incessantly, horses in the moonlight craned their long necks, in search of the moon's shadow.

On the way, she met a long-haired, skinny, bearded stranger, who repeated the words, "Dangerous! It's dangerous!" to her, with a serious expression on his face.

At the time, she concluded that he must be mad. There are lots of mad people walking about the streets of London, no one would look at you twice even if you wore your shoes on your head, so she didn't pay overdue attention to him. She

---

* As Yoyo tells us, at Mid-Autumn Festival when the moon appears larger than at any other time in the year, families reunite, and where unable to physically reunite, they all look up at the moon from wherever they are. It is primarily a festival of reunion and appreciating family.

only recognized vaguely to herself that she ought to have been staying at home with Luke for the festival. This was the one day in the year that family ought to be together. And she had left Luke all alone at home. It felt unbearable.

However there was that demonic power pulling her against her wishes, and she set off in the opposite direction to her home in the end!

She had no idea that this would be her last meeting with Thomas. She was quite clear that this kind of relationship would be discovered sooner or later, but she never imagined that it would come so swiftly and unexpectedly.

Only when it had passed did she realize that it all that had been a sign.

The "mad man" had been a wise prophet.

When she arrived, Thomas was already standing there on his balcony looking out. She saw him waiting for her, it added a warm sense of romance. In the desolate moonlight they embraced lovingly. The feeling of love being so pressing, it lessened their physical desire. They did not come together in a storm as they used to. Their bodies wrapped together, like the Milky Way in the moonlight. Thomas slowly kissed her all over her body, as if it was not enough, he pulled her along towards the balcony, in the secretive moonlight their bodies were like a sacrificial altar to love. That endless river of emotion flowed off into the distance, where would it flow to? How many mementoes of love had they left on each other's bodies during their many meetings? They did not make love that night, it was as if they both had a premonition. They curled up naked before the fireplace; the firelight struck their bodies that looked like mournful marble. They gazed upon each other, a despairing air covered them, they felt as if the flames within them were about to go out.

They would go out tonight.

Never again would they be able to lean on each other like this, the firelight expanded the sorrowful scene.

Beauty, that made them powerless.

Qu Shuang spontaneously began to sob.

Thomas gently licked away her tears, as he asked her in a voice full of sympathy why she was crying.

It was the first time that she had cried in front of him. He had wondered if she even had tear ducts.

She looked up at him, her face covered in hot tears and said, "I'm crying because I cannot love you."

She spoke as if to herself, and as if she were speaking to him at the same time.

It was the first and only time that Qu Shuang had expressed her emotions so openly, it was like a disastrous curse.

In the long silence, only their heartbeats were audible.

Qu Shuang looked up at the inky blue night sky and asked once more, "So, is there such a thing as perfection?"

Was she asking the sky or Thomas?

Thomas looked at Qu Shuang for a long time and said, "We know that nothing's perfect, that is why we pursue perfection. It is that bitter searching that we call life."

Qu Shuang looked into the flames without a word, she felt as if she were about to depart, about to disappear into the firelight.

They hung onto each other like that until late into the night, she pushed back going home one hour, then another hour. She knew that the crisis between Luke and her might blow up at any time, but she was already beyond caring. They kissed for a long time, Thomas and her, bidding farewell on the street in the middle of the night, they said dozens of good-byes without actually parting, in the end it was Thomas who drove her back to a street near her house, it was as if they were rehearsing a final farewell scene in a tragic play.

Luke watched it all silently, maintaining his dignified silence. He was the kind of highly intelligent man who would never get himself unnecessarily involved in a matter, he knew the danger of seeing smoke where there was no fire. He was clear about what was going on between Qu Shuang and himself, it wasn't difficult to figure out. Sometimes the logic of life is not very complicated at all. He had heard too many stories of that kind, but he was unwilling to accept what was happening in his own home. Supposing he did face up to that reality, it would be a blow to his dignity. As a man he could not possibly accept that, whereas by overlooking the matter, he showed the magnanimity of a real man. He was even less willing to start following her, spying on her correspondence and other such low acts. He saw that as a demonstration of inability that would only cause a person to lose their mind. He decided that for the time being he would not look into it, that he wouldn't ask too much, and see how things went. He knew that he couldn't fool himself for long, but he was unwilling to be the first one to break through that boundary of paper.* Even if it proved to make a cuckold of him, he would not make the first move to destroy their home, he knew how difficult it was to establish a home in this big wide world as it was. He had worked hard in this mixed-up world, his home was the only place where he could catch his breath. In truth, he was unwilling to admit the most important fact of all, which was that he loved his wife. "Home" became the shield behind which they hid all of their inexpressible emotions. How many difficulties had they invented for that shield? Why must their "home" turn their love cold? No longer exhilarating, lifeless, just existing. This world has already fallen to a point where it is ashamed to speak the word "love", even husbands and wives cannot bring themselves to use the word honestly and frankly, they only make love, they don't dare express their love. They mistakenly believe that that is one way to express their love, when that's not necessarily true. People have already forgotten the simplest definition of love as given by Pangu, creator of the heavens – which was "speaking of the emotions and talking about love", it is a thing that must be spoken and talked about.

The twentieth century is a time that has lost the ability to love.

---

* This Chinese saying refers to older days when windows were made of paper stretched over a wooden frame. The boundary exists, but is easily broken. It refers to situations where there is a thin covering of decency or dishonesty over something that everyone knows but is unwilling to tear away the final veil.

When she got up in the morning, Qu Shuang felt a dizziness akin to weightlessness, she had felt that way for several days now. She seemed to have a premonition, but at the same time she didn't really think it possible. She had always been so careful not to let that awkward situation happen. She couldn't be sure of her premonition. But, to be on the safe side, she went to the hospital. The results left no room for doubts, she was pregnant. This was totally unexpected. The earth beneath her feet was shaken as if by a Richter 7 earthquake, tearing her to pieces. She was so giddy she could barely walk out of the hospital doors, she hung onto the hospital walls, reaching with difficulty a bench where she sat down, worrying the nurses so badly that they ran to fetch her water and asked if they could call a relative for her. She waved her hand and said that there was no need, that she'd be fine in a moment.

How could she tell Luke that she was pregnant? She knew that Luke would be happy to hear the news. Luke would be a great father, his nature determined that he would be the best. The problem was that she could not be certain who had produced the life in her stomach. It would hurt Luke so much if she told him that, it might put an end to their relationship. That was the result that she desired least of all, she was indivisibly tied to Luke, they had fallen deeply in love with each other in China, and shared the struggle of leaving the country. Could she wipe out ten years spent together in one fell swoop? She didn't quite understand how she could hurt Luke when he was the most important person to her, the person

202

that she absolutely could not bear to be parted from? This was her calamity; she could not escape her inexorable fate.

She walked out onto the street blankly, holding the test result paper that proved she was pregnant in her hand, her head was a knot of confusion, she thought carefully about her days with Thomas and Luke, but still she could not be sure. She was as full of sorrow as it was possible to be. She wasn't feeling sorry for herself, but for that new life. She hated herself for being frivolous, she thought that everything has a cause and a effect in the world; if you do wrong you will be punished; now God was finally punishing her. Qu Shuang was not someone who analyzed things in terms of standard morality; but in this case she knew that she was guilty, and that what she had done was awfully wrong. She did admittedly belong to the generation of new women, but she hadn't made the decision not to have children. In truth, she wished in her heart to have a child, but she always felt that it wasn't the right time, she thought that she would do some more of her own things in her thirties, and then settle down and have a child with Luke, and live happily ever after. The current situation ruined all of that. This life that had appeared like a bolt from the blue, not only failed to bring her joy, it was a destructive blow.

To face telling two men that she was pregnant!

It wasn't hard to imagine how awkward that would be.

How would Thomas act? She couldn't be sure. She had never discussed the matter of having children with him before. She pictured the scene of such a discussion with Thomas, if he threw up his hands and said that it had nothing to do with him, that would be a blow to her, her self-respect could not take such a scene. Supposing he was wildly happy then, she would be out of the frying pan and into the fire, because she was not in the least sure whether or not she actually wanted to live with Thomas, her doubts were rooted in her basic cultural makeup. She was a mature woman after all, which was different to the passion of a girl in her youth. She cared more about the practical elements of life, and not the romance of a few days.

Did she even want to tell Thomas? That was a question that hung, undecided, in her mind.

She had heard of too many marriages hurried through because a woman had gotten pregnant. That sort of forced marriage would lead to such unhappiness at home, endless complaints, with the adults arguing and the children crying in a vicious circle. She did not want to play the role of a woman who was out to entrap Thomas. The problem was that her situation was much more complicated than that. It was not a question of wanting to trap someone; it was a question of how she was to escape herself? She had not imagined that she had put herself in such a low position. She was like the most false of women, not even able to tell who the father of her child was. What an insult to that little life!

She imagined a third possibility, that was to give up her home and living with Thomas, to bring up the child alone.

She did not know whether or not she had that kind of courage. She had a modern mind, but a weak resolve and in this frantic world, Luke was her anchor. She was afraid of biting the hand that fed her, that would leave her feeling insecure about the future. If her child was deprived of having a father, it would affect their psychological growth. She was deeply concerned with the long term upbringing of her child, she felt that a good upbringing was crucial—at which point, she quickly dismissed the idea completely. What was she to do now? Blame god? Cry to the heavens? It wouldn't help much. She herself had sowed the seeds of this bitter fruit, and she would have to bear the consequences alone in the end, there was nothing else to say.

She decided to tell no one, she would undertake everything alone.

She finally picked a plan out of her entangled and complex feelings.

The first stages of pregnancy are hard to endure, she threw up until she felt dizzy. But she could not divulge the cause of her morning sickness, all she could do was try her best to hide it. Fortunately, Luke was rarely at home during those days. When Luke was away, she would run to the bathroom time and again and vomit to her heart's content, as if she were trying to throw her very heart and stomach up. Occasionally when Luke was at home, she would excuse herself saying that she was going to the library to read, when in fact she went to the park nearby, and walked along the road vomiting as she went. On her way back she would put the plastic bags into which she had vomited the disgusting stuff in the rubbish bin on the street. The symptoms were especially violent in the morning. In order to keep him from realizing she rushed to get up before Luke woke. She said she was going jogging, she said that she had been feeling listless recently, that she wanted to get some exercise. When she went out, the gusts of the morning breeze certainly did make her stomach feel much better.

Qu Shuang had laid this trap for herself; she knew that she had no other choice. She had to suffer it with as much strength as she could muster. She felt strangely towards the little life in her body. She would often sneak a feel of her stomach, which was still quite flat, and speak to that little life. At such times she felt extremely fragile. She spoke to it with her face covered in tears. She didn't blame that little life in the least for giving her such an unspeakably hard time. She could not get used to calling herself "mum" to that little life, she was always saying, "I've let you down, my dear." Perhaps she was not brave enough to call herself "Mother". A mother was a tremendous person, she felt herself to be dirty and insignificant. She didn't deserve to be called mother. She asked quietly, "Can you forgive me? I know that I don't deserve to be forgiven." When she said those words, it was as if she were saying them to Luke, at the same time it seemed that she was speaking to that little life, and to Thomas as well. She hadn't thought of Thomas for a long time, she had focused all her attention on that little life, like an animal in the natural world, when the female realizes she is pregnant she doesn't pay attention to anything else. Is that the nature of women? She decided that for this period of time, that little life would suffer nothing, she would look after that little life, afraid that the slightest shock from the outside world might harm her, she would not let anything interfere in the slightest with that little life.

She became serene and content. Ever since she returned from the test at the hospital, she had had no more marital relations with Luke, she was close and tender to him, but it was a tenderness that kept him at a distance. She became pale and she ate little. She always had food prepared before Luke got home, she felt sick as soon as she saw food, but she couldn't always leave Luke alone at the dinner table, she had to pretend that she was eating with him. Every now and then, she would leave the table and dart into the bathroom. Fortunately, the bathroom was just at the other end of the kitchen, inside she covered her mouth as tightly as she could, afraid that she would make a noise. When she had rinsed her mouth out, she walked out again as if there was nothing wrong. Luke asked after her with concern, she said that her stomach had been playing up recently. Luke carried on eating as he asked if she wanted to have it checked out, to which she said there was no need. Luke was the kind of person that cared deeply about his own interests, but was disinterested in anything beyond himself, he was unkind in that way. Although he was her husband, he was very slow about women's biology. Qu Shuang was familiar with Luke's character, as long as she didn't actually throw up in front of him, he wouldn't notice anything.

Qu Shuang suddenly changed her way of life, she went back to going out very rarely, she stayed quietly at home, silent as the grave. Luke did not know what had happened, when he asked her, she merely laid her head on one side and smiled, saying nothing was wrong. It was obviously a lie, her quiet unnerved him; he did not know what had happened to her. Now her actions were not in the least sneaky, she barely set foot outdoors, she had very little contact with the outside world, this only added to her air of mystery.

Qu Shuang still went to the hospital for her monthly check-up like any other pregnant woman. The first time she went to the hospital she filled in the many different forms and bits of paperwork: name, age, nationality, home address, marital status and the like. In the box for marital status, she filled in 'Married'. After that they took blood, tested urine, took her blood pressure, listened to the heartbeat—she didn't know whether the doctor was listening to her heart or the fetus'. Then they allocated her a doctor to see regularly and asked her to come back again next month.

This time, the doctor had told her that the fetus was healthy, that everything was progressing normally. She insisted upon having an ultrasound. On the screen she could see the movements of that little life clearly, she had already become a complete body, her head looked big, out of proportion with the rest of her body, there were two small black dots on the sides of her head, they were the baby's eyes. She looked so adorable, she kept moving all the time.

The doctor told her it was a girl. That was Qu Shuang's most ardent desire.

"My daughter!" she shouted out in her head.

She put her head down and her shoulders shook as she began to weep silently.

The doctor was very kind, and was clearly moved by her passionate tears. The doctor embraced her shoulders benevolently and said, "The first child is always a concern, but there's really no need to worry, you will know how to be a good mother."

The more the doctor comforted her, the harder she wept.

She spoke through her tears, asking the doctor, if she was to have an abortion, what was the latest the fetus could stay in her body?

The doctor looked at her in confusion and said, "I don't understand what you mean."

She had stopped crying, she said that she wanted to have an abortion.

The doctor replied in greater confusion, "Then why have you come for the scheduled tests? Why didn't you get rid of it sooner? It's not a very smart move."

She looked bitterly at the doctor, "Please just tell me, how much longer can she stay inside of me?"

"It's a very healthy child, you ought to keep her. You're at the most ideal age for child-bearing. If you don't have children now, in the future it may be too late." The doctor coaxed her with sympathy.

"I have to warn you, if you have an abortion, it may induce habitual miscarriages in the future, it could be very bad for your body." The doctor finally said with a solemn look.

Qu Shuang hesitated for a long while. "Please tell me, what is the final deadline for an abortion?" Qu Shuang practically begged the doctor.

The doctor looked at her sternly, and said hesitantly, "I don't understand why you don't want this child. Of course, it's your right to choose. After three months we can only perform an induced miscarriage, it will be very painful."

Qu Shuang told the doctor that she would like to make an appointment.

"If you've decided, you ought to do it sooner rather than later." The doctor's eyes were full of reproach.

How could Qu Shuang speak of her inner pain? She could not explain a word of it. She could only bear the punishment, perhaps she deliberately chose this most cruel of methods available just to teach herself a lesson. She knew that the baby could not remain in her body for long, but she wanted to keep her flesh and blood until the very last moment, until she had no choice but to have it taken away. With this thought in mind, her heart broke with grief, she added to her feeling of guilt, she recognised the fact that she was a slaughterer, a killer, she had no choice but to kill her daughter. And so, she chose an extreme method to punish herself, this was the price of her games, a cruel lesson for being irresponsible in life. A wound that would never be healed.

She had not had any contact with Thomas during those days. Thomas knew that it wasn't his place to phone her, so he had always phoned her very rarely, it was usually she that phoned him. This time though, Thomas couldn't wait for her to call, he did not know what had happened, he felt uneasy and had no way to seek her out, his only choice was to make a phone call to her home. She answered it, in a strange tone of voice. She merely stated in very simple terms that he was not to call her for the time being, that he would receive a letter in a couple of days. And the phone was hung up. Thomas did not know what to do, faced with that cool and emotionless phone conversation. As far as he could work out, something serious must have happened between Qu Shuang and Luke, it could be no worse than that. Although Thomas was very concerned, he thought that the most sensible thing to do would be to keep his distance.

Two days later a letter did arrive. It was as concise as a telegram. There was only one line of writing which said, "I will come to you when the time is right."

There was no opening line and no signing off, just that sentence that provided practically no information.

Thomas stared blankly at the piece of paper, and gave a helpless shrug of his shoulders. His mouth twisted strangely at the corner, as if there were something he wanted to say, but he did not know where to begin. That woman's behavior was just as full of twists and turns as her name implied, unintelligible. He had asked her what her name meant once, Qu Shuang had explained, "A twisting, turning pleasure." Thomas asked her how to say "difficult" in Mandarin, Qu Shuang taught him the sound "NAN" by exaggerating the shape of her own mouth. Then he said, "You ought to be called 'Qu Nan', the twisting, turning difficulty."

He had said that in English.

At the time Qu Shuang had smiled with delight, "You could be a sinologist; you're pretty good at linguistic games already."

Is it possible that a person's name can determine their character?

At that moment, he wondered where his attachment to that Oriental woman had come from, primarily? How many times he had asked himself this question, but in the end he would always conclude that it was down to her character. Her character was decidedly odd. She never said anything clearly, her language seemed to hide her meaning behind a screen, releasing a pale mist that entangled him about, which continued to carve its way into him. She was soft, but within her softness there appeared a terrible toughness. It was that that left Thomas totally confused. He had not heard a word from Qu Shuang in the last three months, Qu Shuang had just disappeared out of his life without the least explanation. He was angry that this unreasonable foreign woman could be so heartless.

One morning, when the sky was exceptionally clear, the air as pure as could be in that ever-soiled capital, it was almost an unimaginable miracle.

It was like a sign.

Thomas had lived in London for five years, and he had never seen such wonderful weather. The clear blue sky seemed to be beckoning to him; he felt a premonition. Ever since he mysteriously lost touch with Qu Shuang, he had thought about her many times. He even went to the bar where they had their first date to wait for her, thinking he might bump into her there. Only when the bar closed its doors for the night did he understand that he was wasting his time.

Today he felt differently. He looked at a piece of porcelain on the mantelpiece: It depicted two intermingled bodies, expressed in an abstract primordial state, yet seemingly distorted. It had round, full curves, rough modelling; it had been produced by a skilled hand and was powerful. It didn't look like it could have come from the hands of a female artist. Qu Shuang gave it to him. She said it was inspired by their relationship; she left it to him as a memento. The piece was very different than its creator; it established a contrast. It was the only thing Thomas ever received from her; he didn't even have a single photo of Qu Shuang. She was not like most self-obsessed women who loved the lens, with lots of photos of herself all over the house. She avoided the camera like the plague. Once they went for a long walk to stretch their legs outside the city, when Thomas pointed a camera at her; she cried as if she had seen a ghost and ran away. Afterwards, she explained to Thomas that she was terrified of the camera lens; she wouldn't accept her photo being taken unless there was absolutely no other choice. How strange, Thomas thought, How could a modern individual be afraid of cameras? It was the first time he'd come across such a thing. He thought it must be a psychological impediment. He asked her why. She said she couldn't explain, she was just afraid of it. Her eccentricity enticed him to understand her better.

Thomas walked over and touched the rough surface of the sculpture and shook his head; he was still unable to explain that strange woman. He walked over to his cello, and sorrowfully began to play Beethoven's Sonata in F, Op 5; his fingers touched the strings as if they were Qu Shuang's body. The sound the cello produced was melancholic and distant. Thomas liked Beethoven's late chamber music best of all: The great sympathy for the human condition, the boundless understanding of humanity perfectly embodied in Beethoven's music; the irrepressible sympathy for mankind, transcending the understanding of all things—one feels no need to complain ever again! That is the pinnacle of Beethoven's later music, a most wonderful contribution to humanity. To the present day, there is no one who surpasses Beethoven.

At that moment he could do nothing other than pour his emotion into his music—music was his only hope. Whether pain or happiness, he expressed everything through music; he found release through music—he would search through music.

Music took him to Paradise.

He called to her through his music.

Dry leaves outside the window tumbled in the wind, slowly falling down to earth.

He finished one movement, and turned around to look for another piece of sheet music when he saw Qu Shuang standing right in front of him. For some reason he wasn't a bit surprised; he knew she would come. That morning, the moment he opened his eyes and saw the brilliant sky, he knew she would come.

And she had come.

She wore a long, grey gauze dress that fell to her feet and a black Scottish shawl draped over her shoulders. She looked very slender and more feminine. A rare, red aura glowed upon her face, casting a pale pink light over her; she looked full of tender mystery. Of course, he had no idea that it was caused by hormones released during her pregnancy.

She walked quietly in and closed the door gently. She remained standing, keeping her distance from Thomas. She said that she had never asked anything of Thomas before, but today she wanted him to play Bach's Requiem for her.

Thomas didn't say anything. He paused for a moment, then walked over towards the window, sat down, got into position, and began to play the third movement of St. Matthew's Passion: It was spiritual, quiet, deep and inspiringly beautiful.

All rivers run into the sea.

The soft, deep and graceful music of the cello floated through and filled the room. Qu Shuang stared at the familiar hand, its tapered fingers ravaging the cello's strings, as if all his feelings had poured into his fingertips. The bow swayed back and forth on the strings, creating a bitterly sorrowful, ponderous sound. It was spiritual, eulogising the rebirth of life, calling for the return of the spirit. She did not know whether this dissipated spirit could be saved.

The only audience under the sky, she listened enthralled to the music, as if in the vaults of heaven she indistinctly saw the deepest azure blue appear.

She would be like all other mothers, she thought to herself, and give the baby inside her its first prenatal music lesson. The following day that life would leave her body forever; she wanted to see that little life off and bring peace to her soul. She wished that little life, on its way to another world, a safe journey.

The music reverberated in the air, ever rising; Thomas shut his eyes tightly, intoxicated by the cello music. He had never put so much into his playing as he did that day. The spiritual music guided him to Heaven; he forgot the pains of the profane world, dissolving in the air with the music, no longer bound to the material world.

There was only his cello, his music.

At the end of the piece, Thomas looked around: There were two keys placed on the side. He understood that this was a lasting farewell from that Asian woman, a permanent full stop.

Dusk fell, and he walked out of the room full of memories.

D

ONE MAN'S DECISION TO BECOME A TREE

决定做一棵树

Mo Shen and his City

Mo Shen* finally moved to another city, and it was only after an inhuman effort that he eventually found himself a battered apartment. Looking at the extremely bare walls, he thought to himself, "What am I to do with these?"

His experience of life had left him with rather unhappy memories. He hoped that this time he could turn over a new leaf, but he felt lost when he tried to think of where to start.

Although Mo Shen was already approaching middle age, he had endured all of his days in bitter solitude. He never really understood the true nature of his problem; it was indeed true, as they say, that "self-knowledge is the most difficult kind". To put it another way, he was quite incapable of knowing who he was. So often he felt himself the last to know. He had been deposited on the boundaries of human society and his nature determined he would spend his life alone.

---

* Yoyo subtly incorporates language reminiscent of the final chapter of the *Laozi* or *Daodejing*, describing a peaceful state where residents are aware of neighboring states but never travel there. A stark contrast to the itinerant life of Mo Shen. The *Laozi* is the core text of the Daoist school of philosophy.

He had spent a long time on his own; you would think he ought to have accepted it by now. The tragedy was that he made persistent efforts to remove himself from his isolation, but each attempt was to end in failure. He didn't know what the moral was in all this, or where exactly the problem lay. Time and again he regrouped for battle, and time and again he gave up in exasperation. He wasn't willing to face up to it. One thing was obvious in his sorrowful face; long-term spiritual depression had carved its lines there. That face, full of suffering, could no more attract members of the opposite sex than it could command respect from his own gender. However, he was unwilling to believe that it was his own innate qualities that were sabotaging his attempts.

He had never put up a fight, on top of which, he was terrified of confrontation, and so all he could do was give up.

Escapology became his strongest suit. It was the only magic charm he possessed. As a result he went about with his tail between his legs, avoiding all sorts of situations. He could hardly help becoming the loneliest man alive.

He often thought that it wasn't so much that he had chosen life, but that life had chosen him. He could not help but feel some regret, he felt that rather than having chosen this particular way of life, he felt that he had been given no choice in the matter. No matter how he sought to escape it, solitude pursued him as always. After that, loneliness became like a shadow that he could not shake off, that he would not be rid of for the rest of his life.

Despite that, he did find moments of enjoyment amongst his days of solitude. Listening to music, for example, any sound is basically a means of dispelling loneliness, whether you understand it or not. At any rate, all music was performed by a living person, so it has a little feeling of humanity about it. He would feel as though he were surrounded by a group of people. He could quite well imagine that he was sitting in a crowd, exchanging glances with a certain girl across the dimly lit space. It was a source of stimulation for him. However, this detached tenderness was not enough for him. He desperately wished for a visible and tangible figure to move before him, music was too abstract for that; the music floated in the empty space. There was something substantially lacking, such as a touch, an exchange, a look. Without these things he felt regret. This alone is sufficient to tell us that Mo Shen was a normal and healthy individual; he did wish to have human contact in his life.

At 2.16 in the morning, he was still sitting in a broken armchair whose protruding springs dug him in the bottom. He stared at the cracks in the ceiling, and he still felt empty, lacking. He listened to the empty drifting notes of the music and felt that his understanding of them was very limited. You could say that he was not listening to music at all, but creating a noise that would fill the space, just so that he wouldn't feel so alone.

Running away was the way of life that he chose, and he chose it on purpose. All along he had put himself in this very awkward position. He was stuck between a rock and a hard place. This was his reality. It wasn't that he didn't want to change, it was that he was unable to. Three days ago he was struck by the feeling that things were absolutely fine just like this, then just one hour ago he was suddenly overtaken by a vacant, empty feeling that sent a chill through him.

What was he afraid of?
Afraid of loneliness?
Not only that, and yet, yes, that was it.

Hadn't he lived by himself for a long time? Surely it's not possible that he hadn't gotten used to it yet. He told himself over and over, "You must learn to get along by yourself. You simply must learn to get along by yourself." He repeated those pale and insignificant words to himself constantly as if they were a mantra. The hands on the alarm clock, with its two big metal ears, indicated 2.33 am. In that short space of nineteen minutes he had experienced a deep feeling of negativity about himself.

Mo Shen looked at the alarm clock on his windowsill. It was the only thing he'd brought with him from place to place as he moved. The alarm clock was the most treasured gift he had received as a boy. His father had brought it back for him once when he went on a business trip to the South. His father, who was a man of few words, had said, "You'll be sixteen soon, time waits for no man, so work hard at your studies." His father didn't say that it was a birthday present; it was still one month and sixteen days 'til his birthday when he gave him the clock. He was so happy with it, for several nights he slept cradling it in his arms. If it weren't for the incredible racket it made in the morning, he would have happily gone on sleeping with it in his arms each night. The alarm clock was from Shanghai, a big and prosperous city. It was also the most expensive thing his father ever gave him in his life.

Throughout his adolescence, Mo Shen tried to throw the alarm clock away several times. One time he rode his bicycle out to the river and lifted the clock high in his hand. He very nearly threw it in, but he just loved it too much! His father's early death left a deep, deep scar on Mo Shen. All of a sudden he was the man of the house, the only man left. He felt as if a great wall that had stood behind him had collapsed. Mo Shen himself did not have the characteristics to become head of the household; his mother often complained of his weaknesses, sighing to herself that she had failed to give birth to a good strong son who could reach the stars and take care of everything for her. His mother and father were completely different characters. His mother was always creating a racket at home, she would often tell his father off as if he were a puppy that she must discipline. His father appeared to have no means of defending himself. Five months after Mo Shen's sixteenth birthday, his father washed his hands of the human world; he had died of cancer of the liver. Mo Shen didn't even know that he was in the terminal stages; he just noticed that his father had grown pitifully thin. He never saw his mother take special care of him at all. Later, Mo Shen came to believe that his father had died of depression. He thought to himself that he had inherited all of his misery from his father's innate qualities. He thought that if he could rid himself of his father's gifts, perhaps he would be able to rid himself of that legacy. Indeed, while he was alive, his father had never been particularly close with him. Yet his reticent gaze was always full of tenderness.

At night, his father would sit quietly in the dim light waiting for Mo Shen to finish his homework. At that time children were given a lot of homework, most days he would stay up until gone eleven under the light of the 18 Watt lightbulb. And his father would sit on their cheap and rather uncomfortable sofa waiting for him. Once, Mo Shen had unconsciously raised his eyes and happened to catch his father's gaze. Only ten years later would Mo Shen perceive the weight of that gaze meeting him straight on. His look concealed an infinity of words, a father's hopes for his child; that look contained a father's concern and love for his son.

Now Mo Shen is glad that he didn't throw the alarm clock into the river. That alarm clock was the only decorative article in the whole room; at the same time it was a way for him to remember his father.

Now, the minute hand and the hour hand piled up over the three. Mo Shen gazed at the alarm clock that was already beginning to look a bit old and battered. Then he turned back to the room and continued to regard it with terror.

Surely he wasn't about to go down this road again?
Would he sink back once more into the way things used to be?
Where would he find a reason to move to yet another city?

It must be lovely to stay put in the place where you were born and grew up, growing old alone and dying peacefully of old age. That's one way of living. But he couldn't resign himself to that fate. He hoped that in the latter half of his life he might really turn over a new leaf. He hoped that this time he moved things would be different.

Hopes and reality often go against each other. In his heart of hearts, Mo Shen knew that he was beyond all hope.

In fact he was constantly moving. Each move was absolute, as if he uprooted himself and moved on. Sometimes he would forget the date, the time or where he was. Sometimes he was so confused that he would lose all sense of direction. He did not know where in the world he was. He did not know whether he was at home or abroad, in the city or the country. With no idea where he was, or what the time was; he felt the very reality of his existence was in question! That was his current predicament.

He did not know what he hoped to achieve by moving about from place to place for no apparent reason. He moved for the sake of moving. He thought that something might happen if he stayed on the move. In the end, it didn't solve his problem, but made it worse and worse. In order to travel lightly, he had no choice but to leave behind objects full of memories for him. As a result, he only became more alone. His frequent moves became second nature to him. Before long he could not stop himself. Mo Shen moved so often he didn't even know anymore if he was on the move so as not to rest or resting so as not to move. Such deep philosophical questions only left him confused. His own philosophy was very simple: just to get on with life.

At about that time, he passed by a shop and saw the owner sitting inside looking bored, waiting for customers. Those shop owners could sit there all day every day for a whole year and not see a single customer come in their shop. Right then, Mo Shen understood what boredom was. In that moment, a little confidence sparked in his breast. but that confidence vanished quicker than lightning. His confidence quickly turned to self-doubt, "What right have you to laugh at other people? Don't you sit there killing time in exactly the same way?!"

Perhaps, to begin with, he did have one reason for moving about: to escape the surveillance of his neighbors, to disappear from the field of vision of his friends. Strictly speaking, he didn't really have any friends. It had already been years since he had written a letter, not because he didn't want to write one, but because he had no one to write to. Who could he write to? Who needed a letter from him? If no one was going to read his letter, there wasn't much point writing one in the first place. He had enjoyed writing letters in the past, but that was a long time ago. That was so long ago, the memory itself seemed to have become fossilized.

He looked at the big locust tree outside and thought, "if only I could be like him: No feelings, no desires, he doesn't worry about being lonely, he just stands there like that forever."* As the thought crossed his mind, he realized that he had been living alone for a very long time. He wondered if we would still be able to adapt to living with another person again. Never mind with a man or a woman, just to live as a normal person would. Even if he kept a cat, dog or a snake, that could be called companionship. The word "companion" in English has a very broad meaning.** It doesn't necessar-

---

* Yoyo's description of the tree "free from desires" is reminiscent of the treatment of trees in several places in the Zhuangzi (See Zhuangzi's Dream of a Butterfly in The Reincarnation of Dreamer), where trees have been depicted as beyond the trials of life and unassailable through their vast uselessness.
** Similarly, the Chinese word "things" or wu 物 also has a broad meaning, often remarked upon by scholars of Chinese philosophy, for including humans, animals and plants without a strong differentiation between these categories.

ily mean a human, it could indicate a bird, a monkey, a fish or anything. In that case, you couldn't say that Mo Shen had always been alone. He had kept pets and grown plants. If you go along with the English understanding of the word, he had lived a very full life. He couldn't really be called a loner, in that case. The trouble with Mo Shen was that he placed too much emphasis on his 'companions' and forgot the importance of people. He placed those voiceless, living things above all else. According to his logic, people, animals and plants were all equal in the sense that they were all endowed with life, and they were of equal value and importance in terms of that life. He thought it certain that animals and plants have their own language, it's just that people have not yet advanced to a high enough level to understand them. The explanation of his state was that he was a step ahead of the rest of mankind. Apart from that, his patience with people was extremely limited; they threw him into a deep depression, his previous experiences taught him that at least. This is what led to the monotony of his life, and monotony leads others to despise a person. The people around Mo Shen didn't care about him at all, they treated him as if he were nothing but a dog. Only he was not as faithful to man as a dog would be. That's not wholly his fault, the reason is—he's not a dog but a man! There's nothing surprising there, don't people turn on each other just as easily as that? That's the difference between men and dogs. Only a man abandons his dog, a dog will never abandon its owner. He'd never heard of the latter in all these years. Besides that, Mo Shen was too quiet. That alone will arouse curiosity amongst people who can't mind their own business. His neighbors couldn't help but wonder, how can he bear the day-in-day-out monotony of his life? How can he not go mad? And yet not only does he remain sane, but the skin on his face is as smooth as if someone had run an iron over it—quite dubiously smooth and fresh-faced. It made some people think of the early stages of leprosy or syphilis. Apparently when leprosy is in the early, latent stages, the face will appear fresh and pink as a peach flower, as the rotting flesh beneath swells it out. In that state they'll look quite glorious, that's an initial trick of the light. As for Mo Shen's complexion having some special qualities, naturally that was the hysteria of those around him. And as for whether or not he really did have leprosy, there was no way to say. It was his eccentricity that led them to speculate about him. Quite a few times people in the village saw him meditating before a filthy wall. It is said that that kind of meditation is pretty difficult to master, if you get it wrong you'll go straight down to the fiery depths of hell.* In the end, people put Mo Shen's meditation down as evil practice. "As virtue rises one foot, vice rises ten"**, otherwise why should he appear so different to everyone else. However, apart from being solitary, he didn't seem to possess any other special abilities. He didn't join the immortals, nor did he have any powers over the spirits, you could see that from his monotonous way of life. It was really only his abnormal behavior that aroused

* Voicing a familiar folk caution around spiritual practices, that if you meditate 'wrong' you'll go too far or mad. However, Mo Shen's contemplation of everyday objects is also reminiscent of the study of objects promoted in the Song dynasty Neo-Confucian practice known as gewu 格, where great knowledge could be imparted by gazing and reflecting upon objects.
** A Chinese aphorism stating that evil will always win.

people's suspicions. Firstly, the wall he chose to meditate in front of was incomparably ugly. Apart from the intermingled piss-tracks of men and dogs, there were several other dubious stains and some marks that might have been blood. This layer of filth only added to the general condemnation of the wall. It naturally led people to think of murder and smuggling, the kind of shady business transactions that go on in such poorly lit corners. Although this wall was overlooked and ignored by people time and time again, it was in fact a part of the ancient city wall. It had a complex history and had managed to survive damage during times of war and remained standing until the present day. The older generations used to lay fresh flowers and grasses there, but people today don't care for all that. Even though that wall had borne witness to all the changes of this city. It was an ancient pharaoh, whilst practically speaking it had become insignificant. As it could not be put to any use, there was no reason to pay any attention to it.*
Practicality is a very important subject in this day and age. People forgot all about the glorious past of this wall. It had been rejected, and seen as a shameful object. It only left them puzzled. Why would Mo Shen pick this broken down wall in particular? It wasn't a great looking city certainly, but there were places with a great deal more appeal than that one, like the flowerbeds in the streets—but he insisted on going to that godforsaken place. Each time he went there, they would see him approach the wall slowly, in no hurry. Then, as if it were an act of worship, he would be silent for three minutes, lost

* Echoing Zhuangzi's story in the "World of Man" chapter, about a tree so unremarkable and useless that it lives for years and grows large, because no-one is able to recognise its use.

deep in his thoughts, breathing deeply with his head lowered. His back would be straight, chest out, stomach in, both legs bent in a position as if he were straddling a horse—it was not a comfortable position to maintain, but he stood there without moving an inch. He gazed at that blank wall as if gazing out at the ocean; his spirits soared. There was no comparison for the peace and quiet he found there, precisely because it was forsaken by all. That was the reason that Mo Shen chose it. People spread the rumor amongst themselves that Mo Shen would often take up a seated position in his house and go three months eating nothing but a single kiwi fruit to sustain him, and only taking a drink of water once every ten days.* As for the details of his bowel movements during that period, they didn't go so far as to ask. They had no way of finding out how far this meditation business went, whether or not he could really go without human sustenance, whether the whole thing was true or not. They were only interested in their debates. Within the monotony of a small town, these debates were necessary to their lives. Otherwise how would they prove that they were alive? Even a small town has its rules of operation. And whoever breaks those rules will come to no good in that town.

---

* In both Daoist and Buddhist practice, one of the aims of dedicated meditation practice is to no longer need nutrition from food, being sustained only by meditation and universal energy.

Mo Shen and his animals

Monotony is a form of eternity; it is a complex thing. People continue to live on by respectfully perpetuating that monotony for generations. No one breaks that rule. If anyone did so, they would have to pay the price. There can be no doubt about that.

Mo Shen was doubly monotonous within that monotony. He didn't speak to anybody, which didn't mean that his speech was impaired in any way. To begin with he could speak, and then he found that speech was superfluous. Especially speaking to people. He gradually stopped speaking altogether. His loneliness certainly appeared to be somewhat eccentric. Of course he did speak sometimes. He would take his leftovers and give them to the stray cats and dogs that came by. As he watched them eat, he said, "Take your time, it's all for you, no one's going to fight you for it, look how hungry you are, you didn't run away from home did you? Were you abandoned, then?" There was a stray cat who at first, would only look timidly at him with a cold and hungry look in its eyes, without dropping the food in its mouth for a moment. The cat miaowed as it ate. Only an animal will instinctively give off such a noise as it experiences pleasure. As the stray cat perceived that the man before it was not a threat, it gradually began to relax, and its eyes grew friendly. Mo Shen stroked its black-gray fur and said, "Oh, look what a pretty fellow you are after all, you look lively now that you're eaten and drunk your fill, go on, eat, eat." Mo Shen spoke to the cat as if it really were a human companion. He found it much easier to speak to these non-human creatures; he didn't see them as animals or plants at all. They were living beings, they had their own means of communication and the most significant thing about their part in their exchanges was that they listened patiently to Mo Shen speak. Theirs was a non-linguistic form of communication. He wondered why he lacked that tacit understanding with people. When he spoke with other people he often found that he was cut short, misinterpreted and sometimes the person he was speaking to didn't even have the patience to let him finish a single sentence. Sometimes the misinterpretations became quite hostile. He couldn't resolve their hostility, and he could not get his point across, so he was left with no choice but to hold his silence. He was human, but he was stuck with a total inability in social interactions. It wasn't the fault of other people either. The problem lay most definitely with Mo Shen himself. However, he was stubborn as a mule, he didn't want to change, so his problem became laughable, he could not be anything other than alone. In fact, Mo Shen truly hungered after interaction of some kind, otherwise why would he go trying to communicate with animals? The trouble was that he was a human being who had no capacity to communicate with other human beings. It was a kind of misunderstanding, but who could make up for it? Only after many years of life did he realize that his life was a preparation for death, sometimes it was even more painful than death because he was still a conscious being. He thought certain things over and over in his mind, but he didn't have the language to express them. Before other people, his vocal organs became paralyzed all of a sudden. This problem didn't exist with animals. He would go on and on talking to that black-gray stray as if there were no tomorrow. If anyone passed by at that moment he would instantly cast his eyes aside and stare off into the distance, as if at a landscape that didn't necessarily exist. At that moment he would fall silent, he was even afraid of letting someone hear the sound of his voice. That was how stubbornly he insisted on keeping his silence before other people. When he discovered the possibility of communication with animals, he began to go out regularly every day with all kinds of leftovers. Sometimes he even went out especially and bought some cheap bones and scraps of meat. He went out punctually, and when he arrived at a corner of the block of apartments, there were already several stray cats following him, or some dogs that were all skin and bones. The starving cats and dogs could not get along, they were like fire and water, there was no way for them to be around each other. They would often fight bitterly over one piece of food. The stray cats were no match for the dogs, and would always lose the battle. Mo Shen tried to distribute the food evenly in order to keep these kinds of fights under control. He would indicate a spot further away to one cat or dog, and that dog or cat would obediently go and wait there. But even this method relied on his being fair in distributing the food. Mo Shen could not imagine himself as a well-trained Drillmaster and he had no idea about animal psychology. These scenes provided him with great excitement. He was filled with a sense of achievement hitherto unknown to him. It was as if he were commanding two troops of soldiers. Their gains and losses were in the palm of his hand. He had never experienced successes like this in the human world. This only gave him all the more reason to keep going. He had never had this experience with people, so he loved these homeless animals all the more passionately. But there was trouble in paradise. Before long stray cats and dogs from a radius of several kilometers around were gathering around about the simple apartment buildings, they lay in ambush about the buildings, waiting for their "god" who was to appear at any moment and save them from starvation. The orderly proceedings were ruined by the newcomers, the worst of it was that those stray cats and dogs had begun to cry and howl at night. Especially in April, the cats in heat shrieked incessantly, like a Siberian gale. The neighbors began to loathe Mo Shen. In fact, the noise of the dogs and cats had begun to seriously affect his sleep as well, at that moment he too would detest the animals, but when he remembered that they were faced with the threat of starvation, he managed to put up with it. In that moment, he would feel as if he was surrounded by cats that rubbed to and fro against him. Only the ginger tabby cat was really close to him. To begin with, the ginger tabby had been very timid, she would always hide away in the distance and look at Mo Shen with tearful eyes, emitting thin little cries. The look in the little cat's eyes along with her feeble voice made Mo Shen especially fond of her. Mo Shen would always find something special for her. He would carry a saucer of milk out and set it before the little cat. The cat looked nervously about her as she lapped up the milk with her pink tongue. Mo Shen stroked her gently and the cat gave a shudder and shot off to the corner where she looked up at Mo Shen with curiosity. Mo Shen thought, "She's used to being hurt, I ought to protect her."

Mo Shen spoke softly to her, "Don't be afraid, come over here, come and have a bit more to eat, you must be hungry."

The ginger tabby made her halting way over, eventually testing the water by rubbing her tail along the bottom of Mo Shen's trouser leg, then ran away again. She progressed in this way, gradually getting closer and closer to him and within a few days had relaxed her guard completely. After that, the ginger cat was always the first to run up to Mo Shen when he came out, with her tail sticking up poker straight, and she would rub her body affectionately against Mo Shen's legs. The cat began to miaow in a very tender fashion. It was a tenderness that Mo Shen had never experienced before. Each time he laid his hand upon the soft fur of the animal he was filled with warmth. His own physical craving for contact was obvious to him, but he would never be brave enough to get fanciful about attaining similar contact from humans. He felt that these cats and dogs gave him much more than he could ever give them in return. Therefore he became more and more devoted to those forsaken animals.

His concern for homeless animals soon incurred the anger of the residents of his building. One time, one of his neighbors walked straight up to him and said furiously, "If you want to open a care shelter, you'd better hurry up and move out of here!"

Mo Shen just stared at the fat woman who shouted at him, without showing any emotion, silent as usual.

That woman stared at him through squinting eyes, like the eyes of a chicken. She lowered her voice and enunciated clearly, "Pretending you're deaf and dumb, what exactly do you hope to achieve?" Mo Shen didn't make any appropriate response to her rough words. He was thinking to himself, "Why does a chicken's gaze always look so aggressive?" As a rule he liked the eyes of animals, and having paid attention to the look in different animals' eyes he had found that dove's eyes were peaceful, giraffe's eyes were melancholy and full of doubt, camel's eyes are tender yet miserable, dog's eyes are pitiful and begging, they rely on people their whole lives, but are often forsaken. Horse's eyes are full of benevolence, and their fidelity is rewarded with punishment. Sometimes cat's eyes can be fawning, but you cannot help but love them. Sometimes, Mo Shen found himself quite moved by their eyes alone. He had already reached an age when he was not easily moved to emotion, yet sometimes he would get quite protective of these animals. Only chickens' eyes sent a chill down his spine, he found their eyes greedy and savage, a thoroughly chilling aspect. Mo Shen remembered this very clearly even as a child, he had never eaten chicken in his life. He thought that the look in a chicken's eyes was pure evil. He was caught up in his thoughts about chickens as the woman turned her great backside upon him and walked away. Even the shadow that fell on the ground behind her looked oily and dirty. He thought, "Perhaps it's eating too much chicken that has done that to her."

Ever since that day, people began knocking on his door. At first, they just knocked lightly a couple of times, quite restrained and polite. Mo Shen pricked up his ears and listened, he felt surprised; who would come and visit him? It had been ten years or so since the second pair of feet had crossed his threshold. In the very beginning, he had desperately hoped for company. As one year passed and then another and no one came, he gradually lost faith in the idea and with that, all desire for it. He no longer asked anything of life. He knew that no one would come to see him. He did not dare to ask too much. He therefore decided not to open the door. Then the knocking grew more urgent, and finally became a heavy pounding. The harder they knocked, the less attention he paid to it. It was already loud enough as it was; there was no need to pay attention to it, it made him feel angry enough as it was. He thought, "This heavy knocking sound is an act of violence. I won't stand for it." He felt confused as to why nearly everything he did was opposed by other people, including his silence. He had thought seriously about it before, but it only gave him a headache, and he still didn't understand it. Where was he going wrong? Could it be that the mistake was his existence as a human? Why do some people take to life like a duck to water? What is it about them? He envied people that had a gift for communication. He had tried to practice to become like them, but with little success. He practiced in secret as he entered his adolescence. When he was alone he would rehearse flashing his teeth in front of the mirror. As far as he could make out, people that really had the gift of the gab always possessed a wealth of expressions. He stood in front of the mirror exaggerating his every look, making wild gestures with his hands. His eyebrows leapt, his face twisted into knots. He had noted that important people never stood still, and he practiced accordingly. He stood before the mirror practicing with all his might, but it came to no good. Try as he might to discover his talent for speaking, or at least to encourage such skills before the mirror, it only made the situation worse. At the dinner table he made eyes at his mother and his little sister—his inflammable gaze burst out of a face full of unsolicited attentions. His mother told him off loudly; she told him to sit quietly and eat his dinner, and not go copying other people's bad habits. He had thought he could practice on these two, his only audience. He hadn't imagined that his mother would put such a swift end to it and then there was the weird way that his sister looked at him for the next few days. She avoided him as if he were a criminal, as if he might set upon her and rape her at any moment. When Mo Shen listened to other people speaking happily in public, he would think to himself, "If I were the one talking about that, I could do much better than him." Yet when he came to try and get his point across he became tongue-tied, his pulse raced and he could feel a little devil's fork pricking him all over. As a result he completely lost his bearings. He felt his temperature rising in his face, that was what he feared the most—once he blushes red all over all is lost, no matter how well thought out he had it in his head, no matter how philosophical it had been, it simply came out as nonsense. All he wanted then was to draw the failed conversation to as swift an end as possible. In time "speaking" became his complex. The moment he thought of speaking in public he would break out in a cold sweat across his forehead, his pulse would quicken. He detested the fact that he couldn't express himself. It was always the same, no matter how he tried—his nature decided his fate! Why was he so terrified? Was his present incarnation a mistake? Then what was he in his previous life? A dog? A cat? A mouse? He did seem like a mouse, just because of how timid he was. The only thing he was certain of was that he hoped he was not a chicken! He truly envied those guys who could just casually open up and talk away. What spell did they cast to get people over to their side to listen to their endless discourses? He could not hold a candle to them. In fact, he would like to be the center of attention, he hoped that when he began to speak other people would put down what they were doing and turn to look at him, as if they were listening to the speech of a great man. He had the mentality appropriate for leadership! He thought of a hundred ways to fulfill his ideal: "Never to rest until my words have moved the world"; he wanted his every word to be worth its weight in gold, but he just did not have that way with words. No matter how spectacular his thoughts were, language emerged from his lips bland and uninteresting. The more he went over and over the first sentence in his mind to get it just right, the more he felt it was impossible to open his mouth. Privately he thought that speaking was like writing an essay: The most important thing was a good beginning; if the first sentence caught your attention the whole essay would certainly glow. That was what he hoped to achieve, but every time the moment came to speak, he couldn't come up with anything good to say which made him furiously embarrassed. He began to turn against himself; he tested himself. The more he wanted to get an idea across the more difficult it became. In the end, he stopped speaking just to spite himself. This rebellious attitude gradually became his reality; he could not turn the situation around. He felt that life had no need of him, and yet here he still existed. His body was a real object, only by eliminating the physical could you eliminate the spirit. If he wanted to disappear from reality, he would first have to destroy the physical; if the body didn't exist, then the spirit didn't exist. Only in the case of great men does the spirit linger on long after the body's destruction. Although he subconsciously hoped to be a great man, in conscious thought he didn't even dare to dream of achieving such greatness. He knew he would never be a great man, therefore his spirit would not live forever! Up until now he had not been brave enough to destroy his physical body. Therefore, he had continued to live in this predicament. It made him feel utterly hopeless; everything was overcast with shadows. Under several such attacks, he regressed to an attitude of rabbit-like quiet.

The knocking at the door grew louder once more, the rhythmic knocking sent his train of thought steadily downhill.

He had had some human contact before, but that was already a long time ago. After leaving secondary school he agreed to become pen pals with a classmate of his. He Xiao26 was the only person who respected his silence. Not only did she not look down on him for his lonely character and frugality with words, it instead seemed to make her all the more friendly towards him. They would walk home together in long periods of silence. When He Xiao asked him something, he would make the most succinct of replies, "Yes, No, Maybe, Perhaps, Okay, Good," and so on. In truth, he wanted to pour forth words, to grab the attention of this girl, the only one who was interested in him; but he could not forget the painful lessons life had taught him. The more complex he wanted to make his responses, the more simple his thoughts became. He felt his mind becoming blank; where were the contemplations he was usually full of? No matter how much he wanted to say, he just couldn't find a suitable place to begin. He wasn't aware that he was suffering from a psychological complex, it was as if he had already taken his inability for granted. And He Xiao was extremely patient with his boring ways. Mo Shen was deeply moved by that; yet he lacked even the ability to express his gratitude, that is to say, he wasn't accustomed to doing so.

* The name means, "How does she know?"

One day, He Xiao told him that her family would be moving to another city.

"That's impossible!" Mo Shen said, in surprise.

Then he asked, "When?"

"Soon." He Xiao replied.

Mo Shen had his back to He Xiao. There were many things he wanted to say, but he didn't know where to begin. They stood for a long time in a stretch of grassy wasteland. Mo Shen grew inexplicably nervous; his heart was pounding. He knew that he ought to say something, but the words stuck in his throat all the worse as he became nervous. It was He Xiao who broke the stalemate by saying, "Let's write to each other."

Two weeks later He Xiao's letter arrived. Mo Shen had expected that she would eat her words, he hadn't really been very hopeful of her fulfilling her promise. When her letter came, Mo Shen's faith had its first taste of encouragement. In her letter, He Xiao described her new home and the new city she lived in. Mo Shen wrote back straight away, he described the city he had grown up in as a pit. He said that he was crawling along a long tunnel looking for a way out, but all he could see were tall ranges of mountains, he could not conquer their heights. He tried to climb over them, but the black clouds in his body obscured his vision. The black clouds wrapped around him and he didn't know where to go. He wrote, "I hate those black clouds, where did they come from anyway?" As he wrote more and more he found that it was much easier to communicate with people on paper than face-to-face. He was happy that he had found a means of communication. He Xiao replied soon after and told him that he was too 'dark', she said 'darkness is not right for people our age'. Mo Shen wrote another letter to her describing his two cats: He called one "Chatterbox" and the other "Cloth-ears". He anthropomorphized these two animals: He described Chatterbox as an opportunist who never missed a chance to express herself and as a result was spoiled by one and all. Even though he could see through Chatterbox's craftiness, he could not resist her powers. He was willingly duped time and time again. Chatterbox had spirited eyes, she was a slippery character, and people are easily fooled by good looks. As for Cloth-ears, he was a dreamer. His nature was like that of a stoner; totally unreliable. Cloth-ears didn't care about the outside world. He just floated along dreaming his dreams. Despite the fact that he was a cat, he would attempt to take wing as birds do. He climbed to the highest branches of the tree, as he thought this way he was nearer to the heavens, he imagined that he could spread his wings and fly from tree to tree just like a bird. Whereupon he spread out his two front paws, in place of wings, and sadly came crashing down to earth. After that, he was lame in his right front paw for several weeks. Chatterbox, who was so skilled at taking every opportunity that arose, took full advantage of Cloth-ears weakness as a dreamer to get him into trouble. (Actually, the nature of a dreamer is a charming quality, but reality often plots to eliminate this excellent characteristic.) For example, when it's clearly Chatterbox that wants to eat the meat that's cooking in their owner's pot, she will trick poor Cloth-ears by saying, "Can't you smell that delicious meaty scent? You really don't feel like having a try? If we could only have a try, I'd only take a little bite out of the left-hand side, and you'd take a bite from the right. I'm sure the lady of the house won't even notice." To begin with, Cloth-ears had been lost in his own laziness. He didn't have any inordinate ideas about the fragrance in the air. At Chatterbox's prompting, the fragrance became an utterly irresistible temptation. Chatterbox was perfectly clear about Cloth-ears' nature in this matter. In the end Cloth-ears went bounding up like a bandit and knocked over the pot. He offered that piece of beef to Chatterbox without the least hesitation. By the time Cloth-ears moved in to have a taste himself, Chatterbox already had three mouthfuls beginning to digest in her stomach and was miaoing out loud with delight. That night, Cloth-ears met with a harsh punishment. He received two vicious blows to the back of his skull with mother's flashing stainless steel ladle. Then he was driven mercilessly out of the house and spent the night out in the elements. Meanwhile, Chatterbox lay there shamelessly in the greatest of comfort, snoring on mother's lap. Mother continued to stroke her, her extra shiny fur no doubt a result of the extra beef that she had eaten. Her expression was so peaceful; it was as if the matter had nothing to do with her at all. Chatterbox was a pure instigator to trouble, and she had eaten rather a lot herself. Each time she would use her wits to make the best of a situation, find just the right thing to say and when it was all over she made a quick getaway. One more story can fully illustrate the trickery of Chatterbox the cat. Chatterbox's clever ways had caught the eye of the tom cat next door who had sought to win her heart many times. Chatterbox always stopped short of definitely refusing or accepting his advances. She preserved a thoroughly indistinct attitude to him. Therefore, this fine example of a proud tomcat always imagined he had a thread of hope, and often did his best to please her. One day Chatterbox spoke coolly to Cloth-ears, "We've lived together under the same roof for a long time now, even if you don't love me, we at least have a kind of sibling affection, don't we? You can't just stand by and watch whilst an outsider takes advantage." In fact, she knew full well that Cloth-ears had had the snip, and couldn't possibly be her lover even if he wanted to. She went on in an inflammatory manner, just to get his male pride up. One blazing hot afternoon, Cloth-ears went storming out of the house like a mounted knight to seek out the other tomcat that was twice his size and have a duel. Within half an hour Cloth-ears came dashing back home, his face dripping with blood; half-shredded by his rival. Mother cleaned up his wound and scolded him as she did so, "Why must you always be so naughty? Can't you be more like Chatterbox? You must learn to fight with words, not with fists." Cloth-ears thought to himself, "If I had the gift of the gab like Chatterbox, I wouldn't be in this state now." He was in such a great deal of pain that he cried softly as he looked piteously over at his companion. He was hoping for some of the sympathy and support that he deserved, a few words of pity would have been enough. Chatterbox showed no sign of compassion as she sashayed past whistling to herself, without uttering a single word of comfort, as if this matter had nothing to do with her anyway.

Previously, He Xiao had written to him in moderation. Mo Shen always wrote much more frequently than his counterpart. The contents of his letters spanned many subjects. He often wrote twenty or so pages. By comparison, He Xiao's letters were much simpler. This time He Xiao wrote back very quickly to praise his style of writing. She wrote, "I never knew your language could be so powerful. Each letter is a gem—you're full of talent! Why don't you express yourself like this usually? You'd do so well if you could. You ought to develop this talent of yours. Perhaps you'll become a famous writer! I really think so." Mo Shen was very excited when he received that letter. He never imagined that anyone would praise him so lavishly. As a result he couldn't stop what he had started. He began to bombard He Xiao with reams of letters. He rapidly exhausted the treasure trove of ideas that he had amassed over the years. He Xiao didn't know quite what to do with him, but Mo Shen didn't care, he went on and on. He wrote back telling her that thought and reality are two very different things; he could not bring the two together. He admitted quite objectively that he found his mental life more interesting than reality, but that he had no way to make his real life more interesting. In the end the ennui of his real life was victorious over his spiritual values. He wrote, "I cannot overcome the boredom of reality, boredom is like a long, long shadow following me, no matter how hard I try I just cannot shake it off. I don't know how other people manage to battle through their boredom, just because the weather is nice, perhaps? Or by making mountains out of molehills just to pass the time? Just like my mother, every day she makes a big thing out of what we'll have for dinner that day. She feels like she's toiled away over this matter her whole life. If you think about it, she's not wrong in principle, "Eating is the religion of the people,"* as they say. But to live your life just for eating is just pitiful." Their communication continued for five years, and those five years of writing letters suddenly ended just like that, for no reason. Mo Shen didn't expect any explanations from his pen pal. He felt that these five years of correspondence were enough joy to last him a lifetime. In fact, it was not so much that He Xiao understood him completely, but that she was his only devoted listener, and quite frankly he was more satisfied with the latter. Along with this feeling of satisfaction he developed a tiny thread of expectation: He hoped that one day he would hear someone come and knock on his door, and when he opened it there would be standing that girl, the only one who ever understood him—He Xiao. He spent his life waiting for that day, it was the only dream he had.

The sound of knocking was thunderous. He still refused to open the door. He then received the final communiqué demanding that he cease his ministrations to stray cats and dogs immediately, otherwise he would be driven out of the building on

---

* A saying originating in ancient Chinese historical texts, but that has remained popular. Its modern popularity may be in part due to its being quoted and referenced by Mao Zedong, as well as it aligning well with the Chinese cultural significance of food and eating.

the spot. It was a strongly worded petition signed by all of the residents in the building. They left him no room to maneuver, the letter announced that if he did not stop immediately they would take action and on his head be it. It would appear that his actions had infuriated his neighbors. This was very serious, suppose he ended up like the stray animals, driven out of his home to live on the streets? He didn't want to let things get to that stage, so it seemed all he could do was to give up. In all honesty, his feeding the stray animals had nothing to do with ideas of right or wrong, he was only seeking to alleviate his boredom, to cope with his loneliness. But who could he turn to? People? After successive failures he found that this too was an impractical idea. Animals became a possibility, but he never imagined that it would cause so much trouble.

Soon afterwards, the residents implemented a movement of viciously beating the stray cats and dogs. The beatings that were intended to drive out the animals were administered in a completely automatic fashion: Any animal that wandered into the area was driven off with a wild beating. The animals had no idea what was going on, they would gather as usual on two sides of the building waiting for their master to come and feed them, when suddenly what appeared instead were sticks and beatings. The men and women, young and old who were participating were waving sticks and yelling at the tops of their voices as they chased after the animals. Little children looked as if they were taking part in a festival of some sort, throwing rocks with delight, they weren't about to be soft-hearted with the adults egging them on. When Mo Shen went out of his apartment, some young boys even threw stones at him and shouted, "Get that idiot! Get that stupid dog!" When Mo Shen turned angrily upon them, they scattered, then, as he turned to leave they crept up behind him shouting, mockingly, "Hey, you idiot, weirdo, you're a big stupid dog, go sleep with the bitches." Mo Shen shook his head in disbelief; the children's games were no less hurtful than the cruelty of the grownups. This was certainly sufficient evidence to illustrate the character of human beings: As soon as you posed the least threat to their happiness there was no reasoning with them. The fate of any animal before humans was the same—to be cruelly driven to death. An animal stood no chance of winning this battle since humans had sufficient brains to outwit them. The strays soon realized their fate. At the same time, they felt critical of the man who had so carelessly abandoned them. Why did he not come to save them? They had no choice but to look for another solution.

The block of apartments stood towering in a desert of solitude. It had regained its peace and quiet. It did not want the blast of the wind or the drumming of the rain. It stood at rest under a layer of clouds without moving a muscle, shut off from all communications.

Mo Shen and his plants

His interaction with animals was put to an end just as cruelly as that and Mo Shen went back to living with one foot in the grave. Every day he watched the sun rise and set again, with the same thought grinding through his mind, "Since I can't keep animals, I'll just have to think of something quieter to occupy myself, that's all." He thought and he thought and began to take action.

Before long his neighbors found that that gormless individual was up to something new. He was constantly seen moving all sorts of plants into his house. His apartment soon resembled a forest; he was hemmed in by plants, which gave him a feeling of security. They were the barricade that separated him from other people. Never again would he be disturbed by the outside world; he felt as if he had put on a suit of armor, that he had become impervious to all blows. He was deeply moved by this feeling of confidence previously unknown to him.

Mo Shen regained his sense of the meaning of life. He was in high spirits, especially meditating in his little thicket of plants; that was just beyond description. He felt he was approaching paradise, as if he were walking on clouds. He had never reached that state of mind before. He no longer had to leave his house to go and meditate before that piece of city wall that everyone hated so much. They wouldn't need to call him a weirdo any more. He could reap all the benefits of meditation without leaving his home. He was all the more fond of his plants because of that. Every day when he got up, the first thing he did was to greet his plants, "Hey, Good morning to you all!" he would say in a loud voice. He felt that they too made their greeting to him. It was as if he stood before a group of refined gentlemen, with one hand tucked behind his back he bowed ever so slightly returning their salutation with gentlemanly respect. Soon he became an expert horticulturist, carefully examining each plant in turn, carefully touching each leaf, inspecting the path of their veins, and judging the direction of their future development. Next he would bend down and rub the soil at their roots, plunging his beautiful hands deep into the dirt without the least qualms. He checked the temperature of the water, and misted them with a humidifier. He moved the plants that did not like the sun into shady spots. He never watered them in full sunlight, knowing that that was tantamount to cold-blooded murder to plants. He was very meticulous in giving the correct amount of water to each plant, as well as the right amount of fertilizer. He knew that too much water not only did no good for plants, it could actually kill them, just like if you overfed a child on chocolate, it wouldn't do them any good, they would grow obese and die of a heart attack.

Ever since he began this collection of plants, his fingernails grew black as soot; they were full of dirt. He had always taken good care of his hands; they were white and finely shaped. His fingers were long and tapered; it always looked as if his very soul were housed within his fingers. His hands were extremely expressive, his fingers were always moving about hesitantly, hanging in midair, revealing his ponderous character. When he was younger, both women and children had displayed curiosity towards his hands. Young children would often grab his hands with interest, and turn them this way and that and ask, "Do you eat with these hands?"

"Of course I do," he would reply, smiling.

"Then, do you work with them too?"

He replied, smiling, "Of course I do."

"They look as though you never did a thing in your life."

He smiled as he replied, "I only wish it were so."

One particular kind of child would enjoy playing with his hands, as if they were delicate playthings. As for the women that developed an interest in his hands, that usually bordered on a fetish. They looked at him with eagle eyes as they snatched up his hands. "He must be either terribly fascinating or terribly boring," the women contemplated to themselves. Once in a bar a woman had suddenly asked him, "Do you write poetry?"

He gave the middle-aged woman an odd look, "Why?"

The woman was still intrigued, "Because you have the hands of a poet."

In the end, he had to disappoint her.

When he got home that night, Mo Shen lay on his bed and looked at his hands. He said to himself, "Do I have the hands of a poet? Do I really?" He had never noticed such a thing in his own hands before. Never having written a single poem in his life, he became even fonder of his own hands. Now that he was going against his nature by dirtying his hands he was making no small sacrifice. Yet, when he looked upon his flourishing plants he felt an incomparable comfort. He looked after that bunch of plants as if they were babes in arms. He placed his trust in them. With those plants he had a future— life had meaning. The group of plants were his "circle": He spoke with them, he sat amongst them to read, to eat, to take a nap. He was a part of them. He didn't feel in the least bit lonesome. He was very happy with his discovery; he wondered how he had gone so long without discovering this source of happiness? As a result, his purchasing of plants soon grew out of control. He collected more and more interesting specimens and wild flowers. He scanned the streets for the particular species of plant he was looking for, he became selective in the kind of plants he collected. He wasn't interested in just any kind of plant, he showed a clear preference. He turned his attention to unusual broad-leaved plants, like the large-leaved cheese plant, rubber plants, Japanese banana trees and the like. He liked plants with odd shapes. He liked plants from the desert that could weather a drought, they usually grew very slowly, plants like cacti, mother-in-law's tongue, desert roses. Then there were plants from the Columbian tropical rainforest. Deep greens and purples appeared on their leaves. They disliked the sunlight and preferred shady corners. If the sunlight fell upon them they would curl up their leaves and look hard done by. There was another special flower, an ugly and odd-looking one. It looked like a cluster of ringworms, but it had one special ability. When flies or mosquitoes flew past it would emit a special fragrance to entice them to alight, then the stamen would make a jellyfish convulsion, it was an extremely sensual movement and the fly would quite happily be sucked head first down the little hole. Before long the fly disappeared and that is how the plant dealt with that. The fly is dissolved in the little cave and no one knows where it goes after that. At first Mo Shen felt it was a little frightening. He wondered if he should throw the plant away. But soon he was entranced by the flower's delicate movements, it reminded him of Chatterbox with her silvery tongue; remaining favorite of the house despite all the black marks against her name. In his nostalgia, he stopped thinking about whether or not it was cruel to the flies, and gave it pride of place on his windowsill. He had read in a book that that rare plant loves the sun, that it can make its enticements only when it has had enough sunlight. It was the first time in his life that he'd seen a plant eat an animal: The carefree act of cruelty left him rubbing his eyes in disbelief. This unique method of nourishment piqued his curiosity. He was wild with delight that such a precious plant could be found in this little backwater of a place!

To begin with he arranged his plants about the sitting room—what was called a sitting room, of course no one had ever come to sit with him there before, even for a second. "Now it comes in handy," he thought to himself. He was so excited he could hardly sit still. He moved his pots of plants to and fro, trying to find the most suitable place for them. The plants lived warm and comfortable lives under his protection. Later, he went ahead and made the sitting room into a greenhouse, making the plants the owners of that room, they exercised their rights of ownership there. And he, Mo Shen, was only there to complement them. He was perfectly happy to think of it like that. It was difficult for him to express the joy that his plants brought him. He was willing to make this sacrifice for them.

Owing to his mad obsession with buying plants, it soon became obvious that there was simply not enough space in the sitting room. He soon had no choice but to move some into each room in his apartment, including his bedroom. He knew that it wasn't fitting to share a room with plants. Plants will fight with a person for oxygen during the night, which is not very healthy for the person. But now that his bed was surrounded by plants of every size, he felt as if he were sleeping in a tropical rainforest. It was very exotic, he felt as if his heart had come into bloom. He thought now he had no need to go off on a long voyage to Africa, and there was no need to go off traveling to Southeast Asia. Just sitting at home was like sitting in a primaeval forest. It was a wonderful feeling! And he needn't worry about other people turning against him over it: These quiet plants couldn't possibly bother anyone. His neighbors had no right to interfere with him on this one. It was as if these plants had awarded him his freedom. He felt as if there was light at the end of the tunnel, and that the road ahead was broad and straight. He had already made his decision to spend the rest of his life with these plants. He no longer felt lonely. At night he could feel the plants breathing along with him. The breathing of another within these walls was a new experience for him. Whilst he felt it a little strange, that feeling was accompanied by a kind of novelty and excitement. He was extremely satisfied with this bunch of plants of his. They would never do things to disappoint him; they were just as quiet as the man who looked after them. However, he was rarely quiet before them, he was always muttering something to them. He looked at the great big fellow from Africa and said, "My, big guy, you're growing too fast, you're going to burst through my little room soon, aren't you?" Then he turned to examine the rubber tree once more, "My goodness, how did you grow such big leaves overnight?" Each leaf was as big as a palm fan. Usually you'd have to grow this kind of plant for eight or nine years before it would reach this size. Plants of this kind are pretty delicate and don't adapt well to a human environment. Even those that don't die often have dry, wilted leaves and grow poorly. The proverb says, "A Dragon tree may grow for a thousand years before it blooms", but his dragon tree had flowered in two years of his raising it. It was a real rarity. His Ganoderma* was especially fresh and healthy looking. It blushed pink like the cheek of an eighteen-year-old girl. The only strange thing about it was the magical speed at which it grew. In six months it had already grown as big as an umbrella, it was simply miraculous. Mo Shen was very pleased that he had discovered he had green fingers. Since he had no luck getting on with people and had been attacked for keeping pets, at least growing plants shouldn't get him into too much trouble. His plants didn't let him down either, with his dedicated care they grew furiously and soon took over all the space in his apartment. Soon he could only move about by squeezing through in the spaces left between them. He had to sidle between them to get from his sitting room to the kitchen, there was no other way to get through. He had broken teacups, plates and bowls on several occasions due to it. Branches and limbs of plants struck his arms and obscured his vision as he carried crockery from the kitchen into the sitting room so that it was all he could do to keep from dropping and smashing things. Several times he tried to carry his dinner into his greenhouse area so that he could enjoy his meal with his plants, only to be tripped up by a vine beneath his feet and drop the whole lot on the floor. At such times, he had no choice but to go to bed on an empty stomach. The Oleander grew particularly quickly. It soon reached the ceiling of his room. Mo Shen was a bit worried about it. He did not know what to do with these plants that were growing so ferociously.

---

* A fungus believed to bestow health and longevity; it is often made into tea or used in cooking.

One day, when he was sitting reading beneath the spreading Cheese Tree (he had to regard this plant as a tree, it had grown so tall) he suddenly noticed that cracks had appeared between the walls and the ceiling of his room. He was scared. If things carried on at this rate the plants would soon burst through the roof, and then the people upstairs would have something to complain about. He had to go and buy a saw, and a ladder. He carried them back home dripping with sweat from the exertion. He propped up the ladder and climbed up to saw the branches down in length. His delicate hands were tormented worse than ever before, several blisters appeared on his palms. No more than a few days had passed when he found that the tree had reached the ceiling once more. He could only continue his hopeless pruning of the tree. He was already exhausted and the idea of giving up on these plants crossed his mind. The wild plants grew together into a densely woven net that covered his apartment. His movements were seriously restricted. With each step he had to lift up the leafy branches before him, as if he were an explorer moving through a real forest. His own living space grew ever smaller. Soon only the space on the bed was left to him, he did feel that something wasn't quite right, but he didn't see it as an invasion, the devouring of his space went on in secret. Without his realizing it, they were taking over his territory. A fine Cheese plant was constantly producing shoots and sprouts, they stretched in all directions as if it were baring claws and teeth, they coiled on the ground like snakes. Mo Shen had to go carefully by them to avoid landing on the ground with a crash. At night he felt increasingly short of breath, he was often trapped in the grip of nightmares. He would wake up afraid of suffocating, and experience difficulty breathing. He felt lacking in oxygen. He knew that this was the result of fighting the plants for oxygen. He could only resort to opening the windows. Previously, regardless of season he had always left the windows open a crack. But there was another problem: Some plants required a certain temperature and humidity. Mo Shen had to bow to the needs of those more delicate plants. One night as Mo Shen was sleeping soundly he suddenly became aware of something cool slithering about his neck, he stretched out a hand subconsciously to touch it: Something was entwined about his throat. He pulled hard at it but couldn't pull it away. He switched on his bedside lamp in a state of panic, only to find a creeper wrapped snake-like around his neck. He felt both fear and surprise. He was bemused. The frequent odd occurrences were beginning to make him think that something peculiar was going on. Surely he wasn't going to have to give up his plants as well? he said to himself. He quickly drew a negative conclusion to that question. That would be too cruel to him; he obviously could not withstand such a blow. He lay still for a while, then switched off the light and went back to sleep. But he still found it difficult to breathe, he felt suffocated. He opened his mouth wide; he opened his eyes. In the darkness, he made out innumerable mouths opening on the leaves of the cheese plant, the little mouths were open wide and gulping down oxygen. Mo Shen threw himself out of bed and ran towards the window. He tripped over a plant pot and nearly knocked his front teeth out. He opened all the windows in exasperation, only then did he begin to feel a little more comfortable.

When he got up in the morning, he found that the mushroom-shaped Ganoderma he was growing had produced magnificent colored spots. Dots that were an orange-pink color, it was quite lovely. In a moment, he decided that all that had happened the night before was nothing but a nightmare. He began to get his breakfast ready, when he suddenly became aware that the upper half of his body was itching beyond all relief. He lifted his vest to have a look and saw that his body was covered with red spots, just like the spots on the Ganoderma. Those same spots looked particularly striking upon his own snow-white skin. He was terrified, he left his breakfast untouched and rushed straight out to a local pharmacy. When he arrived at the pharmacy, he hesitated. He managed to ask the pharmacist if they had any ointment for itching. The pharmacist began to speak in a professional tone of voice, "That all depends on what kind of irritation you have." Mo Shen described his symptoms most unwillingly to the pharmacist. In fact, all he needed to do was to lift up his top and show the pharmacist his rash and he would be able to find the right medicine. Mo Shen felt an irrational fear of other people finding out the root of his problems. He felt that if they knew what the cause of his illness was, he would be besieged once more. He would rather suffer in silence. His life was a case history of that. The pharmacist could only prescribe some common anti-inflammatory creams for him to try. There wasn't much to choose between them, he had no choice but to give it a go, it probably wouldn't do any good. Mo Shen left the pharmacy with two different types of ointment, doing his best to avoid bumping into his neighbors. Returning home, he quickly applied the ointment to his body. After three days he showed no signs of recovery, if anything his symptoms were getting worse. He itched beyond all relief; and finally started losing sleep. In the end he had to go and consult a doctor. He chose a private clinic especially far away from his home. When he lifted his top up the doctor took one look then made an unnecessarily detailed inquiry into Mo Shen's living conditions. He begrudgingly admitted that he did grow some plants. The doctor told him that what he had was a kind of rash caused by an over-humid atmosphere. An excruciating expression flashed across Mo Shen's face as he begged the doctor to keep his secret. The doctor looked at him in bewilderment. It was only a standard case of sensitive skin, nothing like syphilis or warts. There was no awful reason behind it; he really had nothing to hide. It was rather Mo Shen's slightly disturbed nature that would give you cause for concern if anything. The doctor went on to prescribe some medicine, pills and ointment. Just as Mo Shen was about to walk out of the clinic, the doctor cleared his throat and delicately said that it might be best to move some of his plants elsewhere, as it would be advantageous for his recovery. In fact, Mo Shen was already clear in his heart of hearts where the roots of the problem lay, but he wasn't very willing to admit the truth. In the past few years, he and his plants had come to rely on each other. They had made it through many a dark and lonely night together. His communications with his plants were the only thing that prevented his total degeneration of speech, he was filled with an unswerving gratitude towards them. He believed that it was the plants that had saved him and not that he had nurtured them. He was willing to do all he could for them. If they were to be taken away, that would be equal to taking away his life. He felt troubled. What was he going to do with his plants? He thought about it all the way home and reaching home he felt thoroughly despondent. When he looked at those plants that were increasing, growing all over the place, his hands were tied. He didn't care if two and two did make four. He took the pills the doctor had given him. Before long he began to feel drowsy. He walked over to his bed where plants and their pots lay entangled together. Just as he was about to lie down he found that his sheets were covered with great big leaves. They had finally invaded his bed! That was the last little space he had to himself, his last remaining private space! He threw the leaves on to the floor in a rage and stamped upon them viciously. He had never been so rough with his plants before. He recalled how excited he was when the first tender shoot had trailed itself about the head of his bed and he felt as if he were lying in a cradle, as if he had entered a Utopian realm. He thought of how the plants had repaid his careful tending. He had lived on a desert island, what more could he ask for? He felt very lucky. He thought he finally understood the meaning of "happiness"! Who could have imagined that the rapid growth of the creepers would make him feel unsafe? He was impossibly confused. But he could not raise a hand against his plants. He felt a kind of satisfaction amid his helplessness. He felt rather confused about his current predicament. On the one hand he was thoroughly pleased with himself; on the other hand he couldn't help but feel a little concerned, his hands were tied in the matter. At that particular moment, the medicine made it impossible for him to continue turning the matter over in his mind any longer and he slept. He slept very deeply and in his dreams the Ganoderma grew enormous and filled the whole room. The four walls were gradually pushed away into the distance. All of the plants were encroaching upon him, their movements were no longer furtive, they were openly invading his space. He was pushed onto the bed where he was made to make no sudden moves. His space was now restricted to the bed. When he stretched his legs out down the bed, a creeper tied down his hands and feet. The Venus Flytrap that he had fallen in love with, mercilessly sucked off half of his little finger. Their actions seemed to be a warning, "This is our world. We want to exercise our rights, that is what you promised us." When he woke up, the room was very muggy. It was so damp he felt as if mildew were attacking the bones in his body. Mo Shen recalled the details of his dream carefully. He was oppressed by a distinctly inauspicious feeling. He felt that a disaster was about to happen. He began to consider the true nature of his current predicament.

Mo Shen Gives Up

One evening at dusk when the rain had ceased, Mo Shen's neighbors once more saw that weird man moving his plants one by one downstairs, to the side of the road. He was muttering away to himself as he tossed them out. Once more his neighbors were surprised by his abnormal behavior. At first they only lifted their curtains to steal a look at him, wondering what stupid things that idiot was up to this time. When they discovered that Mo Shen was throwing out such expensive plants they rushed downstairs and fought each other to take the plants back to their own homes. They thought, this kind of free giveaway is a rare opportunity! His neighbors were laughing at him behind his back, the more stupid he gets, the better it is for us! Several elderly residents stopped to watch Mo Shen. He lurched back upstairs, he seemed to have aged greatly in the space of one night; his once-pampered hands seemed troubled. He stood in his spacious apartment, full of a desolate feeling. Suddenly he felt a lurch, normally he would busy himself looking after his plants; he would always feel better looking at those thriving green beings. Looking before him now, the wall rushed up to meet his gaze. He looked back at himself, he cast his eyes over his own body, dry and withered, lacking in vitality; he looked like a natural born loser. His body swayed from side to side in the spacious room, he was in danger of falling. He explained it away as exhaustion. Now a desert spread before him. He had constructed an oasis with his own hands then destroyed his desert island with those same hands. He heaved a sigh. He thought, now there was nothing to bind him there, he could set off on the road with no worries. He didn't know what "setting off" meant. He was running away. Where was he running to? He wasn't at all sure, he just wanted to get a good night's sleep first before he set off. Those fiendish plants had tormented him so badly that he hadn't gotten a good night's sleep in months, he thought to himself as he walked over to his bed. The bed covers were damp, and smelt unpleasant. He pulled all the covers and sheets off the bed and threw them down onto the floor. He lay down on the bare boards of the bed and looked at the ceiling. Before long he fell asleep. He didn't know how long he slept for, but when he woke up he felt energized. He stretched out his hand to touch his nose; to his surprise he found a spring onion growing there. His eyebrows had become two palm fronds, whilst his legs had turned into the thick and sturdy roots of a rubber tree, the finer roots of which were continuing to grow outwards. His arms were two towering branches, covered in burgeoning leaves, full of life. Everything had changed except for those tapered fingers of his. Mo Shen was frightened half to death by this transformation. He had become an extremely rare breed of plant! These plants had become a part of his body, they went everywhere with him. Wherever he went, there they would follow him. If he took the smallest step, the leafy branches on his upper body would begin to sway in a lively fashion. Full of terror, he walked to the window and closed the curtains, afraid his neighbors would catch sight of him. He ran in circles about the room, trying to shake off the leaves that covered his body. But that only created a whispering susurration as they swayed along with Mo Shen's movements. The leaf-covered branches soughed and swayed. Usually Mo Shen would have pricked up his ears to listen to such a song-like sound, but in that moment, Mo Shen grabbed the saw in a fury and attempted to chop off the branches. He felt an extraordinary pain in his left arm. The branches were already a part of his flesh and blood. There was no getting rid of them. Mo Shen looked at his ridiculous body and felt total despair! What was he going to do? What could be done with this one-of-a-kind body? He stormed up and down his apartment. He couldn't even leave the house now, let alone go out shopping. He would have to stay put indoors and wait for a miracle. His situation could not possibly get any worse. However, there was something else weighing on his mind: What would happen if the plants started to grow rapidly (he had after all seen the like), if one day he broke through the roof, he would be exposed to broad daylight. There would be no keeping his secret then. He would be a monster known to all in the area. How embarrassing that would be. Everyone would come to look at him: He would be the greatest oddity in the world! He had been trying to escape his whole life; in the end he would become an exhibit before the masses. This was nothing less than the greatest satire of his nature, it would be shaming to him. Could it all be bound to end like this? Who was it that was poking fun at him? The joke was beginning to go too far, it was totally unacceptable! He was terrified; he was at his wit's end. He buzzed about the room like a bluebottle, complete with his 'coat of armor'. He thought he would try to kill off the plants by not drinking water. However, he experienced no desire except the desire to have a drink. He persisted for five days and five nights through sheer willpower. He refused to let a drop of water pass his lips. On the sixth day cracks appeared on his skin in a tortoiseshell pattern. He could hold back no longer, he went despondently to the tap and drank without the least hesitation for a good half an hour. He felt his heart burst into bloom, he was in a fine mood. Just then, he saw that his ten beloved fingers had put forth delicate little green shoots. They were lovely! All of a sudden, he asked himself, "Why shouldn't I become a plant? Since I'm so uncomfortable in the human world, isn't this a rather wonderful opportunity I've been offered?" And so, he decided that he would just become a tree! All things considered, it was really the most ideal option available to him.

Aus dem Programm von PalmArtPress

Yang Lian
Erkundung des Bösen
ISBN: 978-3-96258-128-2
Lyrik, 86 Seiten, Hardcover, Deutsch

Carmen-Francesca Banciu
Ilsebill salzt nach
ISBN: 978-3-96258-130-5
Briefroman, 320 Seiten, Hardcover, Deutsch

Patricia Paweletz
HERZBRUCH
ISBN: 978-3-96258-131-2
Roman, 200 Seiten, Hardcover, Deutsch

Martina J. Kohl
Family Matters – *Vom Leben in zwei Welten*
Family Matters – *Of Life in Two Worlds*
ISBN: 978-3-96258-134-3 (DE)
ISBN: 978-3-96258-143-5 (EN)
Roman, 240 Seiten (DE) / 204 Seiten (EN)
Hardcover, Deutsch / Klappenbroschur, Englisch

Fawzi Boubia
Mein West-Östlicher Divan
ISBN: 978-3-96258-114-5
Roman, 300 Seiten, Hardcover, Deutsch

Wolfgang Heyder
Penthesiela / Moabit
ISBN: 978-3-96258-133-6
Erzählungen, 280 Seiten, Hardcover, Englisch

Klaus Ferentschik
Ebenbild
ISBN: 978-3-96258-132-9
Agententhriller, 200 Seiten, Hardcover, Englisch

Wolfgang Kubin
102 Sonette
ISBN: 978-3-96258-104-6
Lyrik, 128 Seiten, Hardcover, Deutsch

Sarah Kiyanrad
dorna
ISBN: 978-3-96258-135-0
Lyrik, 86 Seiten, Klappenbroschur, Deutsch

Wolf Christian Schröder
Fünf Minuten vor Erschaffung der Welt
ISBN: 978-3-96258-113-8
Roman, 320 Seiten, Hardcover, Deutsch

Mechthild Henneke
Ach, mein Kosovo!
ISBN: 978-3-96258-096-4
Roman, 350 Seiten, Hardcover, Deutsch

Ilse Ritter
Weit sehe ich, weit in die Welten all
ISBN: 978-3-96258-074-2
Lyrik, 180 Seiten, Hardcover, Deutsch

Tanja Wekwerth
Seerosenzimmer
ISBN: 978-3-96258-078-0
Roman, 380 Seiten, Hardcover, Deutsch

Denise Buser
Sechs Beine stolpern nicht – *Fakten und Fabeln*
ISBN: 978-3-96258-110-7
Miniaturen, 200 Seiten, Hardcover, Deutsch

Jennifer Kwon Dobbs
Vernehmungsraum
ISBN: 978-3-96258-115-2
Lyrik, 100 Seiten, Hardcover, Deutsch

YoYo, originally from Western China, moved to Beijing in the 1970s. In the 1980s, she worked as an art editor for the Chinese Theater Publishing House and began writing on the side. In 1989, she was invited to New Zealand as a guest lecturer and thus witnessed the Tian'anmen massacre on June 4, 1989, from Auckland. She decided to remain in exile.

Her literature often deals with her multi-layered memories from China, both inspiring and depressing. She has published several books in Chinese, some of which have been translated into other languages.

From 1997, YoYo taught at Eton College in Windsor and at the School of Oriental and African Studies (SOAS) at the University of London. Her artistic work includes performances and paintings, which have been exhibited at Galerie Avantgarde in Berlin, among other venues. YoYo has also been invited to numerous writer-in-residence positions and art projects in China, the US, and throughout Europe. Today she lives in London and Berlin.